LOST TRAILS

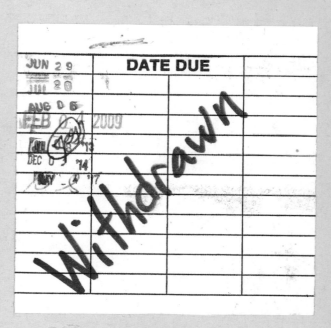

LOST TRAILS

Edited by Martin H. Greenberg
and Russell Davis

PINNACLE BOOKS
Kensington Publishing Corp.

www.kensingtonbooks.com

All Kensington titles, imprints, and distributed lines are available at special quantity discounts for bulk purchases for sales promotions, premiums, fund-raising, educational, or institutional use. Special book excerpts or customized printings can also be created to fit specific needs. For details, write or phone the office of the Kensington special sales manager: Kensington Publishing Corp., 850 Third Avenue, New York, NY 10022, attn: Special Sales Department; phone 1-800-221-2647.

PINNACLE BOOKS and the Pinnacle logo are Reg. U.S. Pat. & TM Off.

ISBN-13: 978-0-7860-1824-6
ISBN-10: 0-7860-1824-0

First printing: May 2007

10 9 8 7 6 5 4 3 2 1

Printed in the United States of America

CONTENTS

INTRODUCTION

When I was a little boy, my father surrounded me with the literature of the American West. Names like Louis L'Amour, Elmer Kelton, Zane Grey, and Max Brand were placed side by side with series Westerns that featured the same hero in a new adventure—and with a new woman or two (or three)—every month. But while I read each of these stories with the unbridled enthusiasm of the new reader who has discovered an untamed land and a clear code of right and wrong, and a mythos of good guys and bad guys that even my young mind could understand, my true hero of the West was, and still is, my father.

It was my father who introduced me to the character of Little Joe—a young boy, always about my age, who grew up (depending on where we lived at the time) on the plains of Nebraska, in the flatlands of Kansas, the rolling hills of Missouri, or any number of other places. Little Joe was tough. He fought off Indians and bandits with equal ease, once using a single bullet shot across the blade of a bowie knife to kill two assailants at once! Little Joe taught me about sod houses, about protecting your family, about doing right, and mostly about the mythic American West. I have been in love with it ever since, and I have had moments in my professional life, being involved as an editor, a writer, a book packager, a publisher, and even a sometime agent, that have transcended even my boyhood fascination with Little Joe.

During those moments, I wasn't just reading about the West, but participating in preserving it through books.

Imagine my pleasure, if you can, five or so years ago, when I was able to arrange, through the good graces of a friend, for my father to appear as a character in a long-running Western series. Imagine when Elmer Kelton happily signed a book for my father a year or two ago, and was willing to personalize it exactly as I'd wanted . . . or when I regularly receive signed copies of novels and collections in the mail, all signed for him by writers who know how much it means to me to able to send them along. Imagine what I felt when I called a few years ago to tell him I was going to be a judge for the Western Heritage Awards.

Imagine, if you will, what it meant to me to be able to call him more recently and say I was editing an anthology of Western stories, and some of the finest writers in the genre—like Elmer Kelton and Loren Estleman and Johnny Boggs—were going to write for it.

I can tell you that I have never been more honored than to have a role in continuing the important tradition of bringing new stories of the West into the bookstores and libraries of our nation. And it *is* important.

For those of you reading this, what I'm about to tell you should come as no surprise at all. The literature of the American West is fading into the sunset much like the lone gunslinger riding away at the end of the movie. Go into any bookstore and look at the Western section. Really look. It's smaller than it was, and getting smaller all the time. With a tip of the hat to Mr. L'Amour—whose estate has graciously allowed a story to appear in this collection—it seems tragic to me *as a reader* that a man who has been deceased for nearly twenty years is still taking up forty percent of the shelf space at my local bookstore. In reprints. It seems equally unfair that another significant percentage of the shelf space is taken by series Westerns like *Longarm* and *The Trailsman*—not because these stories aren't valuable (they are), but because there are so many fantastically talented Western novelists doing original work . . . and not finding a publishing outlet for it because there isn't enough demand.

Now for the part you may not know. As a reader, *you* can make a difference. The publishing market is *reader-*

driven. They will publish what *you* ask for, provided that it's asked for by enough people in a loud enough voice. As a point of comparison, one might think of attempting to drive a herd of cattle alone, which would be a feat nigh on impossible. However, get a group of folks together who know how to ride a horse, how to move the cows, and how to rope, and the herd will go right where they tell it to. Usually. And in the world of publishing, the readers are what drives the publishing herd.

The stories of the American West *are* important. All of them. The old ones and the new ones. The series novels and the original epics. Stories written by famous authors long dead and stories written by new authors you've never heard of before, and every kind of Western writer in between. And should you, the readers, make a point of asking the bookstores, the publishers, the writers, and anyone else who will listen and might make a bit of difference for more books and more stories, this important genre will stay alive. And better still, it will *grow.* There will be more space on the shelves at your local store, and while you'll still be able to find plenty of Mr. L'Amour's work . . . you'll also find new stories.

Now more than ever, there is both a need and a hunger, I think, in our population for stories that remind us of who we are and where we came from. There is no genre of fiction more uniquely qualified for this than the Western. There is, in fact, no genre of fiction more uniquely American than the Western. I learned more about the West, about history, about where our values came from, in reading those books and listening to those stories about Little Joe than I ever did in a history class at school.

Right now there is an entire generation of young Americans who haven't yet read *The Sacketts* or *Lonesome Dove* or *Buffalo Wagons* or *True Grit* or so many other books. This same generation, and the ones that follow it, should read these books and new ones as well, because the literary landscape of the American West has always been free-range country. It is as vast and beautiful as the landscape of the West itself.

In some small way, the collection you hold in your hands represents an opportunity to help preserve our literary heritage. All these stories, with the exception of "The Gift of Cochise" by Louis L'Amour, are original, written specifically to the theme of this anthology—namely, the theme of *Lost Trails*.

I challenged the authors to tell me a *new* story of a famous (or infamous) historical figure from the American West. I'm quite proud to say that all of them responded in ways that have surprised and moved me as a reader and an editor. They have provided stories about Billy the Kid, Wyatt Earp, Jesse James, Blackjack Ketchum, Seth Bullock, Mark Twain, and many other recognizable figures, capturing the *spirit* of these icons, while at the same time, offering up a fictional tale of an adventure that might have been.

Part of the joy of reading stories about the West is in knowing that there *are* gaps. History, in the best of circumstances, is never a complete tale, but only the loosely woven tapestry of the most accurate information available to the teller. The history of the American West has many gaps, and a fair amount of the history comes in stories told by the victors of the battles, and reiterated by the third cousin's uncle twice removed. In so many ways, that is what makes the history both exasperating and (ultimately) a great deal of fun.

We can speculate about those gaps and, in doing so, enjoy a glimpse of where we came from and who we once were . . . maybe even who we are now and who we may one day be.

Without further ado, dear readers, I invite you to take this opportunity to not only read these stories for yourselves but to share them with someone else. Perhaps there is a young person in your family who would enjoy reading about some of the most famous people in our history. Perhaps it will start a discussion about that history. Perhaps it will start a lifetime love of literature, even a love of Western literature. Perhaps the demand for these types of stories will grow out of the simple act of sharing them with others.

And perhaps you will even tell your own stories, though I must warn you that Little Joe is already busy. He's been entertaining my children for a few years now and I think he's got a bit of life left in him yet. Worst case, should I run short of Little Joe memories, I can always call on my father for a new adventure. He's told me that he makes them up as he goes along, which explains all those cliffhanger endings and sleepless nights, when I stayed up worrying about what was going to happen to my hero.

That is the greatest thing about the stories of the West—those collected in this anthology, those that have come before, those told around the family campfire, and those that have yet to be published—these are the stories that can live forever, a part of the landscape of our lives and our memories and our families . . . but they will only last as long as *all of us* ensure that they do.

Enjoy!

—*Russell Davis*
Northern Nevada
Winter 2006

LOST TRAILS

Mark and Bill

Loren D. Estleman

"Samuel Langhorne Clemens, meet William Frederick Cody."

"Buffalo Bill," said the white-haired man in the white suit, committing his hand to the newcomer's oaken grip.

"Mark Twain," said the long-haired man in the buckskin coat, flashing white teeth in his chestnut-colored Vandyke beard.

Their host waited until both men were seated before sitting down himself, then sprang back up to summon the white-coated waiter out onto the terrace. "Libations, gentlemen?" he asked his guests. "I myself am temperate, but do not let that—"

"Bourbon," said Twain, plucking a long cigar from a hinged silver case.

"The same," said Cody, peeling the foil from a plug of chewing tobacco.

"Soda?" The waiter drew the cork from one of an army of vessels on a wheeled cart.

"Bourbon," said Cody.

"The same," said Twain.

The waiter poured. "Mr. Roosevelt?"

Theodore Roosevelt bared his famous grin beneath

the thick mustache. "Lemonade, and keep it coming. I'm as parched as the Badlands. I've been shouting myself hoarse to those fools setting up the Boone and Crockett cabin at the fair," he confided to the others. "It seems no one in Chicago knows how to care for a wooden building since the fire."

Cody said, "I stole away while Miss Oakley was performing, for a glimpse of the exhibit. Splendid job. A fine homely contribution to that antiseptic circus. You know, the fair's directors turned me down when I offered to bring the Wild West to the White City. They said it was incongruous. So I rented the lot across the street and set up there."

"A regrettable decision on their part," Roosevelt said. "Your exhibition has been steadily outpulling the World's Fair ten to one. Have you been to either, Mr. Clemens?"

"I intended to go to both, but fell ill. Today is the first day I've felt sound enough to quit my room. The prospect of a ride on either Mr. Ferris's wheel or Mr. Cody's Deadwood Stage still turns me a festive shade of green. And tomorrow I must go back East."

"A pity. I'm sure America is champing to hear your observations on both phenomena." Irritably, Roosevelt signaled to the waiter with his still-empty glass. The fellow shook himself out of an apparent trance and reached for the pitcher of lemonade. As a mere member of President Cleveland's Civil Service Commission, Roosevelt made a feeble impression on the serving class in the presence of America's greatest humorist and the hero of Warbonnet Creek.

"I shouldn't wonder." Twain blew a chain of smoke rings that was swiftly torn apart by the wind off Lake Michigan. "America never knows how it feels about a thing until it's received its instructions from me."

"America knows a great American when it hears him," Roosevelt said.

"I am not a great American. I am not *an* American. I am *the* American."

Cody chuckled. "You're an entertaining hoss, Mr. Clemens. I once heard Jim Bridger explain how he roped a cyclone and rode it out of a Blackfoot ambush— 'Square knots only,' he said; 'a Dakota twister'll slip right out of a bosun'—but he warn't a patch on you when it comes to exaggeration."

"I return the compliment, Mr. Cody. I'm on record in opposition to the decline of the fine art of lying, but it's in no peril as long as you walk the earth."

An uncomfortable silence followed this remark, broken only by Cody's reflective chewing and the popping of Twain's lips on his cigar. From the terrace of Roosevelt's suite, the trio could just make out the white spires of the Court of Honor, the centerpiece of the 1893 Chicago World's Fair, dominated by the revolving structure George Ferris had designed for the amusement of those courageous enough to board one of its gondolas and travel to the top of the world.

Cody's cud bonged into a cuspidor provided by the waiter. For Roosevelt, an enthusiastic amateur in the sport of prizefighting, it sounded like the opening bell to the first round. "Which lie are we discussing? I've told my fair share and seen a heap of 'em in print."

"I recall an account attributed to you of a shooting contest between yourself and the late-lamented James Butler Hickok," said Twain. "You took aim simultaneously at the same prairie dog at a distance of forty paces, fired an instant apart, and placed both slugs through the unfortunate creature's left eye, one right behind the other so the orbit was not enlarged."

"The account was inaccurate," Cody assented. "It was the right eye."

Roosevelt yelped his high-pitched laugh. "Bully! He's a match for you in the well-placed jest as he was for Wild Bill in marksmanship."

Steel glittered beneath Twain's shaggy black brows. But Cody spoke first, waving a well-tended hand at the end of an arm fringed in leather.

"I wouldn't presume," he said. "Let's agree I'm as handy with powder and a ball as Mr. Clemens is with his wit and a quill."

Twain demurred. "Strictly speaking, anyone with sufficient eyesight and a steady hand can learn to shoot a glass ball thrown by a man on his payroll. It's quite another thing to raise a snigger in an auditorium packed with Pennsylvania Dutchmen. I nearly started a riot the last time I spoke in Allentown, after sixty minutes of excruciating silence."

"The Dutch appreciate a pleasantry once you've found their range. I'd admire to see you try your hand with a band of Missouri bushwhackers."

"Ten words at the expense of a Kansas Jayhawker would place them in convulsions. I'd venture to wager I'd render every last one to a mound of quivering jelly before you managed to drive a half-dozen nails into a timber with your best six-shooter."

For answer, Cody drew a beautiful Colt revolver traced with silver from his hip, took swift aim, and blasted the cork from a squat bottle of brandy perched on the portable bar. Roosevelt barked a mild oath; the waiter leapt back three feet from his position beside the cart. Twain alone did not react. He drew on his cigar, blew a plume of smoke into the blue exhaust from the revolver, and asked the waiter to inspect the bottle. The man hesitated, then stepped forward and with a shaking hand lifted the vessel and peered at its neck.

"Not so much as a chip." His voice quavered.

With a flourish, Cody spun the weapon on his finger,

offering the butt to Twain. The humorist accepted it and examined the ornate engraving. "'Presented to the King of the West by the Queen of Great Britain and Empress of India,'" he read aloud.

"Victoria put it in my hands personally when we played London," Cody said. "I'd just bested a visiting French count in a shooting contest. He's said to have killed ten men in duels of honor. That grand lady commands the greatest army in the world, and knows her firearms. It's the finest in my collection."

Roosevelt gulped lemonade. "You might have found a less unsettling way to demonstrate your point."

Twain laid his cigar in a heavy tray, slid a handsome slim rosewood box from an inside breast pocket, opened it, and withdrew an elegant gold-plated implement with a nib inlaid with ivory. Cody took it and peered at the barrel. "'To Mark Twain, from Thomas A. Edison,'" he read aloud.

Twain said, "It's a prototype, not yet available on the market. Edison invented it. It requires no dipping; a reservoir inside the barrel furnishes the ink automatically. The Wizard of Menlo Park challenged me to amuse his young friend, a clever machinist's apprentice named Ford, born to a farming family in Michigan of Irish and German stock. Edison had never seen the fellow crack a smile, but I reduced him to tears with a simple anecdote about Jewish immigrants. That was my prize."

"It seems a splendid instrument." Cody handed it back.

"It leaks something fierce. I gave up on it after it expectorated over an entire page of *Roughing It.*"

"Then why carry it?" asked the frontiersman.

"For occasions such as this." Twain returned the pen to its box and the box to his pocket.

Cody emptied his glass and glanced at the waiter, who

refilled it and Twain's, which lacked an inch of vacancy. "I heard something about a wager."

"My bump of humor against your trigger finger?" Twain sipped and flicked drops of bourbon from his mustaches.

"A series of increasingly difficult targets against a queue of mountingly humorless listeners," Cody said. "When one misses, the other must score, or forfeit the contest." He tossed down his drink in one motion and slammed down the glass on the table that separated them.

"And the stakes?"

"My part of one week's proceeds from the Wild West in Chicago to three months' royalties from your latest literary effort."

"One month," Twain said. "It isn't *Ben-Hur*, but it's kept my loudest creditors silent."

Cody dismissed the matter with a gesture. "Who shall hold the stakes?"

"Friend Roosevelt, who is too honest to cheat and far too wealthy to corrupt."

"I accept!" The commissioner's broad face flushed with excitement; then he cleared his throat and adjusted his spectacles. "I must, however, insist upon a more appropriate venue. Hotel personnel are notoriously unreasonable about indoor gunplay. May I suggest Colonel Cody's exhibition grounds?"

Twain put out his cigar. "His advantage would be too great. The gallant South made that mistake when it took the field at Gettysburg. We are but a few hours by rail from Missouri, where a man may shoot all day and not disturb so much as a mule."

"But knock a chip off a statue of Mr. Clemens in every direction," Cody said. "I fought with the North, but fortunately was not present at Bull Run. I have an alternative, provided civilization has not crept that far."

When he identified the spot, all three men touched glasses and drank. The waiter hastened to refill them.

"Hideous!" Roosevelt, clad in tweeds and high laced boots, scraped a foul mess off one heel onto a plank. "To think that such a sordid place should exist in the midst of one of the greatest cities of the world is shameful. If someone does not come forward to reclaim this land from its inhabitants, I shudder to think what the twenti-eth century will hold."

Buffalo Bill Cody, who had exchanged his soft bleached buckskins for rougher hides stained with old sweat and darkened from smoke, thumped his chest with both fists and breathed deeply the scents of Blue Island, a neighborhood neglected by all but derelicts and the sa-loonkeepers who lived off their thirst. "Where you see only decay and despair, I see my youth. It was here that Ned Buntline and I recruited Indians for *Scouts of the Plains* fifteen years ago."

"The Old Pepper tribe, I suspect." With a toe, Mark Twain nudged an empty bottle whose label advertised that pungent brand of whiskey. He was careful to avoid contact with the rubbish and horse offal with his white linen cuffs. He alone was attired more fittingly for a lec-ture hall than for the dregs of a city.

"We sold out everywhere we played, from here to Albany," said Cody.

"It's gratifying to see you earned enough to afford real Indians."

"Spare your ammunition," warned Cody. "The contest hasn't begun."

The location, originally a sandbar in one of the canals fed by Lake Michigan, had been built up over the years by deposits of garbage and manure scraped from the streets. Clusters of saloons stood upon it, ramshackle affairs without foundations, but a spot where one had burned recently and its remains scavenged for firewood offered space and an unobstructed view of the lake, where expired rounds could fall to rest without causing casualties.

Roosevelt alone had come without the support of acquaintances. Cody was accompanied by reloaders from the Wild West; a number of genuine Sioux and Cheyenne from the exhibition, resplendent in tribal trappings; some unidentified parties; and a young man named Johnny Baker, a protégé who wore his hair long like Cody, dressed in buckskins, and specialized in launching and setting up targets. Twain had brought along an amiable band of admirers, men and women whose eyes twinkled even as they picked their way carefully among the topographical hazards and whose lips quivered perpetually on the edge of laughter. "Even the finest pump requires priming," the humorist had explained.

"Quite proper," Cody said. "One warms up with the easier marks. However, I shall select the audience."

"And I shall select the targets."

Simultaneously, the two contestants produced bank drafts—Twain from a pocket, Cody from inside the sweatband of his great Stetson—and held them out to Roosevelt. The pair averred that the totals were averages only, to be amended later should protest arise.

The commissioner placed the drafts in a flat wallet and slid it into a pocket. "Surely, this is not just a matter of material gain."

Twain said, "In the words of my creditors, 'It ain't the principle of the thing, it's the money.' There is, however, a question of pride."

"The gentleman from Missouri has struck the critter square betwixt the eyes," said Cody. "He's claimed for himself the championship title without raising so much as a pistol or a fist in its defense. I'm challenging it.

Henceforward, the winner of today's match will be known exclusively as 'The American.'"

"Satisfactory, Mr. Clemens?"

"The gentleman from Missouri" slid the band off a fresh cigar. "Mr. Roosevelt, Mr. Cody, it suits me right down to the ground."

The contestants and their parties retired to opposite ends of the narrow island to practice. Young Johnny Baker drew specially blown glass balls from a trunk he'd brought along and hurled them over the lake while Cody, using a Deluxe Winchester 1873 carbine with gold plate on the receiver, burst them first one by one, then in twos and threes, levering fresh rounds into the chamber with lightning speed. His group met each success with cheers and applause, not counting occasional exceptions: The Indians observed the spectacle with impassive expressions, their arms folded beneath their blankets, while a stoutish, middle-aged woman wearing an abundance of clothing and a hat with a veil remained glum-faced.

On his end, Twain, puffing his cigar and hooking his thumbs inside the armholes of his snowy vest, related a succession of stories from his childhood in Hannibal through his adventures as a riverboat pilot on the Mississippi for his increasingly appreciative audience. As with Cody, not all were voluble: A leathern man in a rumpled suit smeared with tobacco ash, his fingers stained with ink, stood silently, scribbling with a stub of yellow pencil on a thick fold of newsprint.

At length, both competing parties announced that they were ready to begin. One of Twain's companions handed him a flask of brandy. Twain slanted it Cody's way inquiringly. The other demurred. "That which fuels the storyteller's engine clouds the sharpshooter's eye."

"A metaphor well and truly mixed." Twain swigged. "Defer to me the art of oratory and I in turn will keep my paws off your guns."

Cody bared his teeth. "Choose a target, sir."

Twain held out the flask for his companion to take, then cast his glance up and down the length of the island. Finally, he turned his attention toward the lake. After squinting against the sun's glare for most of a minute, he took the cigar from his mouth and used it as a pointer. "Yon piece of flotsam, to start."

All stared in that direction, Cody holding up his hat as a shield against the brightness. An elongated section of driftwood, bleached white and rounded at the edges like soap, bobbed in the swells sliding toward shore. From that distance it seemed no larger than a needle.

Cody looked at Roosevelt. "Sixty yards?"

The man addressed raised and resettled his spectacles, scowled. "I'll accept your word. I myself can see nothing but blue water."

"Fortunately," Twain said, "politics is one of the few professions where shortsightedness is no obstacle." His coterie chuckled.

"Wait your turn, sir." Cody put on his hat, bent to scoop up a handful of loose earth, and cast it with the wind. He accepted his Winchester from Johnny Baker, worked the lever, shouldered the weapon, and pressed the trigger; he seemed hardly to aim. The pale target stood on end, spun, and fell back to the surface with a smack. A hoot went up from his admirers. The Indians and the woman remained silent.

"Well done," said Twain. "The choice now is yours."

Cody's gaze swept both groups. It rested momentarily on the grim visage of the woman in his own party. A bitter smile touched his lips. Then he shook his head and clapped a hand on the shoulder of the leathery fellow in the wrinkled suit. "Samuel Clemens, Prentiss Ingraham. A journalistic colleague of yours. He's my official biographer and a permanent fixture of the Wild West."

"How many biographies of you has he written?" asked Twain.

"Fourteen," snarled Ingraham before his employer could respond.

"And is the fourteenth life of Buffalo Bill a patch on all the rest?"

Both parties broke into laughter; Cody's ending in embarrassed coughs. The Indians, the woman, and Ingraham were stony.

"I should warn you, Mr. Clemens, that Ingraham has written more than two million words, is familiar with every witticism ever spoken, and is utterly impossible to amuse."

Twain blew a ring. "Is that true, Mr. Ingraham?"

"I had my bump of humor removed at an early age." The biographer's tone was parched, as if he seldom used his voice. "I've never missed it."

"Who is your publisher?" Twain asked.

"Street and Smith."

"Who publishes you abroad?"

"Every damn rag with a staff that reads, and I don't get a cent."

"I'm confident that when Geronimo is President we'll have an international copyright law."

Ingraham grunted. Twain turned his cigar in his fingers, regarding him through narrowed eyes. Just as his silence brought nervous coughs from his listeners, he removed the end from his mouth and said:

"The Pope, it's rumored, ascended to Paradise, where St. Peter conducted him to his quarters, a monastic cell with a narrow cot and no window. On the way, His Holiness noted one of his neighbors resting beyond the open door of a palatial suite in a Morris chair overlooking all of blessed eternity, with Helen of Troy preparing a mint julep for his consumption. Quite understandably, the Pope was curious and asked Peter who the gentleman had been in life. 'A publisher,' came the reply; whereupon the newcomer asked to speak with the Holy Father. Having been duly conducted into the Presence, the Pope asked why he, the spiritual leader of earth, should be put up so meanly whilst a mere publisher was treated with all the luxury of an Oriental potentate. God considered, then responded: 'This is Heaven. I'm up to My chin in popes, but when the first publisher made it through the pearly gates, I decided to pull out all the stops.'"

Ingraham's face reddened with some suppressive effort, but he could not sustain it. Presently, he threw back his head and guffawed. Twain, sanguine, pulled on his cigar while both groups applauded his success. Cody acknowledged the feat with a sardonic bow, then proceeded at his opponent's request to pluck a nuisance of a seagull out of the air with a single shot.

"Poor creature!" exclaimed the stern-faced woman, interrupting the accolade.

The frontiersman glared at her, a muscle twitching in one cheek. He opened his mouth, then shut it with purpose and shifted his gaze to one of the silent braves in his entourage. He made a sign to the man, who stepped forward with slow dignity. The Indian was tall, with the features of a Roman senator engraved in red marble. His blanket was intricately woven and his headdress was fashioned from spotless white eagle feathers tipped with black.

"This is Stands with His Lance," Cody told Twain. "He was one of the victors at the Little Big Horn. The Sioux appreciate a good jest as much as the next man, but I've toured two continents with this fellow, and I can attest that mirth does not repose within his breast."

Twain studied the man—both their profiles were hawkish and challenging. "Does he understand English?"

"If he does, he refuses to acknowledge it. He has no

love for our nation. His only reason for joining the exhibition is to donate everything he earns to the reservation in South Dakota."

"That seems unfair," Roosevelt put in. "Mr. Clemens can hardly be expected to relate an amusing anecdote in the Sioux language."

"I anticipated that argument, and have brought along a mission-school graduate to interpret." Cody signaled to a youthful Indian in store clothes with a white man's haircut. Twain, however, halted the young man with an upraised hand.

"His services won't be necessary. I upended an entire Russian colony in Eureka, California, without uttering a word."

He asked to borrow Cody's hat, coat, and the belt containing his showy revolver, which he requested be unloaded. Amused, Cody complied. Twain handed his cigar and linen jacket to a dark-haired negative of himself in a black suit who turned out to be his brother, Orion, and climbed into his challenger's rig. Sniggers arose when despite the humorist's bushy abundance of hair, the big Stetson slid past his ears to rest on the bridge of his nose. Unfazed, Twain drew himself up, expanded his chest, and strutted in a circle, sweeping off the hat in an exaggerated gesture reminiscent of Cody's in response to his cheering audiences. Cody's smile set hard as iron. Members of his group cleared their throats restlessly. Stands with His Lance watched the spectacle, not a nerve showing in his face.

Suddenly, Twain let out a whoop, scooped the Colt from its holster, and twirled it with an ease that astonished all those present, squeezing the trigger just as the muzzle pointed down. When the hammer snapped on an empty chamber, his shout turned into a yelp. He dropped the weapon and hopped around on one foot, holding the other in agony as if wounded.

The victor of the Little Big Horn let out a surprised bark, as of air pent up for years. He doubled over, hooting and slapping his knees, tears streaming down his face like water running off a rock. His blanket slid off his naked shoulders. Most of the others joined in, including the Indians and even Prentiss Ingraham, his facade demolished now. The woman in Cody's assembly lowered her chin briefly but was impassive otherwise.

Buffalo Bill's face was scarcely more mobile. His eyes were steely as he accepted the return of his gear. Dusky red spots glowed high on his cheeks.

He appeared, however, to have composed himself in time for Twain's next challenge: the ace of spades from the humorist's own deck, nailed to the wall of a vacant shop and observed by way of a looking glass with the Winchester pointing backward and resting on Cody's shoulder. The spectators were still; but he'd succeeded many times in placing similar trick shots in the center ring.

They gasped collectively when the bullet pierced the cigar Twain was smoking, leaving the tattered stump clamped between his teeth. The playing card, of course, was untouched.

Shouts of concern and outrage, evenly divided between the two groups, drowned out the echo of the report. Roosevelt lunged to catch Twain when his legs wobbled, but Cody reached him first, seizing his shoulders. "Ole hoss, you hit?" His voice shook.

Twain turned his head and spat out the stump. "You owe me the price of a cigar."

Both groups melded, gathered around him, with Cody's stammered apologies rising above the jabber. Twain cleared space around him by igniting a fresh cigar and laying down a cloud like fly spray. He silenced the frontiersman with a palm, tugged down the points of his vest, and said, "Your choice now, sir."

Roosevelt polished his spectacles with a handkerchief.

"Under the circumstances, I think it best we postpone the rest of the competition, or cancel it altogether. Can we not agree that we are in the company of the two greatest Americans, and leave it at that?"

"This is a contest, not an accord. Now that my esteemed opponent has faltered, is it your wish to rob me of the opportunity to triumph?"

"It seems a small thing against the risk."

"That's merely a question of timing. Had I gone up with the boiler of the *Paul Jones* in fifty-seven, the event would have attracted little notice, but the loss would have been far greater. I had not yet published a line. I would rather go out at the height of my powers—and a lurid exit would certainly pose no threat to future royalties. However, I don't intend to tempt another stray round. I'm a titter away from claiming the title I came for."

Cody's face darkened during Twain's speech. Now he showed his fine white teeth, swept off his Stetson, and bowed to the severe-looking woman in the veiled hat. "Madame, would you honor us by stepping forward?"

An opening appeared around the woman, who began to shake her head, then lifted her chin and approached the contestants at a stately pace, lifting her skirts slightly to avoid dragging them in the dust.

Roosevelt placed a hand on Twain's arm and turned him away, lowering his voice to a near whisper. "I advise you to forfeit this challenge."

"Come, come, Theodore. She's a dragon, I confess, but I've faced worse."

"The woman is Louisa Cody. Buffalo Bill's wife."

"Ah. The enemy. You saw how I handled Ingraham."

"Ingraham did not introduce himself to the desk clerk in Cody's hotel as Mrs. Cody, only to be told that Mrs. Cody had arrived already with her husband."

Twain drew twice on his cigar. "Why, the old goat. I wonder she agreed to accompany him today."

"Appearances. There is rumor of divorce proceedings. Surrender the point and start again as from the beginning. It's preferable to a complete and humiliating failure."

The humorist laid an arm across Roosevelt's shoulders, steering him from the group. They strolled along the edge of the lake. "Pray tell me everything you know of Buffalo Bill's indiscretions."

Roosevelt's broad face flushed. "That would be indelicate, as well as a breach of my impartiality as a judge."

"Is the information confidential?"

"It is a subject of conversation in every gentleman's club in New York."

"Tarnation. I should be more sociable. Is it a sign of your impartiality that you have allowed Cody to bring along as much ammunition as he requires to make a contest while you deny me the same privilege?"

"I hadn't considered the situation in those terms."

The pair circled the island, Roosevelt muttering, Twain listening, and stopped at last where they had begun. Twain made a ceremony of extinguishing his cigar and bent from the waist.

"I'm powerfully pleased to make your acquaintance, Mrs. Cody. You outshine the White City."

Louisa Cody was silent. Without changing expressions, she lifted a limp hand in a black silk glove. Twain took it and bowed more deeply, brushing the air just above the knuckles with his lips. He lowered his voice to a murmur. "May I trouble you for the loan of an ear?"

She frowned, withdrew her hand. After a moment, she nodded slightly and turned her head a quarter to the left. As the others watched, one group now, straining in vain to catch a syllable, Twain whispered in her ear. She hesitated, then shook her head. He pulled back to rub his nose, then leaned in again and whispered.

For a moment after he straightened away, observers were certain Mark Twain had failed. Then Louisa began to tremble, as if from an onset of the ague. Something escaped her lips that some thought was a cough. Hastily, she opened her reticule, withdrew a handkerchief, and brought it to her mouth, but not in time to quell the explosion from deep within her bosom. It was hoarse at first, but climbed to a shrill note that rang across Lake Michigan like the merry squawking of birds in their bath. Peal after peal followed, and she turned away and absolutely cantered straight at Cody, weeping and laughing with arms outstretched. He reciprocated. For a season after, she shook in his embrace, her mirth muffled against his chest.

Roosevelt was the first to shake Twain's hand. Then the dam burst and well-wishers poured in from Twain's entourage and Cody's, wringing his hand, slapping his back, and demanding to know the source of Mrs. Cody's glee. Twain refused. "A conjurer must be let his secrets."

Cody loosened himself from his wife's arms, kissed her cheek, and strode toward his conqueror, hand outstretched. "You are *the* American," he said, "and I am but a poor showman."

Twain met his grasp. "Poorer, in any event. I'd admire to spend part of the prize on supper with you and your remarkable wife."

Cody accepted, but was alone that night when he met Twain in a private room in the Palmer House restaurant. Both men were in formal wear, Cody's chestnut curls spilling well past his starched collar.

"Louisa sends regrets. She took the train home an hour ago, with an earnest request for me to join her when the exhibition closes here. She's eager to put the house in shape for my return. I believe I have you to thank for our reconciliation."

"A minister would have been less expensive," Twain ordered bourbon for them both.

"And for your entreé?" asked the waiter.

"Brandy," said the pair in unison.

When they were alone with their drinks, Cody asked Twain what he and Roosevelt had discussed on the island.

"He did most of the talking, at my insistence. He mentioned the shopgirl in New York, the opera singer in San Francisco, and the baroness in London. I disremember the others."

"That rascal. He'll go far in politics. I don't reckon he overlooked the little fracas here."

"Why a man should want a wife is a mystery," Twain said. "Why he should want two is a bigamistry."

Cody laughed. "I drew that fire right enough." He started to drink, then set down his glass. "Just between us, what did you say that busted her corset?"

The other shook his head, taking a cigar out of his case.

"If it's that last shot's got your hackles up, I'm sorry all over again. I admit I was stung by that show you put on for Stands with His Lance. I won't say I missed that ace on purpose, but I'd never do a man intentional harm unless my life was threatened."

"I knew that. If Buffalo Bill wanted to shoot Mark Twain, he'd be attending my memorial service in the morning."

"We're tight, then, and I won't be offended. You saved my marriage, ole hoss, whatever it was you said."

"I asked her if she knew why certain men referred to their private parts by pet names."

"I'd bet my best saddle she didn't know."

"She didn't. I explained it was because they didn't want complete strangers making most of their decisions."

Cody's sun-burnished features turned a deeper shade of bronze. When at last he opened his mouth to laugh, every patron of the restaurant knew of it, and their waiter spread the curtains to investigate the source of the disturbance.

Mark Twain and Buffalo Bill glared at the man. Then Cody looked at Twain, who inhaled smoke, let it out, and said, "Can't a couple of Americans dine here in privacy?"

After Blackjack Dropped

Karl Lassiter

"That's about the damnedest, stupidest thing I ever heard," the judge said, staring at the defendant.

"I protest," cried Thomas "Blackjack" Ketchum's lawyer. "You're malignin' an honest man."

"Nuthin' honest about him," the judge said, then spat accurately into a cuspidor at the side of his desk. "You." The judge pointed at Frank Harrington. "Tell me again about what Ketchum did." The judge glared at both the defendant and his lawyer to silence them.

"Yer Honor, I worked as conductor on the train. We been robbed twice before and this time I was ready for anything. When Ketchum—"

"A point, Judge," called the defense attorney. "You are trying the wrong man. This here's George Stevens and—"

"Don't give me any guff," the judge growled. "That's Tom Ketchum, not some first-timer who didn't know his ass from a hole in the ground. Now shut up and let Mr. Harrington finish. We all got better things to do. I want to get home for dinner 'fore it gets too late."

The lawyer subsided and the conductor continued his recitation of the train robbery.

"He jumped onto the train just this side of Folsom,

then forced the engineer and fireman to stop." Harrington grinned savagely and smoothed his mustache. "Where we stopped was real tight, sheer rock faces on either side of the tracks. He couldn't get back and uncouple the mail and express car like he planned."

"What did you do?" the judge asked.

"I heard him walkin' on the roof of the passenger car on his way back, so I grabbed my shotgun and got to the express car 'bout the time he did. He saw me, and damn but he was quick. He got off the first shot. I let loose with my scattergun and missed. I fired the second barrel and got the varmint that time."

"Damned well blew my arm off!" Ketchum cried. He held up a bandaged stump before his lawyer could stop him.

"Didn't blow it off. Not entirely," Harrington said. "But it was danglin'. Heard tell they caught him when he run off."

"Never did," Ketchum said. "I was too weak. Flagged down the next train and surrendered. Sheriff Pinard took custody of me at Folsom, kept me on the train to the Trinidad hospital where they lopped off my arm." Ketchum glared at the conductor. "You done me in, you son of a bitch." He waved his stump around some more, but the judge used his gavel to silence him.

"I'm sorry I didn't blow off yer head!" the conductor shouted. "You wounded *me*! That shot you got off hit me in the left arm!"

"Silence!" bellowed the judge. He straightened papers in front of him on the desk and continued. "Think that 'bout wraps it up. Not much left to say other than guilty!"

"Your Honor!" The defense attorney jumped to his feet. "I protest!"

"Protest this," the judge went on. "On this day of September 11, 1899, I do order Mr. Thomas Edward Ketchum to be hanged by the neck till he's dead. Sheriff Garcia, take the guilty party to the jail. Clayton, New Mexico's 'bout to have its first hanging." The judge brought his gavel down with a ringing bang. The few men in the courtroom let out a shout of glee that drowned out Ketchum and his lawyer's protests.

"I'll get an appeal, Tom," the lawyer said. "They can't hang you for robbin' a train. You didn't kill anyone."

"Not this time," Ketchum said. "Did before, over in Arizona. But not this time. Nuthin' went right with the robbery. I was a damn fool to try it all by my lonesome, but bad luck's been my mistress since my brother Sam was killed by that posse. I shoulda been with him. Together, we coulda got away."

"Keep your voice down, Tom. Don't go givin' the deputies anything they can testify to in court."

"How long?"

"Until they hang you?" The lawyer shook his head. "Months. With luck we can keep 'em jumpin' like fleas on a hot griddle till they come to their senses and let you go. Or at least reduce your sentence to a few years in the Santa Fe Penitentiary."

"Don't want to go there," Ketchum said firmly. "That's where they took Elzy."

"You mean McGinnis?"

"Elzy Lay. Don't matter what name he got convicted under. He's still locked up like an animal. And fer life. The son of a bitch shoulda looked after Sam better."

"You won't be dead."

"What's it matter? You ever seen a one-armed gunfighter?" Ketchum waved his stump around. "I can't use my six-shooter fer shit with my left hand. I can't escape and I botched killin' myself twice. Why don't they just let me do myself in?"

"It's only August. I'll get onto gettin' you out of this

lockup. They got you confused with another Black Jack. You were never called that, and they confused the pair of you. That'll be good for an appeal." The lawyer stood and paused at the cell door. He turned and looked back at Ketchum. "You got money, don't you? Your last heist was more than forty thousand dollars, gold and silver."

"All spent. That bother you?" Ketchum looked at his former lawyer with desolate eyes, and knew it did.

It was bright and sunny in April, but George Otis, M.D., was an old man and felt his advanced years constantly from arthritic joints. No matter what he wore, he could never wear enough of a coat to stay comfortable. Still, Union County was warmer than back in Washington, D.C., this time of year. For all the cherry blossoms and hints of humid summer to come, the city was not this warm. Otis shuffled along, peering at signs through rheumy eyes until he found the sheriff's office.

He paused, rubbed his hands on his thighs, and removed the last of the nervous sweat there. Otis always felt this way when he neared another addition to his fine collection. One day his long years of study would pay off, and Professor Virchow would be vindicated.

And Dr. George Alexander Otis would be hailed as one of the greatest forensic scientists in American history.

He was almost bowled over when the lawman came rushing from the office.

"Sorry, mister. Didn't see you." The sheriff peered at Otis, evaluating him and immediately discounting him as a threat.

Otis didn't mind. That was the way it always was on the frontier. Dangerous, deadly, though not as fierce in 1901 as it had been even twenty-eight years earlier when he had received some of his finest specimens. So much work had been done since then, so much.

"Eh, that's quite all right," Otis said. "You are the sheriff? Sheriff Salome Garcia?"

The stout lawman's bushy eyebrows arched.

"Do I know you?"

"Uh, no, Sheriff, you do not, but I know of you. May we talk?"

"I was on my way to the saloon. A fight's gonna break out any time now."

"I am sure it will wait a few more minutes. I am with the Army."

"You?"

"Not those fine soldiers who ride forth to do battle, no, not them. I am a licensed doctor of medicine and work for the Army Medical Museum."

"Never heard tell of such a thing," Garcia said. He glanced toward the still-quiet saloon, obviously hankering more for a drink than to break up a nonexistent fight in the middle of the day.

"It is not well known, true, true," Otis said, rubbing his hands together to keep them warm against the spring breeze whipping down Clayton's main street, "but nonetheless important. We are affiliated with the Smithsonian Institution. I am sure you have heard of that organization."

"Reckon I might have," Sheriff Garcia said. "What's that got to do with anything in Clayton?"

"Your prisoner. The one about to be executed."

"You mean Ketchum? We'll get around to stretchin' his neck sooner or later. Been havin' a run of bad luck with this and that. Truth be told, we've postponed the hangin' three times already."

"I had not heard that," Otis said, frowning. The wrinkles on his high forehead vanished among those naturally there. "Will the execution be forthcoming?"

"You mean will we do it soon? I've heard rumors that some of his old gang might try to break him out. If they try, well, all I got's one deputy. That means the judge'll have to either approve another deputy or two or let me get a citizens' committee organized."

"Come along, sir, and let me tell you of my work and how you might aid it and the future of law enforcement."

"Something to do with Tom Ketchum? He's a killer, that's for certain sure, but what's your interest?"

The old man took the sheriff's elbow and steered him in the direction of the saloon, where he had wanted to go anyway. It didn't take much to guide him inside the almost-deserted gin mill.

"Looks as if your fight has taken care of itself," Otis said. "Let me buy you a drink while I tell you of my research."

"Go on," the sheriff said, pulling up a chair near the door so he could look out into the street. He might be taking a break, but that didn't mean he could ignore his job entirely.

The barkeep brought a quarter bottle of rye whiskey and placed it on the table. Otis poured, his hands a trifle shaky.

"To crime," he said.

"To catchin' the damn robbers," Sheriff Garcia corrected, downing his shot.

"That's what I do. Or rather it is what I help fine, up-standing lawmen like you do, Sheriff," Otis said. His eyes glowed with an inner light. "I run the U.S. Army Surgeon General's Indian Crania Study." Otis saw the sheriff's blank look and hurried on with his explanation, taking time only to pour the lawman another drink. "We have endeavored to collect more than forty-five hundred skulls."

"Indian skulls? Why?" The sheriff looked perplexed. Otis was used to this reaction. It was more common than revulsion, though he encountered that also, especially in the upper circles of polite Washington society.

"I am a phrenologist. I examine the bumps on the head in an effort to predict behavior. If the red-skinned savages' nature can be determined, we can predict the behavior of those on the reservations."

"You mean predict which're likely to go raidin'?"

"Yes!"

"Suppose that'd be a good thing," Sheriff Garcia said, "but I don't see how that means a danged thing to me."

"Your prisoner. Thomas 'Blackjack' Ketchum, is one of the worst, is he not?"

"Can't say he's *that* bad. A killer, yeah, but not as bad as some I've heard tell of."

"I want to examine his skull. Think of how this would reduce robbing and killing! If I can predict a man's behavior from the phrenologic patterns, you would know the men who would commit crimes before they did so!"

"Don't take bumps on a head to figger which one'll turn bad," the sheriff said. "Right here in Union County, now, we got three or four I'm watchin' real close. They're just itchin' to rob something. I can tell."

"What if your feelings were vindicated by scientific proof? You could prevent murders and robberies."

"Folks'd like that, not gettin' themselves murdered or robbed," Garcia allowed.

"Exactly. All I would like is the chance to examine Tom Ketchum's head after the execution."

"You could do it 'forehand," the sheriff said. "He's just settin' in his cell feelin' sorry for himself. He might like the attention of somebody other 'n the priest or a deputy."

"You misunderstand. I want to take his head with me. Back to Washington where I have a laboratory with measurement equipment."

"That's not gonna happen," Garcia said. "Look, I'm a bit antsy about this execution as it is. I never hung nobody before. And the chin music around town is that Ben Owen might be thinkin' on gettin' Ketchum free."

"A gang member? Could I examine his head too when you catch him?"

"Look, Doc, I want this done with, and you can't have the head. We ain't like them cannibals in Africa."

"I am empowered to offer a suitable fee in exchange for the cranium."

"You'd pay for it? Nope, no way. The judge's order says I'm to hang him and bury him. That's all. I just want this over with as quick as possible."

Garcia half-stood, hand going to his six-shooter when the doors slammed open. He relaxed when he saw his deputy in the doorway.

"Sheriff, surely am glad I found you. Paco Fuentes just said he spotted a suspicious fellow nosin' around. A real tall stranger and Ketchum signaled to him out the window of his cell."

"The gallows 'bout built?"

"As ready as it'll ever be, Sheriff," the deputy said. "We need to test the drop. Otherwise, we're all saddled up and ready to ride."

"Send Billy Gilligan to the judge and get a firm date—as quick as possible—to hang Ketchum." The sheriff pushed back from the table and tried to compose himself. He looked down at Dr. Otis and said, "I got official business to tend to. You can stay in town, if you like. Even talk to Dr. Slack, but Tom's gettin' buried right after the hangin'."

"Slack is your town doctor?"

"Undertaker, sawbones, anything else that turns up. Truth is, he's better with horses than humans, but that don't stop him none." With that, Sheriff Garcia left George Otis sipping another shot of whiskey and making his plans.

* * *

"What do you figger he weighs?" Sheriff Garcia poured sand into a burlap bag balanced on the grain scales.

"He's a big one. Maybe two hunnerd?" The deputy pushed back his floppy-brimmed hat and scratched his head.

"Sounds 'bout right," Garcia said, adding more sand until the scales registered two hundred pounds. "Help me get this to the gallows."

The two lawmen hefted the bag of sand and staggered along to the gallows built next to the jailhouse where Ketchum could see the structure and repent for his crimes. They got it to the trapdoor. Garcia fastened a rope to the bag, then stepped back.

"Let's see if it works all proper," the sheriff said. He took the loop of rope off the trigger for the trap and let it open. The structure shuddered as the bag fell four feet and then swung about underneath.

"That's not much of a drop, ain't it, Sheriff?"

"Want this to go smooth and don't want to have nuthin' go wrong," Garcia said, sucking on his lower lip. "I ought to put some soap on the noose so it'll slip over his head easy once I got the hood on him. And maybe yer right 'bout that. We kin lengthen the drop a foot or two. Just enough so's his feet don't hit the ground under the gallows." They worked for another hour, until after sundown, making certain the gallows was ready for the next day.

"It's all legal and proper, Tom," the sheriff told the condemned. "The judge has given the go-ahead for a one o'clock hangin'."

"Just as soon have you do it now, Sheriff," Tom Ketchum said. "The waitin' is worse than the doin'."

"I got to agree," Sheriff Garcia said. "My nerves are killin' me."

Ketchum laughed harshly. "And it's gonna be your noose that kills me. But that don't make us even."

Garcia looked at his prisoner uneasily, nodded once, and left to check the gallows for the tenth time. He stepped into the bright sun and pulled the brim of his Stetson down to shade his eyes. Looking around, he saw most of the businesses in town were closed and the crowd was already gathering around the gallows, although the hanging wasn't for another couple hours.

"Git yer tickets fer the best seats. Git 'em while I got 'em!"

Garcia pushed his way through the crowd and found his deputy taking money and passing out slips of paper with numbers scribbled on them.

"What 'n hell's goin' on?"

"I thought to make a few bucks, Sheriff," his deputy said. "Why not sell front-row seats to the hangin'? This is the biggest thing that's happened in Clayton since . . . since forever."

"What're those?" Garcia pointed to a box of sticks. He pulled one out. A crude doll with a string around its neck was hung from the end.

"Me and Mr. Kincannon are sellin' souvenirs."

Garcia saw the owner of the mercantile going through the crowd with a handful of the gruesome toys, selling them for a dime apiece.

"Hope you get plenty for your enterprisin' nature," Garcia said, shuddering a little. He looked up the steps to where the wind caused the noose to swing fitfully. It wouldn't be much longer before that noose was filled and a dead man swung at the end. Garcia took a deep breath and remembered all that Tom Ketchum had done. The judge had pronounced the verdict, and it was up to the county to carry out the sentence. And Salome Garcia would because it was his duty. It didn't hurt much that he got a ten-dollar bonus for the extra work.

* * *

"It's one o'clock, Tom. Let's go," said Sheriff Garcia.

"About time." Ketchum swallowed hard, then straightened his shoulders and marched out. Garcia followed a pace back, hand on the butt of his six-gun, but Ketchum made no effort to escape. Just outside the jailhouse door stood the deputy with a scattergun. He looked as nervous as Garcia felt. The only one not the least excited or nervous was the condemned. Ketchum walked with a slow, even stride, paused at the base of the gallows, then mounted.

The crowd cheered and jeered as Ketchum allowed the sheriff to fasten a rope around his upper arms and tie his feet together.

"Because you were found guilty of 'felonious assault upon a railway train,' it is my sorry duty to hang you, Thomas Edward Ketchum. You got any last words?" Garcia shuffled his feet nervously as he ran his fingers over the noose he had soaped to make it easier to slip over the condemned's head when he had the black hood on.

Tom Ketchum looked out over the silent crowd, saw the toys and the way the deputy and a couple merchants passed through the crowd selling concessions. He heaved a tired sigh and said, "Hurry up, boys, get this over."

Garcia placed the black hood over Ketchum's head, then pinned it to the front of the man's shirt before sliding the noose down and snugging it tight. He didn't want the hood coming off and Ketchum's death expression giving the crowd more than they had bargained for. The sheriff looked out over the throng. Some waved their dangling effigies of Ketchum and others were rapt. Most attentive of the lot was George Otis, seated in the front row. Garcia wondered if he had bought the seat or wheedled it out of the deputy.

The sheriff stepped back, hefted his hatchet, and without fanfare, swung it to sever the rope holding the trap-door closed. In his nervousness, he twisted the blade slightly and the edge skittered along the rope. Garcia drew back and chopped again. This time he cut the rope.

The trapdoor snapped open. And then came another snap. A more sickening one followed by a gasp from the crowd.

"His head!" someone cried. "It done popped off!"

The sheriff blinked. A photographer worked his magic to capture the scene.

"Get on back. Don't crowd now. Let me see what's wrong."

Salome Garcia hurried down the steps and went around under the gallows where Dr. Slack was already working on the body—the headless body all trussed up and lying on the ground.

"Sweet Mother of God," Garcia muttered. Ketchum's head had come off and lay in its black hood some distance from the body.

"You shouldn't have put soap on the noose," Slack said. "Made the rope like wire. Sliced right through. And the drop? It was way too much. Old Tom here, he don't weigh but one eighty-five, if that."

"We figured for two hundred pounds," Garcia said weakly.

"Don't much matter to Tom now. Help me get him into the back of my wagon."

"Will you say something to the crowd?" Garcia thought they should be told that the beheading was accidental, but didn't have the words. He was still too stunned by the sudden decapitation.

"Reckon I can. What do you want me to say?"

"That it wasn't supposed to happen like this."

Dr. Slack shrugged his bony shoulders and snorted like a hog, then made his way around the gallows and stepped out into the afternoon sun.

"Ladies and gents, the sheriff wants me to relate what went wrong with the execution."

Garcia closed his eyes and tried to push away the faintness welling up inside. He had never heard of a hanged man losing his head like this. When the vertigo passed, the undertaker finished with: "So let's all give the good sheriff a round of applause for the show this afternoon."

Garcia found himself taking a bow and almost enjoying the accolade given him by the townspeople. This passed when the gravity of the situation hit him.

"Get on back to work, all of you," he said. "The doc and me, we got work to do." The crowd slowly dissipated. When everyone was out of earshot, he said to Slack, "Is there anything you can do, Doc? I mean, it's not right to bury a man like that."

"I can sew his head back on, if that's what you want."

"It is."

"Be an extra dollar."

"Done," Garcia said, willing to pony up the money from his own pocket just to have it done.

"There's only one problem," Slack said as he rounded the gallows.

"What's that, Doc?"

"There ain't no head to sew back on."

Sheriff Garcia pushed the undertaker aside. Sure enough, the body lay where it had fallen, but the head wrapped in the black executioner's hood was gone.

Garcia and his deputy looked across the embalming table at Dr. Slack, who worked to get the blood drained from Ketchum's remains—or what remained of them.

"This is the damnedest thing I ever heard tell of," the deputy said. "Who'd want to steal a man's head?"

"I know who," Garcia said, a tight knot in his belly. "That old geezer from Washington. George Otis."

"Why'd he want it?" The deputy scratched his balding head and looked puzzled. Garcia stared at Slack.

"He talk to you, Doc? The old man from back East?"

"Nope, didn't say a word to me, but I know who you mean. That withered, bent-over fella I seen going into the saloon with you earlier on?"

"That's the one. He stole the head. I'm sure of it."

"Did he, Sheriff?"

"What do you mean?" Garcia stared at his deputy. "You know somethin' I don't?"

"I was just thinkin'. . . ."

"Always a danger with someone like you," Slack muttered, but the deputy plowed on.

"If this Otis did take the head, is it stealin'? It's not like property that belonged to somebody. Rob Mr. Kincannon, say, and you stole somethin' that belonged to him. But the head didn't belong to nobody."

"It belonged to Tom," pointed out Garcia.

"I don't think he's going to file a report, Sheriff," Slack said. He dropped a long silver needle into a tray and took tubing from under the table, preparing to pump in embalming fluid. He stopped and looked puzzled. "If I try puttin' this formaldehyde in, it's going to leak out his neck."

"Hold off a spell, Doc," Garcia said. "I've got a thief to bring to justice."

He left the undertaker's parlor and looked up and down the main street. He hadn't expected Otis to be standing there, holding Ketchum's head like Herod with John the Baptist's, but he had hoped. His stride turning into a fast walk just short of outright running, Garcia went to the town livery stables.

"Bart!" the sheriff called. "You in here, Bart?"

The owner's head poked up from a rear stall. He came out with a pitchfork in his hand. He tossed it aside and wiped sweat from his face.

"Gettin' mighty hot in here. Good thing you came along, Sal, so I have an excuse to take a break. What kin I do you for?"

"The man from Washington. George Otis."

"The doctor fella? He said he was a doctor, at any rate, but he didn't look like one. Didn't even have a black bag with him when he came."

"Where is he?"

"He left, maybe twenty minutes back. Same way he came to town. In a buggy." Bart scowled and wiped more sweat. "Funny thing, now that I think on it."

"What's that?"

"He didn't have a black bag when he came, but did when he left."

"Which way was he headed? Toward Santa Fe?"

"More likely to Folsom. Saw him with a railroad schedule."

Sheriff Garcia wasted no time saddling his horse and getting on the trail toward Raton Pass and Folsom, the spot where Black Jack Ketchum had held up three trains in as many years. He rode steadily, and within ten minutes spotted the dust cloud kicked up by Otis's buggy. In twenty, he was standing beside the old man.

"I'll buy it, Sheriff. I'll pay good money," George Otis pleaded. "Twenty dollars. I'll give you a twenty-dollar gold piece!"

"It's not mine to sell or yours to take."

"It's not doing Ketchum any good now. Bury it and science will lose! I'll give you forty! It's all I have."

Garcia reached past the old man and pulled out the black hood. Stains on the bottom showed where Tom Ketchum's blood had spewed forth, but the heavy cloth was otherwise untainted. Garcia could understand how the livery owner mistook it for a doctor's bag.

With some distaste, he pried loose the corners of the hood and peered in. He had seen some terrible things in his day, but never had he seen a man's head come off like this. The skin had stretched and then the slickened rope had cut right through like a knife through sun-warmed butter. Part of Ketchum's spine protruded whitely. Garcia closed the hood up and stepped away from the scientist.

"I ought to run you in, but I won't. I can't figure what to charge you with. You weren't grave-robbing. We got a law about that, but Tom wasn't buried yet. And there's no law against robbing a corpse of money, much less its parts, if you didn't cause the demise."

"This will be the keystone of my collection. It will reveal the terrible criminal nature. Please, Sheriff."

"Don't let me set eyes on you again, Dr. Otis. I'd hate for you to end up like this." Garcia held up the head.

Otis slumped as if he melted in the sun. Then he turned and climbed painfully into his buggy and drove away slowly. Garcia watched him for a minute, then mounted and rode back to Clayton, Ketchum's head precariously balanced on the saddle in front of him. If he hurried, Doc Slack could sew the head back on and they could finish the funeral before sundown.

Sheriff Salome Garcia wasn't a superstitious man, but he didn't want to take any chance of Tom Ketchum's ghost haunting him because there wasn't a head to go along with the corpse in its grave.

To Shoe a Horse

Don Coldsmith

Author's Note: This is a true story, told to me by an old man who was the son of "Ren" and "Cappie." His opening greeting: "You might be interested that my dad shod horses for Jesse James." The names are changed, but are names of actual people in that time period, some from my own family tree.

Ren wakened, not sure why. . . . Some change in the night sounds maybe. He couldn't recall that anything had actually roused him, but something was different, something he couldn't quite peg down. It wasn't the sort of thing such as wakening to go out and empty his bladder. There wasn't any urgency about that as a rule. Maybe he'd do best to just lie still and listen a little while, till he could get a better feel for whatever it was.

He could hear the soft but deep breathing of his wife beside him, and hated to disturb her while he figured on the situation. Carefully, he eased out of the bed and stood up. The three-quarter moon told him that it must be after midnight. Not that it made any difference.

His gun, a .58-caliber Army Springfield muzzle-loader,

hung on a pair of pegs over the door. He couldn't afford better. But he saw no need to take it down yet. Nothing stirred in the barnyard, as far as he could see. Maybe just a possum or a 'coon.

I'd better be gettin' that watchdog, he told himself for the dozenth time this week. What had seemed an ideal location to settle and operate a smithy had not quite worked that way. . . .

1868 . . . The war was over. There had been a time when Ren had wished he could go and fight the Rebs with his three older brothers. That wish was gone now. Samuel, Jr., the oldest, had died in a Confederate prison camp in 1864. William had lost an arm at Gettysburg, but made it home. John had nearly died with a fever in Arkansas, fortunately missing the Battle of Pea Ridge. John was impressed with the West, and his stories intrigued his younger brother, Ren, short for "Lorenzo," when John returned to Ohio and the home place.

There came a day, however, when Sam Heineman the elder, patriarch, called his three surviving sons together. His health was failing, and his wife had passed away from pneumonia a year ago last winter.

"I ain't too long for this world," he observed. "I'll soon join your mama."

"Aw, Father," protested William, but the old man waved him down.

"Lemme talk, Will. Now, the farm here in Ohio has been purty good to us. Fact is, though, it ain't gonna provide for all of you. Now, your sister Peggy will likely marry that Evans kid down the road purty soon, so she'll be taken care of. William, as oldest, you inherit this place. I'm countin' on you to manage it, and John to work it. It should provide for two families."

He didn't mention William's disability, but he paused and turned to Ren.

"Lorenzo," he said thoughtfully. "I feel bad about this. I done my damnedest, but there just ain't no way to make it work for three families. We mighta done better if it weren't for the war, I dunno. But what I'm gettin' to, you're gettin' purty good with the anvil. You do a better job fittin' a hot shoe than the farrier in town. I'm thinkin', was I you, I'd look at some of the free land in the West. John speaks highly of it."

"That's right," agreed John quickly. "I can tell you about it! Arkansas, Missouri, maybe Kansas."

"You been purty friendly with that Roberts girl, Ren," his brother Will teased. "Gonna take her with ya?"

Ren blushed red and studied the floor without answering. Will was nearer to truth than he might have guessed. Capitola Roberts had been a friend almost as long as he could remember. They had gone to school and to church together. Ren liked her boyish ways and her hearty laugh. He had defended her against teasing about her name, borrowed from the heroine of a current novel at the time of her birth. The Robertses were proud of their education. Ren had shortened the girl's name to "Cappie." Her mother did not completely approve, but tolerated the nickname because she approved of young Lorenzo.

As a matter of fact, they had discussed the possibility of moving West. Cappie's father had approached Ren about his intentions, and had promised a gift of a pair of young mules as a dowry. Ren had not shared that information with his own family yet, avoiding the inevitable teasing. But now . . .

That's how it had happened. Ren had been working as an apprentice to the blacksmith, rounding out his skills. The burly giant was impressed with Ren's self-taught ability. But he also remembered how, in his younger days, the boy would hang around the smithy and watch him work. Sometimes he'd even let young Ren pump the bellows. It was a natural progression.

"If you can fit a shoe hot, and do it right," the blacksmith promised, "they'll come from miles around."

It was a tricky process, forging a horseshoe out of bar stock, then reheating it to sear it into place against the carefully shaped hoof, melting the hoof's edges for a perfect fit. Since there was no space for movement at all after the nails were applied, the horse was more comfortable than with a cold-nailed shoe. It would last longer too. The process was spectacular to watch, the puff of white smoke curling out when the hot iron touched the hoof, but completely painless to the animal, half-dozing in the shade. An experienced horse would come to realize that new shoes could mean more comfort.

There had come a day when the master smith pronounced his apprentice ready.

"You been a big help, Ren, but I know you're plannin' to move on. That's okeh." Many were using this Cherokee word for approval. "Where will you be goin'?"

"West, I reckon," answered Ren.

"Wasn't your brother out there in the war?"

"Yes, that was John. He speaks highly of the country."

"Well, you'll do well. You've got the touch. Some of the tools you've made are better'n boughten ones. Better'n mine even. Take any of 'em with you, to get started, if you want."

Ren picked a few favorite tools, shook the callused hand of his mentor, and set out for home.

His father had ordered an anvil and a forge from back East, "to help ya get started." It was a generous gift.

Ren already had a wagon, which he had acquired early. His brothers had laughed at his "piece o' junk," but Ren had rebuilt and restored it over a period of time. It stood on blocks in the barn, ready to move. The wooden wheels were staked down in the creek behind the barn, to swell and tighten the spokes and the rim against the iron tires and the hubs.

It was a small wedding, at the Robertses' home, the grape arbor behind the house decorated with field daisies from the Robertses' pasture.

There was much more sentiment expressed on the Roberts side than among Ren's family. His sister Peggy hugged the bride, and both girls shed emotional tears, presumably of happiness. The bride and groom changed into garments more suitable for travel, and Ren headed the mules West. It was only mid-morning, and he hoped to travel as much as fifteen miles before dark.

The newlyweds had set out for the West. Ren figured they could cover fifteen to twenty miles a day, with something over seven hundred miles to cover. A month and a half maybe.

That had been only his first miscalculation. He had not counted on the weather and the road conditions. It was late May, with good weather, and on some days they did indeed make twenty miles. But that was the exception, not the rule. Sometimes the delay was blamed on muddy roads, or on traffic. Sometimes, just difficult terrain.

In Indianapolis, they paused long enough to inquire about the best routes, and Ren bought a map. Fortunately, his mother had steadfastly insisted that all of her children must learn to read and write.

With the help of the map, it appeared that their most practical route would be almost directly toward St. Louis, avoiding river crossings. An alternative, traveling by water, was deemed too expensive.

They did cross the Mississippi on a ferryboat at St. Louis, and they asked in more detail about the possibilities for a homestead in the West. An outfitter seemed a logical place to inquire.

Not necessarily. The outfitter tried to sell them "everything you'll need," but soon realized that they were traveling on a shoestring. Ren did get an idea that had not occurred to him before. They could head for Jefferson City, state capital of Missouri. The route seemed, on the map, to avoid many areas of rough country and large streams. Besides, it should be possible to inquire there about homestead land.

That leg of the trip went well, but it was now early July, the summer storm season. They lost several days in camp as the sky pumped itself dry. However, Ren could sometimes shoe a horse for a traveler, to add a little to their dwindling finances.

In Jefferson City, he inquired at a land office as to available homestead claims. The clerk chuckled.

"Don't know where you've been, boy. There ain't much not already claimed. Where you from? Ohio? Well, you got some things to learn."

He went on to describe the devastation due to the war, and the bloody events along the border.

"Which border?" asked Ren, somewhat confused. "Arkansas?"

"No, no, son. The *Kansas* border."

He related how the war was in progress long *before* the firing at Fort Sumter. He described the murders and raids by both factions across the two hundred miles of border between Missouri, with Southern sympathies, and "Bloody Kansas," with Yankees moving in "like flies at a picnic."

Ren's heart sank, but the man went on.

"The good part for you may be that a lot of folks lost their homesteads—got starved out or killed. Look at the map here. Here's Fort Scott, on the Kansas side. And a hunnerd an' some miles north, past Kansas City, Fort

Leavenworth. In between and on south runs the old
Military Road, clear on down to Fort Smith, in Arkansas.
There's a lot of folks had to pull out along that border,
especially around Fort Scott. I'd bet you could buy out
some of those claims. Let me give you a name of a land-
office man in Nevada."

"Nevada?"

Ren was confused.

"Nevada, Missouri, not the state! It's a little town east
of Fort Scott. You can ask this friend o' mine about it.
He'll help you."

And that's how it came about. It was much as the man
had described in Jefferson City. The whole area had suf-
fered. Many of the menfolks had been killed, on both
sides, and others had given up in despair. The Kansas
side of the border had now filled up with Yankees, the
Nevada land-office man explained. His sympathies were
thinly concealed, but the war was over, and he had his
job to do. His advice was much like that in Jefferson City.

The first choice of Ren and Cappie might have been on
the Kansas side, but, as the agent said, little was available.

"There is this one place on this side of the border." He
pointed to the map. "About here. 'Bout halfway between
two towns, and that ain't all bad. You could haul produce
either direction."

"I'll be mostly smithin', I reckon," Ren explained.

"Well, that ain't all bad either! Draw business from
both ways. A smith, eh?"

"Yes, sir. But won't both towns *have* a smith?"

"Don't know. But if you're any good at it, you'll *draw*
business. Lots of folks with horses and mules to be shod
comin' in."

"I . . . uh . . . don't have much money to start with."

"Figgered that. But I saw your wagon out there, and I
also figger you're a hard worker. Somethin' can be
worked out."

The place wasn't in bad shape, but neglected. No one had lived in it for several years. It had been homesteaded, the agent explained, some years before, by "folks from back East." Obviously, abolitionists. They had been virtually forced out. On one corner of the small house, there was a blackened spot. The agent saw Ren studying the scorched logs, and spoke hurriedly. Someone had tried to *burn* this cabin.

"Now, pay no mind to that! War's over, right? Heh, heh!"

"It is as far as I'm concerned, " Ren assured him. "but is this gonna be a problem? Why did these folks leave?"

"There was some trouble, yes. Some of the boys got sorta out of hand, I guess. More or less scared 'em out. But that's behind us, friend. Want to go into town and meet some folks? That's what I'd suggest."

They did so, and found a friendly atmosphere.

"A blacksmith? We sure could use one!"

As the agent had said, there were two towns in the area, each a half day's travel from the homestead. The location of a farm was important, because it must be possible to travel to town and *back* before nightfall to sell produce of any kind. In prairie country, this was obvious in the spacing of townsites.

"Actually, you've got three towns within travelin' distance," pointed out the agent. "Horton, Richards, and Statesbury. And it's only a day's travel from the fort. Fort Scott, that is. You'd likely have business from all directions!"

It had seemed too good to turn down.

In reality business was a little slower than that. He would have to prove himself, and the only way to do that was to *do* some work that would prove his skill.

Gradually, word seemed to get around. A rider would come past with a shoe coming loose after an obviously long and tough ride, and be grateful to find a skilled farrier.

"Glad to see you here! I'll tell some folks."

Everyone in the area knew, of course, that Ren and Cappie were Yankees. Whenever the subject came up, Ren's comment was the same:

"Hey, the war's over!"

People seemed to accept this, and it helped. Cappie was lonely, he was sure. The nearest family was nearly two miles away. But they were young and in love, and together, and made the most of it.

They went to town sometimes, in the wagon. They made friends in the stores, which helped Ren's business, and it began to look more promising. Ren was developing a reputation for his skill.

It was in town that they heard about the bank robberies. Some brothers, who had lost virtually everything in the war, had taken to robbing banks, and sometimes even trains. They had been joined by others with similar losses, and now had quite a reputation. The "James boys," they were called by folks in town, who often showed mixed feelings.

"Them boys shouldn't be doin' this," someone would say. "They'll get in trouble."

"Yeah, but look at what the war done to them!"

It was easy to see both sides of the situation, but to have such things happening in nearby locations was a nervous proposition.

It was just about that time that Cappie shared some startling news with him.

"Ren, I think we're going to have a baby."

"Maybe we should move to town," Ren suggested somewhat frantically.

Cappie laughed at him.

"We don't have much worth stealing," she pointed out. "We're happy here. Besides, you're getting started pretty well."

He was uneasy about it, but had to agree that they

were happy here. Cappie's observation that they were hardly a target for bank robbers was surely true.

There were even stories of the "James Gang" giving some of the stolen bank money to families who were down on their luck, impoverished by the war. There are two sides to everything, Ren thought.

His thoughts were not that philosophical as he lay awake on this night, straining to hear anything other than the night sounds. Maybe he had just been dreaming.

But no. There it was. The soft rattle and squeak of saddle leather and the sounds of hooves on the dirt of the road. He rose quietly and tiptoed toward the window.

"What is it?" said Cappie, wakening suddenly.

"Sshh—don't know yet. Jest be still."

In the moonlight, it now appeared that the space between the house and the barn was full of mounted men. He could hear the rattle of bridle chains and the jingle of a spur.

Quickly, Ren pulled on trousers and a shirt and opened the door, slowly and carefully, keeping his hands in sight. A dark figure was walking toward the door, and stopped a few steps away.

"You the horseshoer?" the man asked.

"Guess so," said Ren.

"Good. We need you to shoe a horse."

Ren's first inclination was to tell them to come back in the morning, but that thought did not last long. A couple of miles from town, from any other people, the yard full of armed and mounted riders who needed a horse shod. What was the logical, maybe the only, thing to do?

"Let me get a lantern," said Ren. "I'll fire up the forge."

The men were dismounting, stretching tired muscles and talking softly among themselves.

Ren quickly explained to Cappie that he needed to

shoe a horse. He brought out the coal-oil lantern and led the way toward the barn.

"Heard you're pretty good at fittin' a shoe hot," said the man who appeared to be the leader.

"I can do it any way you want," said Ren. "Hot shoe?"

"Yep, let's see."

The feet were in bad shape, long overdue for a trim of overgrown hoofs.

"I'll go ahead with the trim," Ren suggested, "and somebody can work the bellows to get the forge heated."

"I'll do it," said the leader, stepping around to take the handle.

Ren could not avoid glancing at the man's face as they positioned the lantern on a bench. The eyes were a striking color, a bright blue, which seemed out of place with his darker hair. What was it he had heard about eyes like that? He hadn't been paying much attention at the time. None of his concern. Now, it was. The description he had heard fit this man exactly. Jesse James!

There were only five in all, counting the leader. Ren tried not to stare. He didn't want to appear to be looking too hard. He had heard that sometimes desperadoes kill potential witnesses.

"Who else is in the house?" asked the leader suddenly.

A cold chill washed over the back of Ren's neck.

"My wife. Please don't hurt her. She's carryin' our baby."

A snort of contempt from the leader was followed by his next remark: "We don't make war on women, son. She ain't gonna do nothin' dumb, is she?"

"I don't think so." *I hope not,* Ren breathed to himself.

The other men, four in number, lounged around the barn, resting while they could. They didn't talk much, but he heard the name "Frank" a time or two, and once, somebody referred to "Cole." Ren tried not to listen. He did not want to know any more about these men than was absolutely necessary.

He worked steadily, and from time to time reheated and bent a shoe to fit better. He was glad that, while he'd waited for some business to occur, he had managed to shape some shoes from bar stock. In this way, much of the forging was already done.

It was still dark, only a graying yellow in the predawn eastern sky, when he finished fitting the last shoe.

"There you are," he said to the leader as he laid the hammer on the anvil.

The blue-eyed man stooped to lift each foot, examined each shoe, and straightened.

"Good job," he stated.

He reached into a pocket, drew out a few coins, and poked with a finger of his other hand, selecting a couple.

"Here," he said. "We'll be back!"

He dropped the coins into Ren's palm, tightened the cinch on the newly shod horse, and stepped up and into the saddle.

Ren stared at the freshly minted gold pieces.

"Wait," he said. "This is too much. You've overpaid me!"

It was at least twice the usual fee.

"Naw, I haven't. Like I said, you done a good job, and *we'll be back.*"

The following day, a lone rider turned off the road and tied his mount to the hitch rail at the barn. Ren put down his hammer and stepped to meet the stranger. The newcomer removed his Stetson, and pounded trail dust from his trousers with the hat.

"Howdy," he said, replacing the headgear.

He wore a silver badge on his shirt pocket. Ren couldn't exactly read the lettering on it. It might have been a sheriff's badge, or a U.S. marshal's. The newcomer didn't bother to introduce himself, but started to ask questions.

"I'm trackin' the James Gang," he said bluntly. "They've been robbin' banks and trains, killin' folks in these parts, an' headed this way. You seen 'em, you better tell me."

Ren was somewhat taken aback by the lawman's approach. He tried to think how to handle this, but the man wasn't finished.

"You're new here?"

It wasn't really a question, but a demand for information.

"Yep," admitted Ren, "not quite a year now."

"Where you from?"

"Ohio."

"Good! I'm sick of havin' people help 'em get away. Damn Rebs stick together. You're a Yank. But if they've been here, you damn well better tell me about it!"

Ren wavered. He'd been getting along well with the locals, knowing that most of them had Southern sympathies. It simply wasn't a common topic of conversation. Some of his best customers had fought for "States' Rights."

Back in Ohio, everybody had assumed that the war was about slavery. Out here, few people he'd met had ever owned a slave. It hadn't been practical, he'd been told, to feed and clothe a slave all year so he could harvest crops for a couple of weeks. To these folks, it was whether the Union had the right to tell the individual states what to do.

Two sides to everything . . .

He had to say something, pretty quick. This lawman, by his talk, was probably not a local sheriff. The man was traveling in pursuit of outlaws; apparently a marshal.

Ren found that he resented the man, but he wanted no trouble, and he'd not be able to lie about it.

From the corner of his eye, he saw Cappie watching, trusting him to do what was best. He took a deep breath.

"Marshal," he said firmly, "I can't help you. There was a couple of fellas, strangers, stopped by a day or two ago. One man asked me to shoe his horse. Didn't say his name. I shod his horse, and he paid me. Said he'd be back. Don't seem likely he's your man, though. Nice fellas."

Cappie, listening at the window, smiled to herself.

For the next few years, it was not unusual to have a knock on the door after dark, and the simple request:

"Need you to shoe a horse."

The stranger never gave any names, and Ren never asked. The war was over.

Dancing Silver

Ken Hodgson

Down in the big cities of Fairplay and Alma, most folks consider me to be crazy. They are all full of crap as the bottom of a year-old bird's nest.

I may be the last resident of Buckskin Joe, Colorado, a ghost town nestled in a rugged canyon high in the Rocky Mountains where each winter lasts until the next one begins, but I have a mighty good reason for staying put. A reason most men should understand fully; I'm waiting on a woman.

Now, before you start thinking I'm touched in the head like those other idiots do, I reckon I ought to go back to when all of this waiting started and do some explaining. I'm going to tell you the facts of the matter about Silver Heels too. A lot of her story has become so bogged in legend that it doesn't even spook the truth of what really happened here over thirty-eight years ago.

My name is Ben Childress and I was a mere lad of twenty-five when I followed the big gold rush west to Colorado Territory. It was in the summer of 1860 that I happened to be in a prospecting party with MacKenzie Phillips when we struck pay dirt here on Buckskin Creek.

Back in those days, news of a gold strike brought a passel of folks in a big hurry. Before the frosts of autumn painted the aspen leaves brilliant hues of yellow and red, a town had sprouted.

Joe Higgenbottom, a beanpole-thin man with a braided beard who wore only buckskins, gave the town its name when he opened the first business. Naturally, the place was called Buckskin Joe's Saloon. The bar was only whipsawed lumber setting on barrels. There were no glasses, everyone took a swig from a tin cup as it was passed around. There was no money either. Joe got to grab a three-fingered pinch of gold dust from our poke for each drink. Since he had bony fingers, most of us figured we were getting off cheap. We all had lots of gold, but whiskey was a precious commodity.

I had lucked onto a rich claim that had both lode and placer gold, so I felt to be in tall cotton for a poor farm boy from Georgia. The War Between the States had begun, which cut off communication with my family. I decided the best thing I could do to help them out was to stockpile gold. No matter which side won, money would be a necessity. This gave me cause to stay here and observe the birth of the boomtown called Buckskin Joe.

"I'm gonna hit it big this time, I can feel it in my bones," Horace Tabor said to me over a drink late that winter. Augusta, Tabor's wife, ran a grocery store they'd managed to put up in spite of snow that reached to the eaves of the only two-story building in town, the Angel's Roost Dance Hall. Horace fancied himself a prospector. By allowing his wife to take care of business, he found time to visit saloons and keep up with important stuff, like where strikes were being made.

"The first thing you'll need to do is venture out of town," I replied with a grin. I genuinely liked Horace Tabor, and didn't blame him for being away from that wife of his once in a while. Augusta had a voice that reminded me of a wagon axle in need of grease. "Darn few strikes being made here in Joe's saloon."

"A man can't look for gold through ten feet of snow." Tabor sipped his whiskey. "I'm putting together a list of where the best places to prospect are. This'll save time later on."

"Phillips has the mother lode staked out. That mine of his is rich enough to make this town into the territorial capital."

Tabor stroked his bushy brown mustache, a dreamy look on his face. "No, Ben, MacKenzie's hit a rich one all right, but I'm going to strike a mine that'll make his look like a piker."

"I hope you do, Horace, I really do." I lit a cigar and looked out the front window at perfect whiteness studded with drab, unpainted wood buildings. "Higgenbottom claims there's over two thousand people living up here these days."

"Likely more than that. Augusta tells me we're running a passel of tabs at our store alone. The only thing keeping us from selling more groceries is bad weather slowing down the freight wagons."

I puffed away at my cigar, only half-listening to Horace Tabor rant on about becoming wealthy. My mind had drifted back to Georgia and peach-blossom memories of Caroline Ames, a girl I once loved, who was now married to a captain in the Army of the Confederacy. I had plenty of money from my mine and couldn't understand Horace's desire for riches. What he had that I did not was a wife, a helpmate with whom to share life's triumphs and tribulations.

Even though Augusta had rougher edges than a bucksaw, I could tell from the look in her eyes that she loved Horace in spite of his faults. To my way of thinking, Tabor was already richer than me by far. I had found the gold I longed for, only to lose the girl of my dreams.

"You're staring out that window looking sadder than if your dog had died," Tabor said, shaking me from my reverie. "And you don't own a dog. Why don't you tell me what's got you in a funk? If it's not woman trouble, I'll eat my hat."

"Reckon your hat's safe," I replied without turning my gaze. "Coming West has cost me my love."

"Is that all?" Horace said with a dismissive shrug. "A dollar spent over in Lou's will cure that problem right up."

I turned to my untouched whiskey. "And Doc Walker will charge five dollars to cure what Lou'll give me. I'd prefer to suffer with only my feelings being distressed."

Tabor cocked an eyebrow. "I can see your point, but you still look sorrier than a starving hound. Why don't you mosey over to the Angel's Roost Dance Hall this evening and shuffle a pretty little lady around for a spell? Sam Castle, who owns the place, don't allow his girls to do more than step on your toes."

"The last time I was there, every gal at the Angel's Roost would cause a grizzly bear to run away yelping from pure fright. Ugly is stacked terrible deep over there."

"You need to get out more, Ben," Tabor said with a smirk. "Sam's got a real pretty new girl, just came in this morning on Lewis and DeAlby's stage. Kitty Clyde's her name. She dropped by our store and bought some necessaries. Augusta wouldn't let me wait on her, for some reason."

"That's because she's got good sense," I replied after downing my shot of bourbon. "But I will drop by the Angel's Roost later on and check out your taste in women."

* * *

Two wagon wheels dangling from the ceiling of the Angel's Roost Dance Hall each held a dozen coal-oil lamps that bathed the interior with wavering yellow light. In the center of the room stood a huge potbelly stove that Sam had built a wood fence around to keep the more energetic or inebriated patrons from scorching themselves. Benches and tables were along three sides, leaving room for a bar across the rear. Smoke from cigars, pipes, and lanterns hung heavy in stale air.

A man known as Big Henry was pounding on an out-of-tune piano while Frenchy blew on some sort of brass horn, squawking away in a futile attempt to keep the few couples on the floor dancing a schottische in time with the music.

I blinked my eyes to focus in the wan light, and began making my way around to the bar, where I would purchase a whiskey along with a few dance cards. That was how it was done in those days. A man gave a card to the lady, who turned them in at the end of the night for pay tally.

Then I stopped dead in my tracks when I caught my first glimpse of Kitty Clyde. Angels normally stay in heaven, but not always. My heart skipped beats as I watched a lithe blonde with ruby lips twirl by, leaving the memorable aroma of spring lilacs in her wake. I know a man must have been dancing with her, but the presence of celestial beauty had rendered him invisible. Kitty had high cheekbones, crowned with a delightful spray of freckles. Her eyes were blue as God's pure sky. My legs felt rubbery when she gave me a wink before spinning away, graceful as a hummingbird.

"She *is* a purty one," Sam Castle said as I approached the bar. "That little gal gets an entire dollar for a dance. I've been hoping for a cute one, helps my business a lot."

"Yeah," I said once I'd found my voice. "A lady like her in a place like this is rare as hen's teeth." I tossed a double eagle to ring on the bar, which brought a smile to Sam's white-bearded face. "Give me ten of those dollar dance cards and a whiskey, the good stuff you keep back for yourself. I'll be spending time here and don't want to burn a hole in my gut."

Sam grabbed up the coin, then poured me a shot of Old Pepper bourbon, which was a vast improvement over his usual rotgut. I was so enamored with Kitty Clyde, I didn't yell when he charged me four bits for the drink and gave my change in shinplasters. I planned on handing it back soon enough anyway.

It took over an hour before I could hold the beautiful lady in my arms. So many men had heard about Kitty Clyde that Sam was forced to draw numbers from a hat to forestall gunplay.

Finally, it came my turn. Kitty demurely thanked me for choosing to dance with her while gathering me close to her alluring form. Never before had I spent time with a goddess. I was thankful to my father, a true Southern gentleman, for insisting I learn the social graces. Our brief dance was a waltz, and I could tell by her smile that Kitty was delighted with my proficiency.

"You're a surprise," Kitty said when the music stopped. "I didn't expect to find a gentleman who is a great waltzer out here on the frontier."

"Thank you, ma'am," I said. Before I could say another word, some burly galoot had swept her away for a polka.

I did not get an opportunity to dance again with the lovely Kitty Clyde that night, even though I hung around until nearly three in the morning. Word of another gold strike would not have traveled so far and fast as did news of this beautiful girl's appearance.

Sam informed me later that many men working at distant mines such as the London, Horseshoe, and Crusader had quit their jobs just to come and hold Kitty in their arms, no matter how briefly.

The lovely girl with sparkling blue eyes and infectious smile entranced all men who gazed upon her countenance. I was certainly no exception. The Angel's Roost became my second home where I awaited, along with every other man in the packed house, a few brief moments of bliss, embracing a goddess who had ventured to this crude and remote mountain town to give solace.

Then came a suggestion from my friend Horace Tabor. "You're going to have to do something special to catch her attention, Ben. All women love getting presents, but in this case, it'll take something really grand."

I knew he spoke the truth, but I had no idea what to buy for the lovely Kitty Clyde. Later, on a warm spring afternoon that set snowdrifts to melting while causing creeks to rise, after assuring myself Horace was in Joe's saloon checking out strikes, I hiked the short distance to the log grocery store and asked Augusta Tabor's advice.

"All girls love getting an unexpected present that was meant only for them," Augusta said with the enthusiasm of a natural matchmaker. "And I have just the thing." She dashed behind a canvas that separated their storeroom and living quarters from the counter area, returning with a dainty pair of high-top black leather button shoes. "I'm betting these are just her size too."

At what I assume was my doubtful look, Augusta continued. "Now Mr. Childress, there is a tinker working out of a wagon two buildings down. His name is Dobbs and he does excellent metalwork. Have him fashion some solid sliver heels for these shoes and they will ring like church bells when your lady dances. I assure you, she will love you for being so thoughtful."

The fancy of angelic Kitty admixed with church bells caused gooseflesh to play along my arms. I quickly signed my name to a tab, then rushed to find Dobbs.

"This thing you ask will take a lot of time," the tinker said, squinting at the pair of shoes through thick glasses. "A very long time, a lot of work."

I knew where Dobbs was going with his complaining, so

I headed him off. "I'll pay you twenty dollars in gold and furnish the liberty dollars for you to melt down if you'll have them ready in two days. After that, I'll pay ten dollars."

The old fellow frowned. "I reckon if'n I work all night, I can have 'em done by then. Hand over the silvers, sonny, so I can get started." He extended a callused hand. "I swan, you young whippersnappers just don't have no patience these days. Now when I was your age—"

"I'll be back to pick them up day after tomorrow," I said, filling his hand with silver. "Make sure those heels are solid and pretty. They're for a mighty sweet girl."

"They're all sweet, until ya marry 'em," Dobbs said as I departed. "Then you're in fer it, sonny."

I paid him no mind; any man smitten by love would have done the same. The old tinker had obviously long forgotten the compelling siren song a beautiful lady can play on a young man's heartstrings.

"Why Mr. Childress," Kitty said happily while slipping on those beautiful new shoes with glistening silver heels. "They fit perfect and are *so* pretty. Please accept the next three dances with me as a small token of my appreciation."

"I would surely like that," I answered. "And I'd like it a lot more if you'd call me Ben."

"Ben is a wonderful name," she cooed. "I'll be honored to address you by your first name." Kitty smiled upon her new shoes. "And thanks to your kindness, from now on I wish to be called 'Silver Heels,' since no other girl has such fine dancing shoes as you have given me."

I studied the scowling faces that surrounded me, and grew grateful that Sam Castle had banned guns after a disgruntled miner from Oro City had shot his pardner in the foot to keep him from dancing.

"*Silver Heels,* that is a grand name for such a comely lady as you," I said, placing a hand on her trim waist.

Big Henry began pounding on the ivories. Silver Heels gave me a look that spoke silent promises of future bliss, slid a soft alabaster hand into mine, and off we danced for the first of three lilac-imbued waltzes that I'd bribed the band to play so I could hold my love close.

Later that night, as I walked to my cabin by the tawny light of a full moon, I paid scant attention to a small herd of sheep being driven into town for slaughter. Little did I know that the very devil himself had come to Buckskin Joe, Colorado, that cold and starry night.

Old Dobbs, the tinker who had fabricated Kitty's silver heels that pealed so delightfully on the worn plank floor of the Angel's Roost, was the first to die of smallpox.

Far too late, we were to discover that the two herders I had seen driving that flock of sheep had spread pestilence among us. Many recalled they were coughing badly when they drank at Joe's saloon and ate breakfast at Link's restaurant. At the time, this was no great cause for alarm since colds in the high country are common as snow. Soon, however, after the sheep drovers had hacked their way out of town and into oblivion, their legacy of death and disfigurement began.

When Dobbs became ill, running a fever and wheezing badly, Doc Walker was called to attend him. It was then that the telltale rash was discovered, along with the terrible realization that we had an epidemic on our hands.

Europe had been devastated many times by dread smallpox. Entire Indian tribes had been wiped out by it. Now this insidious, easily transmitted disease that often left a legacy of deeply pitted scars on those it did not kill had come to our mountain hamlet.

The evening that Dobbs died, an exodus of the frightened—or wise—had begun. Furman Jones, the undertaker, refused to handle Dobbs's body. "Drag him outta town somewheres an' burn him," the gawky, drunken scalawag said, holding a handkerchief to his face. "The ground's froze too hard to dig a grave,"

It was ironic that Jones became the next to become infected. He wheezed his way into the next world around noon of the succeeding day. The undertaker was correct about the ground being frozen hard enough to require blasting, but Doc set some miners to the task.

"Burying the bodies quick will help to stop the spread of smallpox," Doc Walker insisted. To a man, we agreed to do whatever was humanly possible to stem the spread of this horrible disease.

"I sent Augusta to stay in Denver until this is over," Tabor told me over coffee. "Smallpox will strike women and children same as a man. I'm not taking any chances with my wife."

This statement confirmed my belief that Horace loved Augusta, in spite of his constant ogling of every female he came across.

Silver Heels. The thought of her becoming infected stuck me like a bullet to the heart. I had money aplenty from my gold mine, I could well afford to send my love to safety as Tabor had done.

"Are you okay?" Tabor asked seriously. "You look like you've seen a ghost."

"I've decided to send Silver Heels to Denver, like you did Augusta," I said, standing to leave. "I just wish I'd thought of it sooner."

"That's right nice of you. . . ." Horace's words trailed off as I fairly ran to Kitty Clyde.

I found my lovely lady stirring a cast-iron pot that sat on top of the stove in the deserted parlor of the Angel's Roost.

"Hello, Ben," she said. "I'm glad to see you haven't taken ill."

"You are my concern, Kitty. You should pack up your belongings and leave here. I will pay for everything, but please hurry. The stage leaves in less than an hour. Once word gets around there's smallpox in Buckskin Joe, I expect the line will shut down until it's over."

Silver Heels's golden tresses swirled like a swarm of fireflies when she shook her head. "I can't leave here. Sam Castle is in bed stricken with pox, as are a couple of miners. These men need me to care for them. There are several vacant rooms here now that the other girls have gone. I hope with all my heart we won't fill them."

I was so taken aback by her determined demeanor, it took a while to find my voice. "It's not safe for you to remain here," I said feebly.

Silver Heels turned to me, hands on her hips, blue eyes flaring. "What is *not* safe is for me to leave you fellows to care for yourselves. I was raised with six brothers and know firsthand that most men are lucky not to kill themselves with their own cooking. And do any of you know how to apply a mustard plaster or make a camphor asafetida? Of course you don't. All of you wonderful men have been kind to me, far too kind for me to run away when I can be of help. I'll hear no more talk of my leaving."

When a woman gets her mind set on a course of action, it might as well be chiseled on a stone tablet and added to the collection Moses got from the Almighty. My heart was heavy when I realized nothing I could say or do would extricate my sweetheart from the danger of remaining.

"There is something you could do for me, Ben," she asked charmingly.

"Name it," I said.

"Please go fetch Dr. Walker, then drop by Mr. Tabor's store." Kitty reached into a pocket of her apron and brought out a gold eagle. "Purchase a couple of bottles of castor oil along with a jug of New Orleans molasses, some lye soap, iodine"—she hesitated—"and a large bottle of laudanum to help bring on sleep."

I nodded as I waved the back of my hand at the proffered coin. "I'll be right back with what you asked for." I turned and went out, walking in a cold rain to find the doctor. My head began throbbing as if a hammer were beating on it. I ran the errands Silver Heels had asked of me, then went to my cabin and took to bed.

The next two weeks I remember little of, only night-marish sketches of freezing cold alternating with terrible heat. I found out later that Silver Heels had become concerned by my absence and sent some men to check on me. As if in a dream, I recalled her angelic face hovering above while bathing me with the aroma of lilacs.

When my head finally cleared and I found the strength to sit up, Dr. Walker and my friend Horace Tabor came to visit.

"It's about time you quit lollygagging and get back to doing an honest day's work," Tabor said, wearing that sly grin of his.

"I'm surprised you managed to say the word 'work' without choking," I rasped. I then looked to the doctor, who was worriedly stroking his brown Vandyke. "How bad is it?"

"Smallpox epidemics are all terrible to behold. This one, thankfully, seems to have run its course. There's been only one new case in the past few days."

I took a drink of water, then struggled to sit on the side of my bed, which I was told, had been carried, with me in it, to the dance hall.

Horace Tabor placed a steadying hand on my shoulder. "That Silver Heels turned out to be a mighty fine nurse. There was over thirty men brought here for her to care for. I've never set much stock in miracles, but not a single soul she looked after went and died, which is more than I can say for a lot of other good folks hereabouts."

Doc Walker said, "I would sure like to have her for a nurse. That little lady worked day and night, I don't know how she managed. To confound me even more, some of the cures she came up with I'd never heard of before. I can only say that you were lucky to have been brought here. There's been sixty-one die, along with a few that'll be left badly scarred for life."

I blinked matter from my eyes and surveyed the huge room that was now filled with beds. "Where is Silver Heels?" I asked.

Tabor and the doctor exchanged sad glances. After a brief moment, Horace said, "She was the last one to catch the smallpox."

Dr. Walker spoke up, "The crisis has passed—she will pull through, only—"

"Only what?" I said with all the force I could muster.

"The blisters were mainly on her face," the doctor said with sadness. "They were deep and plentiful. I regret to tell you that the scars are terrible to behold—and permanent."

"Silver Heels will always be the most lovely lady in the world to me," I said, feeling a tear trickle down my cheek.

"I'd venture every man in Buckskin Joe feels the same way," Tabor said. "We've all chipped in to try to repay that little lady for what she has done—and for what she's lost. We've raised over five thousand dollars to give her." He forced that sly grin of his to return. "You rest up for a spell. This evening, all of us are going to surprise Silver Heels with the money. I'll come along for you to lean on."

"Thanks, I want to tell her that I love her," was all I could say before the laudanum once again wrapped me in satin darkness.

Even now as I look back upon that time across a deep chasm of years, my heart aches. When we made our way to Kitty Clyde's room, it was vacant. Somehow, my love had found strength enough to pack her belongings and depart. On her neatly made bed sat the pair of dancing shoes with glistening silver heels along with a note, which read:

My beloved friends,

   Please remember me as I once was. I do not wish to become an object of pity. There are many fine doctors in the East. I shall go there to see if my beauty can be restored.

   My heart is gladdened that I was able to help the few I did.

   Tell Ben Childress to take care of my wonderful dancing shoes. I shall return one day to wear them again.

Yours humbly,
Silver Heels

Grizzled miners wept when they read that note, as did I. Dr. Walker eventually made the suggestion that we hire a lawyer to bribe the lawmakers up at the capital to name the towering peak east of town in Kitty's honor.

Surprisingly, the matter was quickly adopted by the legislature. Mt. Silver Heels towers majestically; its snowy crown brushes the abode of God. A more fitting monument I could not envisage, even though no mountain could ever be so large as my love's heart.

At the close of the Civil War, Buckskin Joe died. The mines simply ran out of gold. After that, there was no reason for the place to exist. Within the space of a few weeks, I became the only person in a deserted town to await Kitty's return. I did not mind—the less competition the better.

Horace Tabor went on to fame and misfortune. His story is so well known it does not need repeating by me.

I abandoned my cabin to live in the Angel's Roost Dance Hall, where I reside to this day. Alone, inside that vast empty parlor, memories echo like the spoken word.

Every evening after a cold sun hides its face behind craggy peaks, I build a fire in that great potbelly stove. I then slide a deacon's bench close. The heat feels good on my bones of late. Close by my side are Kitty's shoes.

I sit and watch flames cast ghostly shadows on the walls while I await my love's return. I know she will be back. She said so in the note I hold. Tonight, for certain, or tomorrow night at the latest, Silver Heels will return.

In my mind's eye, I see her coming through the door, bathed in beauty and the sweet aroma of spring lilacs. She runs to me and we melt into each other's arms.

Big Henry begins to play the piano while Frenchy wails on his brass horn. We embrace and dance a waltz just like we did all those many years ago. I once again hear happy laughter and the sonorous peal of dancing silver.

My long vigil is over. I am content.

Bear River Tom
and the Mud Creek Massacre

William W. Johnstone
and J. A. Johnstone

It was a fine summer day in Abilene, in the Year of Our Lord 1870, when I came nigh to losin' a fight for the first time since my days in the prize ring back in New York City.

A few weeks earlier, some of the city fathers come to me and asked me to take the job of city marshal because they knew I was a tough hombre and had wore a lawman's star in a few other places. I accepted, but only after tellin' 'em that the only way I'd take the job was if I had a free hand to carry it out the way I saw fit, without interference from nobody. In them days, Abilene was a mighty wild place, and had been ever since the trail herds had started comin' up from Texas a few years earlier. Sometimes, likkered-up cowboys outnumbered the reg'lar citizens half a dozen to one. So those old boys just looked at me and said, "We don't give a hoot in hell how you do it, Tom, just get it done."

So the first thing I done was to get some signs made up sayin' it was unlawful to carry firearms inside the town limits, and then I put 'em up in the saloons and the whorehouses and other places where the cowboys went, and on the road leadin' into town too. Lord, you never heard such caterwaulin' as when those Texans saw them signs. I thought one or two of 'em was gonna fall down and go to foamin' at the mouth. But after a few of 'em gave me lip about the new rule and I had to crack their heads together for 'em, the rest of the bunch started payin' more attention. Killin's fell off to where there weren't more'n one or two a night. Compared to the way it'd been not long before, Abilene had got plumb peaceful.

Now, my name is Thomas James Smith, but folks has called me Bear River Tom for a long time now, ever since I was the first lawman in a minin' camp called Bear River City, in Wyoming Territory. The people there who prevailed on me to take the job didn't know it, but I'd been a policeman back in New York City, where I was born, after I'd decided that I didn't want to be a prize-fighter no more. I don't mind all that much bein' walloped, but after a while it gets a mite tiresome. My police career didn't end too well, but that's a tragic story and I ain't in the mood to tell it right now. As some fancy perfessor might put it, suffice to say that I left New York and come west, and I been out here ever since and consider myself as much a frontiersman as if I'd been growed here.

Anyway, after a heap of troublesome driftin' around, I lit in Abilene and liked it, and like I said, in the time I'd held the job of city marshal, I'd cleaned up the place considerable. I wore a brace of Colt's revolvers, one on each hip, but I hadn't yet drawed those hoglegs in the line of duty. My malletlike fists were enough to take care of the problems I ran into. I had a big gray stallion called Grizzleheels, and I rode him up and down Front Street when the cowboys were in town, and if any of 'em refused to shuck their guns, I just leaned over and give 'em a good sharp rap on the head. That always made 'em more reasonable about things. Either that or unconscious, in which case they didn't cause no trouble neither.

So there I was, a-standin' on the porch outside the

marshal's office on that fine mornin', lookin' up and down Front Street and thinkin' what a good job I was doin', when a buckboard comes rattlin' along at a high rate of speed, dust boilin' up from its wheels. There was a young woman at the reins, whippin' along a pair of mules hitched to the wagon. The gal seemed so frantic I knew somethin' had to be wrong, so I stepped out into the street and held up a hand for her to stop.

But instead of stoppin', them mules stampeded right at me. I heard the gal yell out in alarm, but she'd lost control of that team and couldn't do anything to stop 'em. I was about to get trompled.

My footwork ain't as fancy as it was during my days in the ring, but I can still move pretty fast when I need to. I needed to then. I jumped back, out of the way of them mules, and reached up to grab the harness of the closest one. Now, I'm a pretty big gent, so when I hauled back on the harness, the mule stumbled. I heaved again and the mule like to fell over. But he stopped and so did his pard. Naturally, the buckboard rocked to a halt too.

"Are you all right?" yelped the gal. "Thank God you were able to get out of the way!"

"I'm fine," I told her, "but you'd ought to do a better job keepin' these jugheads under control."

"I know. I was hurrying because there's trouble— Oh!" Her eyes—which were blue and pretty by the way— had lit on the badge pinned to my shirt. "Are you Marshal Smith?"

I nodded and said, "Bear River Tom, that's me. You say there's trouble?" I was practically salivatin' at the prospect of a fracas, especially if this pretty little gal was gonna be watchin' whilst I dispensed some frontier justice.

"My name is Evie Phelps," said the gal. "My brother Bud and I have a farm south of town on Mud Creek."

I hadn't never heard of Evie Phelps and her brother Bud before, but I nodded like I knew who she was anyway. There were so many folks movin' into these parts that it was mighty nigh impossible to keep up with all of 'em. It struck me, though, that she looked sort of familiar. I reckoned I must've seen her and her brother around town before.

"Go on," I told her.

"A gang of wild cowboys has besieged our farm," said Evie. "They stampeded their cattle through our crops, and I think they wounded Bud. He ran out to try to stop them, and there was shooting . . ." Her voice faltered in a way that was heartbreakin'. When she was able to go on again, she said, "I was already on the buckboard and the team was hitched up because we were coming into town today to buy some supplies. Bud told me to get out of there as fast as I could and to fetch help. Then he drew the fire of those madmen so I could get away. The last I saw of him, he was limping into our soddy, and I don't know how badly he was hurt . . . but I know they're going to try to kill him, Marshal. They'll burn him out, and then they'll shoot him down like a dog."

I didn't blame her for bein' upset, but as tears started to well up in them blue eyes, I said, "Don't you worry, Miss Evie. Things ain't as bad as they seem."

"They're . . . they're not?"

"Nope. Those cowboys'll have a mighty hard time settin' a soddy on fire. About all they can do is burn the grass off the roof. Could get a little smoky, but if your brother's holed up in there, he should be all right. He'll be able to stand 'em off."

"But what if he's badly wounded? What if he's bleeding to death? Can't you help him?"

I scowled. "You say your farm's on Mud Creek? Whereabouts?"

"Two miles south of town."

That was a problem. I was Abilene's city marshal. My jury's diction, or whatever you call it, didn't go past the town limits. But I was also the only law in these parts, so if anybody was gonna help Bud Phelps, looked like it had to be me. I'd just stretch a point a mite. Since Mud Creek ran through Abilene before meanderin' off south, if anybody asked, I'd say that my authority extended on down the creek bed.

Anyway, who the hell was gonna argue such a thing with me and risk gettin' walloped?

"You just wait right there," I told Evie once my mind was made up. "I'll saddle my horse."

"Thank you, Marshal. Thank you so much."

I wanted to tell her to save her thanks until we were sure her brother was still alive, but I didn't risk it for fear she'd go to bawlin'. There'd be enough of that soon enough if ol' Bud had got hisself ventilated fatal-like.

So I went around back of the marshal's office to the shed where I kept Grizzleheels and slapped my saddle on that stallion. Evie Phelps led the way out of town, whippin' those mules into a trot as we headed south.

I couldn't help but glance over at her as we rode along. Even scared and upset like she was, she was pretty as a picture. Her cheeks were rosy and the wind whipped her long yellow hair out behind her head. I ain't the sort of fella what gets carried away rhapsodizin' about feminine enchantments, but if I was, I might've busted into song right about then.

"Did you ever see those cowboys before they attacked your place?" I asked. "Know any of their names?"

She shook her head. "Of course not. Bud and I don't have anything to do with cowboys. Our farm is off the main trail, thank God. We usually see the dust from the herds as they pass by, but that's all."

I thought it might be a good idea to keep her talkin' so's she wouldn't be thinkin' about how her brother might be shot full of holes by now. I asked, "How long have you lived there?"

"About six months," she said. "We came out from Missouri after our folks died and we lost their farm because we couldn't pay the taxes on it. Bud said we could make a go of it homesteading out here."

"How's it been goin'?"

"Fine. We got our first crop in and I think it's going to be a good—" Her voice caught again. "It *would* have been a good one, if those cowboys hadn't stampeded their cattle over it and ruined it."

"Maybe you can salvage some of it," I suggested.

"Not if Bud is dead." She was back to that again. "I don't know what I'll do."

"Now, don't you worry," I told her. "No matter what we find when we get out there, folks in Abilene will give you a hand. You'll be fine, Miss Evie."

I thought she was gonna start sobbin', but she took a couple of deep breaths and settled down some.

I'd been thinkin' on the fact that I'd sort of recognized her there in town, once I got over the excitement of almost bein' trompled by them mules. I sure wished I could recollect where I'd seen her before.

We'd been followin' Mud Creek ever since we left town. It's just a middlin' little stream, no more'n ten feet wide and a couple of feet deep 'cept when it floods, and its banks are lined with cottonwoods. After a while, I saw a little rise ahead of us—there ain't no *big* rises in Kansas—and Evie said, "Our soddy's just on the other side of that hill."

I waved for her to stop the buckboard and said, "Hold on a minute." She hauled back on the reins and brought them mules to a halt, and I reined in old Grizzleheels at the same time. As I leaned forward in the saddle, I listened so hard it brought a frown to my face.

After a minute, Evie asked, "What is it, Marshal?"

"I don't hear no shootin'," I said. "Them cowboys must be gone."

Evie put a hand to her mouth. "Oh, dear Lord," she said. "I hope that doesn't mean they've killed poor Bud!"

Quicklike, I said, "Naw, more'n likely it means they got tired of hoorawin' him and rode on." The wind was out of the south, from the direction of the soddy, so I took a sniff of it. "Don't smell no smoke neither. I'll bet when we get there he's just fine."

"I pray it's so." She lifted the reins. "Do we go ahead?"

"Powder River and let 'er buck." And when she looked at me sort of confused, I waved a hand and said, "Yeah, go ahead."

We moved on toward the farm, goin' a mite slower now than we had on the way out there. When we got to the top of the rise, I saw the dugout in the hillside. Hundreds just like it were scattered over the Kansas countryside. You couldn't get enough lumber from them scrawny cottonwoods along the creek banks to build a reg'lar cabin, and most places there weren't even that many trees. So folks had to dig their homes out of the ground. Some dug up blocks of sod and stacked them to make walls, whilst others hollowed out the side of a hill like Evie and her brother had done. It makes for a pretty sorry habitation, but it beats nothin', I reckon.

I knew somethin' was wrong, but it took me a second or two to realize what it was. Then I reined in and said, "You stay up here, Miss Evie. I'll go look for your brother."

She'd stopped the buckboard at the crest. She looked scared again as she nodded. "Please be careful, Marshal," she said.

"Oh, I intend to," I told her. I clucked my tongue at Grizzleheels and started ridin' down the hill, not gettin' in any hurry. That gave me time to take a long look around the place. I didn't like what I saw.

Or rather, what I *didn't* see. There were no signs of any stampede. Hooves churn up the ground pretty bad, so it's not hard to tell if a bunch of cows have gone runnin' through a place. A few minutes earlier, when I'd been sniffin' for smoke and hadn't smelled any, I'd noticed that there wasn't any dust in the air neither. A stampede raises a hell of a lot of dust, and it takes a while for all of it to settle.

That had made me a mite suspicious, and now the lack of tracks made me even more so. On top of that, I didn't see any crops, trompled or otherwise. Fact of the matter was, even though there had been a farm here at one time, it looked deserted and abandoned now . . . sort of like my heart when I realized that Evie Phelps had been lyin' to me.

But I wanted to find out just what the hell was goin' on here, so I rode down the hill. Sure enough, as I reined in and the sound of Grizzleheels' hoofbeats stopped, a man stepped out of the soddy. He wasn't a farmer, though, and his name wasn't Bud Phelps. It was Axel Skidmore. He owned a saloon and whorehouse in Abilene. We'd had a few run-ins. He didn't like the fact that I'd sort of tamed Abilene down. Sure, it cost money to repair the damages when a bunch of Texas cowboys shot up the place, but those Texans spent a whole heap more than they cost. The reg'lar citizens appreciated what I'd done, but not so much Skidmore and his ilk. They were afraid I'd run off too much of their trade before I was through.

"Skidmore," I said with a curt nod. "You're outta your bailiwick."

"I could say the same thing about you, Marshal," he answered me. "That badge you're wearing doesn't mean a thing outside of Abilene."

"What's goin' on here?" I jerked a thumb over my shoulder toward the rise where Evie still sat in the buckboard. "Why'd that whore of yours decoy me out here?"

"You know who she is, eh?"

"Yeah, I knew as soon as she drove into town this mornin' that I'd seen her somewhere before. Took me a while, though, to recollect that I saw her get off the train a few days ago, all dressed up and wearin' a hat with a feather in it. *You* met her at the station. That right there was enough to tell me what sort of gal she really is."

"Is that so?"

"Damn right. You can wash the paint off her face and put her in a farm dress, but she's still a calico cat. She still purrs . . . for a price."

Skidmore grunted. "I didn't think you'd seen her when she came into town. My mistake."

Truth to tell, I hadn't figured out who Evie really was until I seen Skidmore step out of that soddy. That was when I put it all together, even though I was lettin' him think that I'd known all along this was some sort of trick. When you're dealin' with a slick hombre like that, you grab whatever advantage you can get your paws on.

"You still ain't told me what this is all about."

"It's simple, really, Marshal. You need to ease up on enforcing the law in Abilene. If you keep making it too tough on those drovers, they'll take their herds somewhere else. That would ruin not only my business but a lot of others."

"You know good and well it's gonna come to that anyway, once the railroad lays tracks farther west," I told him. "There'll be some new cow town closer and easier for those Texans to get to."

"When that happens, I'll move too, I suppose. But it hasn't happened yet, and for now, I have a lot of money invested here. I won't have you ruining things, Smith." He got a crafty look on his face. "Cooperate with me and you might start making a little more money than what the town pays you. But if you won't be reasonable, you'll regret it."

I shook my head. "I ain't a crook, Skidmore. I ain't scared of you neither."

"You're sure?"

"Certain sure."

He nodded slowly, and then motioned with his hand. I wasn't surprised when more fellas started comin' out of that dugout. There were four of 'em, and they were all big as life and twice as ugly. I recognized 'em from town. They worked for Skidmore. A couple tended bar in the saloon, whilst the other two kept order in the whorehouse.

"Boys," Skidmore said, "convince the marshal it would be wise to join forces with us."

"Ain't never gonna happen," I said as I stiffened in the saddle.

"Well, then, in that case . . . kill him."

The order didn't surprise me. Skidmore was a ruthless man, and I had a hunch he was responsible for more than one killin' in Abilene. As the varmints who worked for him started forward, I saw that none of 'em were packin' iron. They prob'ly figured on beatin' me to death. Even though it went against the grain for me to use my guns, I reached for 'em at that moment, knowin' that no matter how rough those gents were, they'd back down in the face of a pair of hoglegs.

Before I could touch the gun butts, a shot blasted. I heard the wind-rip of the bullet past my head, and instinctively hunched over in the saddle. I swiveled my head around and seen Evie sittin' on that buckboard seat with a rifle in her hands. It must've been covered up in the back of the wagon.

"Touch your guns and Evie will shoot you," Skidmore said calmly as he took a cigar out of his vest pocket. "You've got a beating coming to you for being such a stubborn jackass, Smith." His teeth clamped down angrily on the cheroot. "The way you strut around Abilene thinking that you're tougher than everybody else . . . it makes me sick. You're about to get your comeuppance. Take him, boys!"

The bruisers lunged at me. I hauled back on the reins

and Grizzleheels reared up, lashin' out at 'em with his hooves. That made 'em fall back for a second, and as the stallion came down, I tried to wheel him around so's I could gallop out of that trap. A couple of the varmints grabbed hold of me, though, and jerked me out of the saddle. I hit the ground so hard it knocked the breath plumb out of me.

I got my second wind in a hurry, though. I knew if I didn't get up, those bastards'd stomp me to death. I rolled over and come up on my knees. A kick grazed my ribs, but didn't do no damage to speak of. I grabbed the foot of the fella what kicked me whilst it was still up in the air and dumped him on his back. Then I came up sluggin'.

Let me tell you, there's somethin' about a good fight that gets my blood to percolatin'. Way down deep in the heart of every man, even the so-called civilized ones, there's a little bit of savage. If you go far enough back, we all come from barbarians, and in the midst of a fight, when your heart goes to pumpin' a mile a minute and your breath hisses hot and fast betwixt your teeth and your eyes get this sort of red haze in front of 'em . . . that's when the old barbarian in us all rises up and commences to smite his enemies. He has a damn fine time doin' it too.

Which explains why I was laughin' as them sons of bitches pounded on me and I waled away right back at 'em. Them malletlike fists of mine shot out to right and left, in front of me and behind me and all around, as I shrugged off the punches landin' on me and gave as good or better'n I got. Blood run in my eyes from the cuts on my forehead; my lips swelled where a fist landed on 'em. Bruises were already formin' all over me from the fists that thudded into my body. I didn't care. One by one, I knocked them bastards down, and when they got up, one by one, I knocked 'em down again. It took a few times, but eventually they stayed on the ground, moanin' and twitchin'. If I looked worse'n they did, I must've been a sorry sight, because they looked plumb whipped.

Then I turned to Skidmore and saw that his eyes were big and scared. He started backing toward the dugout.

"That's right," I said. "You better run and hide, you whelp. You better hunt a hole like the snake you are."

He didn't turn and run, though. He yanked a little pistol out from under his coat instead.

I got my hand on the gun and twisted it aside just as he pulled the trigger. The gun went off with a wicked little pop. My blood was surgin' so much, I didn't even notice until later that he'd shot away a teensy piece of the web betwixt my left thumb and forefinger. I twisted and heard bones crack and Skidmore screamed as he dropped the gun. Then he looked past me and screeched, "Shoot him! For God's sake, shoot him!"

I glanced back, havin' forgotten about Evie and her rifle until then. But I seen her toss the rifle down and grab the reins, and she turned that buckboard around a hurry and whipped up the mules. All of 'em vanished over the top of the rise.

I grinned at Skidmore and said, "Looks like she don't work for you no more."

Then I picked him up, carried him over to Mud Creek, and dunked him in the water until he was half drownded. I finally hauled him out, flung him on the bank, and watched him spit and sputter for a second before I put a boot on his throat and watched his face turn purple.

"I got a feelin' you wasn't in this all by your lonesome," I told him. "I'd be willin' to bet some of the other lowlifes in Abilene put you up to it. I ain't gonna kill you, though maybe I ought to. I'm gonna let you live so's you can go back to town and tell all the other skunks and snakes and varmints that you can't buy off Bear River Tom Smith, and you can't scare him off neither." I eased off a mite with my boot so Skidmore could get a little air down his gullet. Then I bore down again and said, "The only way you can get rid of me is to kill me, and you don't want to do that, Skidmore. You know why?"

He didn't answer. Of course, he couldn't, with my boot on his throat like that. So I answered for him.

"The reason you don't want to kill me is because some other fella will just come along to take my place who's even tougher. Your kind may not realize it yet, but that's the way it is out here in the West. Folks will put up with crooks and cheats and connivers for so long a time, but sooner or later, they rise up and put a stop to such shenanigans. There's more honest, decent folks than there are the likes of you, and that's why you can't never win unless the good people get so lazy they *let* you win. That ain't never gonna happen, leastways not in our lifetime, Lord willin'. So you can go back to Abilene and behave yourself, or you can get the hell out. Your choice." I bore down a little harder with my boot. "Just don't ever look crossways at me again, 'cause if you do, I'll kill you. Write it down in the book."

Then I let him breathe again. The other fellas I had walloped on were tryin' to crawl away. I hurried 'em along with a few well-placed kicks, then caught my horse and swung up into the saddle. I was startin' to hurt now, but I didn't care. I'd done a good day's work and it wasn't even noon yet.

That work weren't over, I reminded myself. I intended to have a cautionary word with Miss Evie Phelps too, if that was her real name. She sure as hell didn't have no brother Bud; I knew that now.

But when I got to Abilene, Evie was gone. The ticket clerk down at the depot told me that a gal answerin' her description had bought a ticket on the eastbound that pulled out not long before I got back to town. When I asked the gent where she'd been headed, he told me, "She said it didn't matter, as long as it was away from here!"

I never saw her again. I reckon a gal like her can make a livin' just about anywhere, if you can call it that, so I ain't surprised she didn't come back to Abilene.

As for Axel Skidmore, he sold his business interests and left town too not long after that. He talked in a croak from then on and never really got his voice back, so I guess I stomped on his throat a mite too hard, which I reckon I'm sorry for. But I was riled up at the time.

Skidmore leavin' town didn't mean that the trouble in Abilene was over, of course. Not by a long shot.

But I've bent your ear long enough, so that'll be a story for another time. That's one thing you can say for the West.

Folks will never run out of stories about it.

Blue Horse Mesa

John D. Nesbitt

Author's Note: The story of the Johnson County War of 1892 is well known in the history of Wyoming, as is the bravery of Nate Champion, who stood off an army of hired guns for the better part of a day until they smoked him out and shot him down. The most eloquent part of the story is his own courage, which had fifty witnesses, but history has also preserved the contents of a little notebook that Champion kept while he was under siege.

Several years back, I heard a less verifiable story from the great writer Frederick Manfred, who in the mid-1950's interviewed people in Johnson County who were close in time and family to the original participants in the conflict. According to Manfred (whose research culminated in his novel *Riders of Judgment*), there was speculation that Nate Champion might have had a child with a woman who was married to someone else. With all respect to a brave man, this story explores that possible lost trail.

Nate Champion rode down from Blue Horse Mesa on a buckskin he called Tag. Of the half-dozen horses in his string, Nate liked the deep-chested buckskin the best for traveling across country. Tag, with his smooth lope, put the miles behind them. Now the horse was picking his way down the southern slope, where the pale sun of late March had melted snow on the rocks along the trail.

Lonely country, it seemed today. In the ten or twelve miles since he left Powder River, he had seen few tracks in the snow. Up on top, he had seen nothing. As he leaned back in the saddle and shifted with the movements of the horse, he felt the pangs of hunger and along with them the downcast feeling that sometimes came at this time of day. He didn't worry about a small thing like that, though; he could ride all day without eating, and he would usually get a second wind in the afternoon.

There was plenty else to worry about. Talk had it that Frank Canton had a dead list of seventy men in the Powder River country. Some said only twenty, and others said there was no such a thing. Nate didn't even know where Canton was, but he figured if there was any list at all, no matter how short, the name of Nate Champion would be on it. That was one thing to worry about—it could come at any time, a bullet in the back like they did to John Tisdale. Nate was a long ways off his regular range for someone to be stalking him here, and he had kept a good eye on his back trail all the way over, but once the big cattlemen got started, they knew no stopping.

The other thing to worry about was Lou Ellen. He hadn't seen her since October. Over a period of months they had met more than a dozen times on Blue Horse Mesa—never for very long, but the feeling ran so deep that he felt it would never end. Sometimes, it took her an hour or so longer to get away, but she always made it to their rendezvous—until the last time, when she didn't show up at all. Since then, he hadn't gotten word one from her. Between that and the trouble with Canton and the others, it had been a long winter.

Down off the slope and headed back west again, he caught the smell of wood smoke. Cottonwood Creek lay up ahead. If he could get a look at the camp, he could decide whether to ride in or go around.

Clearing a rise just enough to look over, Nate saw a picket line with a half-dozen horses tied to it. Closer to the creek stood a low canvas tent with a pile of firewood on one side and a freight wagon covered with a tarpaulin on the other. A gray-bearded man in a wool cap came out of the tent, straightened up, and looked around. When Nate got a full view of the man's face, he recognized him as Ben Jones, the chuck wagon cook. He and another roundup hand, Bill Walker, trapped through the winter, so this would be their current camp.

Nate gave the buckskin a nudge, then rode into plain view and gave Ben a wave. At the edge of the camp, he swung down and covered the last ten yards on foot.

"Howdy, Nate," called the older man.

"Hello, Ben. Havin' any luck?"

"Oh, a little. And yourself?"

"Same." Nate glanced around the camp. "Where's Bill?"

"He's downstream. We'll see about makin' one more set here before we move on." Ben tugged on the bill of his wool cap. "Care for a cup of coffee? Somethin' to eat?"

Nate shrugged. "I wouldn't turn down either."

"Tie up your horse then, and I'll get you somethin'."

Seated on a log with a tin plate balanced on his lap, Nate broke apart a biscuit and poured a dab of molasses on each half. "Well, what's new?"

"Not much with me. Heard about you, though."

"Oh, really? What was that?"

"Heard they come callin' for you one morning, while you were still in bed."

"That they did."

"Heard it was Canton and Elliott and two others."

"I knew Elliott for certain, and I'm pretty sure of the rest."

"Hah!" Ben poured coffee into a tin cup and then took a seat on the same log. "How about that fella that was bunkin' with you?"

"Gilbertson? He's not much of a fighter. I threw what lead I could."

"You didn't get anyone, though?"

"I drew some blood on someone, but that's all I know."

"These big cattlemen just don't want you independents to have your own roundup, do they?"

"If that was all it was. But there's other bad blood, and it just got worse when they couldn't get me."

"You mean Tisdale."

"He had an old grudge against Canton, from back in the Texas days. First thing I did, when I could see they weren't comin' after me again, was ride across country to his place. Soon as I got there, I told him, 'There's goin' to be trouble.' He was worried, I could tell, and there was his wife—she hadn't had the baby yet—but he said, 'By God, if we've got to fight, that's what we do.'"

"And he didn't live to see Christmas."

"No, and sometimes I think it's my fault."

"For goin' to tell him?"

"More than that. Not long after these fellas tried to jump me, John Tisdale and I run into Make Shonsey."

"That two-faced sonofabitch."

"The same. Well, I knew that Shonsey knew who took the shots at me, because I tracked 'em back to a camp right next to the NH, where he's foreman. And he'd been by, all smiles, just the day before. So I knew he knew, and I made him say all four names in front of John Tisdale, in case something happened to me."

"So Shonsey talked?"

"He had to." Nate patted the grip of his six-gun. "But

he hated to say it in front of John, who despised Canton already."

"Well, hell, then, it just gave Frank one more reason to shoot him in the back."

"Seems like it now, and no one doubts that Canton shot him. But you've got a man who salted his alibi every way he could, and eyewitnesses afraid to stick to their story."

"Should be an open-and-shut case."

Nate took a drink of coffee. "Not when you've got all the big mucky-mucks on your side. He walks free on the first warrant, and the governor won't have him brought back from Illinois on the second one."

The older man took out a pipe and began scraping the bowl with his jackknife. "Maybe they think they've gone far enough."

"No tellin'." Nate started on the second half of his biscuit. "How long you been trappin' over this way?"

"'Bout a month."

"Catchin' mostly what?"

"Coyotes." Ben turned the pipe upside down and rapped it on the log.

Nate decided to take a chance. "Seen anything of Spangler?"

"He sold out to Irvine."

Nate stopped with the biscuit halfway to his mouth. "He did?"

"Yep. Sold what he could and moved to Douglas." The older man made a crackling sound as he blew air through the stem of his pipe. "His wife had a little one, you know. He moved 'em into a town."

"Not afraid of the trouble, I wouldn't think. He's careful to stay on good terms with everyone. When did he move?"

"'Long about a month ago."

"Huh."

Ben stuffed fresh tobacco into the bowl of his pipe. "You fellas still gonna go ahead with your independent roundup, eh?"

Nate ran his tongue around to clean his teeth. "I suppose so. You can't say you're goin' to do somethin', and then not do it."

"That's right. And you got Jack Flagg and all the Hat boys behind you."

"Sure. That's all fine and good, if your friends are around. But even when they are, if it comes to the scratch, it's what a man can do for himself. He's got to. He just hopes he gets a chance, more than some did."

The older man lit his pipe and smoked in silence while Nate finished the second biscuit.

"Want more coffee?"

"No, thanks. I should probably move on."

Ben looked at the sky. "Don't let me keep you. Be dark sooner'n you know."

"Hate to be in a hurry."

"Not at all. Make use of the daylight."

Nate stood up. "Well, I thank you for the grub."

"Wasn't much."

"It was good all the same." Nate shook the grounds out of his cup. "If you and Bill get over to the KC, don't be shy. I'm stayin' in the cabin there, and you fellas are always welcome."

"That's not where they jumped you?"

"Nah, that was out on the Bar C. This one's not so out of the way, and it's a little more comfortable. Don't be afraid to stop in."

"We won't." The old man stood up and took a cheerful puff on his pipe.

"So long, then." Nate checked the cinch on his horse and swung aboard. He touched his hat in farewell, then put the buckskin into a trot.

So Lou Ellen got moved to Douglas. There wasn't

much chance of seeing her again on Blue Horse Mesa, and there was no telling if he would see her elsewhere anytime soon. It always seemed like the real thing when he was with her, but after all she was married, and even if Nate didn't care much for Spangler, he didn't like the feeling of doing another man wrong. If he had gone this long without seeing her, maybe it was just as well if it stayed that way.

On the other hand, he didn't like to leave things unresolved. She'd had a baby. He needed at least to be able to ask her about that.

Maybe later. This business with Canton and the others had him looking over his shoulder all the time. When he told John Tisdale there was going to be trouble, he didn't know how much. He still didn't.

Lou Ellen stood at the window and watched the afternoon outside turn gray. One day seemed no different from the next, and she had felt numb, dead of feeling, ever since Chas had moved them to this town. She didn't think it was the baby. Some women talked about a depressed feeling that set in after giving birth, but this felt like something else. It was as if something had died inside her, something that had kept her going.

For the last year she had harbored the guilty feeling that came from knowing she could never love her husband as much as she had loved Nate Champion. But the guilt never outweighed the desire, never kept her from wanting to see him again.

Sometimes he rode a sorrel, sometimes a white horse, most of the time a buckskin, but she always knew him from a distance. She knew his posture, his stocky build set off with a dark hat and a dark shirt. As he came closer, her heart raced. Even with his face shaded by his hat brim, she could make out his full mustache, dark eyebrows, and searching eyes. He reined his horse in and swung down, light as a cat, the white handle on his revolver swaying, the steely blue-gray eyes meeting hers. Then he held her in his arms with all the strength of a man of the earth. When she took him to her, the mingled smells of the felt hat, the wool shirt, and the leather chaps worked like an aphrodisiac.

How many times? She had not counted, and he said he hadn't either. It was all open and free, each time unto itself, with no thought of anything ever being different.

Then she would have to leave. It was always her obligations that brought their meetings to an end. She stretched it, for one minute more, and then she had to hurry away, leaving him there on the mesa standing by his horse and holding the reins.

Back at the ranch house, she would bide her time and count the days until the next visit. Sometimes the thought stole upon her that she might have seen him for the last time, and it chilled her heart. But when the appointed day came around, there he was again, sometimes waiting, sometimes riding across Blue Horse Mesa.

It was always that way, the cycle of guilt and hope and fear and escape, one more time in his arms, until one day Chas told her he knew.

She had broken the news about her carrying a child, and he told her he thought it might not be his.

"You're not going to see him again," was the decree.

"You speak as if you owned me."

"I don't have to. But I'm telling you what you're not going to do."

"And if I decide for myself?"

"Things will happen otherwise. Believe me."

Now she was living in this dusty town, where even the snow was dirty. Chas delivered coal and drank two quarts of beer at home every night. The baby cried. Lou Ellen rinsed the diapers, hung them on the rack to dry, and stared out the window.

She hadn't gotten to see him that last time, not even to explain. She had left him waiting. Worse than anything, she did not have the certain feeling that she would see him again to make things right.

Chas, meanwhile, acted as if nothing had happened. He spoke of Frank Canton, Major Wolcott, and Senator Carey as if they were all old friends. The only one she knew was Canton, who had stopped by the ranch in November. An oily man in a curved-brim hat and a long topcoat, he had a sliding pair of eyes that took in everything. Some friend. If she hadn't begun to show already, he would have laid a hand on her when Chas went to the outhouse. That was the feeling he gave her. Now Chas said that Canton and Wolcott and some others were coming through on the train, and he hoped he got a chance to see them.

A few thin snowflakes drifted past the window. She wondered where Nate was at this moment. Probably out on the range somewhere. A thousand times she had imagined him waiting for her the day she stood him up—pacing, fretting, stretching it out for a few more minutes, then swinging onto his buckskin horse and riding back to the Middle Fork. She doubted he had come back to Blue Horse Mesa many more times, but she had the conviction that he had done so at least once before she left the ranch.

Nate looked out the cabin door and watched the snow come down slantwise. After ten years in this country, he knew storms in early April could be as bad as any. Time to stay by the fire, even if it got a little close with the present company. Nick Ray didn't have much of an odor himself, but the trappers were like others Nate had known. They got so they couldn't smell themselves. All the same, it was good to be able to offer them a place to roll out their blankets, and it gave him some comfort to have visitors. Not that company was any guarantee against getting attacked—he had learned that with Gilbertson—but it kept the mind from feeding on other things.

The old man, Ben, had a fiddle. He would probably play it tonight, and they could sing songs about devil horses and blue-eyed girls.

Snow was piling up on the tarpaulin that covered the trappers' wagon. No chores needed to be done. They had a good stack of firewood inside, and the horses had hay. Still, Nate had a restless feeling, as if he should be doing something.

He closed the door and turned to join the company. The old man sat at the table slicing spuds, and his younger pal, the cowhand Bill Walker, had his stockinged feet propped up on a crate to catch the warmth of the stove. Nick Ray was sewing up a hole on a cotton sack he used for a gear bag.

"Still comin' down?" he asked.

"Kind of bitter," Nate answered. "Good night to be inside."

"Good weather for sleepin'," said the old man. "Bill here would like to be runnin' off to town, but I tell him there's time enough for that."

Bill swayed his head from side to side. "Tells me to keep a wrinkle in it, but that's easier for him than it is for me."

"Time you sell your furs," said Nick, "you'll still have a while to rustle some petticoats before roundup begins."

"That's my kind of rustlin'." Bill stopped, then added in a quick breath, "If you'll excuse my language."

"Hell, no," said Nick. "Bein' called a rustler in these parts is the next thing to a compliment. What it means is, you don't kiss the Association's ass. Call me a rustler, it means no one's gonna mistake me for a friend of Fred Hesse or W. C. Irvine, much less Mike Shonsey or Frank Canton."

Both the trappers gave a little laugh. Nate couldn't blame them for wanting to stay out of trouble. Come spring, they would want to hire on with an outfit, and chances were that they would work for some member of the Association. But on the hired man's level, no matter which brand he rode for, a fellow knew that the Association didn't run things fair and square.

Anyone who wasn't a member and owned cattle was presumed to be a rustler; he was blackballed from working for the big outfits. Members could brand mavericks and divvy them up, but a small operator wasn't supposed to brand even his own strays if they got off his land. That was the thing that galled most—the Wyoming Stock Growers Association claimed the right to rule the open range. Everyone knew it was crooked, but it was nothing for a chuck wagon cook or a circle rider to try to buck against.

Nate awoke in the cold gray of morning. The other men were still asleep. He could hear their breathing and snuffle-snoring. Someone needed to build up the fire in the stove, and he figured he might as well.

He dressed in a minute, put on his hat to keep his head warm, and went about starting a fire. As soon as he opened the door on the stove, the old man sat up in bed, his thin hair wisping out. As the one who always had to get up at three in the morning during roundup, he probably thought he should have gotten up first this morning.

"Go ahead and take it easy," said Nate. "No hurry on anything until I get a fire."

The old man settled back into his bed.

With splinters and kindling Nate got a blaze going,

then fed on some thicker pieces. He broke the skim of ice on the water bucket and poured the last of the water into the coffeepot. The fire was crackling now as it took off. Nate left the door of the stove open and pulled a chair up next to it.

The air in the room warmed up, and the other men came alive. The old man sat on the side of the bed and pulled his clothes on. Nick Ray yawned, then pulled the covers to his chin and lay with his eyes open. Bill called out for an order of ham and eggs.

"You'll get flapjacks if you're lucky," said Ben as he stood up and hunched into his coat. He put on his hat and crossed the room to warm his hands at the stove. "I suppose I should go get us a bucket of water."

"Sure." Nate poked another length of firewood into the heart of the fire.

The other two men got up and started milling around. Bill rolled a cigarette and smoked it, then tossed the butt into the stove.

"I wonder what's takin' Ben so long," he said.

Nate shrugged. "Might be makin' a deposit."

"Well, I'm gonna go take a look-see." Bill, who was already wearing his coat, put on his hat and gloves and went out.

"Let's go ahead and start fixin' breakfast," Nate said. "If Ben wants to make hotcakes when he gets back, that's fine, but we can fry up some spuds in the meanwhile."

He went to the dugout at the end of the cabin, selected a half-dozen potatoes, and carried them to the table. Nick was cutting slices off a slab of bacon.

By the time the skillet had heated up and the bacon had started to sizzle, neither of the trappers had come back.

"I wonder what's keepin' them two fellas," said Nick.

Nate frowned. "There might be someone out there holdin' 'em."

Nick stood up and said, "I think I'll go take a look." He picked up his rifle and headed for the door.

Nate had an uneasy feeling, but as he was busy poking at the bacon, he said, "All right, but look out."

A minute later, he heard the crash of a rifle shot and a hoarse cry. He jumped for his gun belt where it hung looped on the bedpost, and he heard six or eight shots together. With his gun in hand, he ran to the door and peeked out.

Nick was ten yards out from the cabin, on his hands and knees, crawling toward the door.

A shot splintered the doorjamb, and Nate ducked inside. He figured the men were shooting from the stable, so he fired in that direction and sank back. He opened the door to see how Nick was doing, and two slugs knocked chips of wood in his face. He slammed the door, opened it again, and blazed three more shots at the stable.

Nick, still crawling, had made it almost to the doorstep when a shot sounded and his back jerked, and he fell forward. Nate stuck his gun in his belt and leaned forward, and with bullets thudding into the lumber around him, he dragged Nick inside. The man was breathing and groaning, but he could not speak.

"I'm sorry, Nick. We should've known when the other two didn't come back."

A hail of bullets shattered the window and raised splinters on the back wall. Nate stayed low. He smelled smoke, and looking around, he saw where a bullet had punctured the stovepipe. Black smoke was curling up from the skillet as well. Ducking, he scurried to the stove, grabbed a rag from his chair, and pulled the skillet off the heat. He did the same with the coffeepot. He hadn't even had time to put in the grounds.

Another volley came in through the window, and he crouched to reload his pistol. Nick was still breathing in gasps.

It looked like one man against a bunch, and the idea began to settle in that he might not live to tell about it. He felt in his shirt pocket for his notebook and a stub of pencil, and under the date of April 9th he wrote as much as he could in the time he thought he could spare. He told how the attack started, and then he ended his entry:

"Nick is shot but not dead yet. He is awful sick. I must go and wait on him."

Bullets came in at the window again. Nate went to the doorway and emptied his six-shooter, drawing fire. He ducked back and reloaded, then crawled to the other side of the cabin, where his rifle stood against the wall. He stuck the pistol in his belt again and levered a shell into the Winchester.

For quite a while he traded shots, and when there came a lull, he wrote a few more words.

"It is now about two hours since the first shot. Nick is still alive."

Then he had to put the notebook down for a minute to steady himself as another barrage of shots came.

"They are still shooting and are all around the house. Boys, there is bullets coming in like hail.

"Them fellows is in such shape I can't get at them. They are shooting from the stable and river and back of the house."

A stillness in the room caused him to crawl over to where Nick lay, and then he wrote a few more words.

"Nick is dead. He died about 9 o'clock. I see a smoke down at the stable. I think they have fired it. I don't think they intend to let me get away this time."

Nate took a deep breath and looked over what he had written. Maybe Jack Flagg and the Hat boys would get to read this. Maybe not. Even if someone took it off his dead body, though, and burned it, these words would have been written. He could do that much.

He went back to trading shots, now at the window and now at the door, taking snap shots with the rifle and thinking he might have made a hit or two.

Things cooled down then, and a funny noise came at the door. He looked out the window to see someone had taken to throwing a rope. He didn't go for it. While he still had breath, he would put down a few more words.

"It is now about noon. There is someone at the stable yet. They are throwing a rope at the door and dragging it back. I guess it is to draw me out. I wish that duck would go further so I can get a shot at him.

"Boys, I don't know what they have done with them two fellows that stayed here last night.

"Boys, I feel pretty lonesome just now. I wish there was someone here with me so we could watch all sides at once. They may fool around till I get a good shot before they leave."

The ranch yard had gone quiet now—too quiet. As he craned his neck to look out the window from each side, he could see no movement. No telling how many men were out there. At least twenty, and not a flicker.

He sat on the floor by the table and took the skillet into his lap. The bacon, crisp on one side and fatty on the other, was cold on the tongue. The fire in the stove had long since gone out, and he couldn't imagine cooking anything anyway. He ate a couple of slices of raw potato, discolored now, and ran out of appetite. He poured warm water from the coffeepot and drank a cupful.

Time dragged on, and then he heard a commotion of

yelling and shooting, but no bullets came his way. He went to the window and peeped out to see that a buckboard and rider had come by, and some of the gunmen had opened up on them. It looked as if at least one of the men had gotten away, but he couldn't be sure in all of the chaos.

A man came into view by the stable, the only man within range. Nate took a shot, and the man disappeared. Silence settled in again, and Nate took the opportunity to scribble a few more words about the buckboard and the man at the stable. Then he choked at the next words but made himself write them.

"It don't look as if there is much show of my getting away."

Before long, the men outside put the abandoned wagon to use. As it came into view, he saw they had heaped it with hay and chopped-up fence posts, and using the pile of hay for a cover, they were backing it toward the cabin. A rattle of bullets through the window kept him from getting any shots at them.

It didn't look good. They had him pinned down, and now they were pushing a go-devil at him. His heart was pounding and his mouth was dry as he took up the pencil and notebook. As he wrote, a volley of shots would come, then a pause, and then another barrage.

"Well, they have just got through shelling the house again like hail. I heard them splitting wood. I guess they are going to fire the house tonight. I think I will make a break when night comes, if alive."

The gunfire kept him from looking out, but the smell of smoke coming in through the window made his heart sink. He wrote fast.

"Shooting again. I think they will fire the house this time."

* * *

He was right. He could see the flames from the wagon as they licked up onto the eaves, caught the roof on fire, and then worked down the wall. In a matter of minutes, smoke was filling the room, getting thicker and lower. He had time to write one last bit, and then he was going to have to try to run for it.

"It's not night yet. The house is all fired. Good-bye, boys, if I never see you again.

"Nathan D. Champion"

He tucked the notebook inside his shirt and tried to gather his wits. It was a good fifty yards to the ravine south of the house, and his best chance was without his boots. He pulled them off, straightened out his wool socks, pulled on another pair, and crawled to the back door. This was it. He either got away or he didn't, but they weren't going to burn him like a rat. He was all on his own. He hated to leave Nick's body in the fire, but it was the only way.

For one more time that day, he thought of people he might never see again—his brother Dudley, Lou Ellen. They would know he went down fighting. So would Jack Flagg and the boys. But none of them was here now.

He needed to get out of this smoke, or he wouldn't be able to breathe enough to run. With the six-gun tucked in his belt and the rifle in his hand, he pulled the door open and made a run for it.

The black smoke poured out around him, and he felt enormous energy as he took the first few strides. He heard shouts of "There he goes! There he goes!" and his mouth went dry as a tingling went through his shoulders and neck. He was running fine, though, his legs lifting and his lungs clearing.

As he pushed around the bend, a man appeared with a rifle, then another standing nearby, also aiming. Not enough time to stop and draw a bead, everything out of order as he raised the rifle. A bullet tore into his arm and he dropped the gun. As he grabbed for his pistol, he felt three more slams in the chest, and he floated like nothing.

Lou Ellen held the baby in her arms as she looked in the store window at a pair of gloves—men's work gloves, with flared leather cuffs, the kind she had seen more than once on Blue Horse Mesa.

There was nothing left now, nothing but servitude, bitterness, and hatred. She could make peace with her husband and put in her time. She could bite her tongue when she heard him and others talk about the rustler war. She could hate the cattlemen and their hired guns for not having to answer for what they did, for having the governor and the senators on their side, for doing as a group what none of them would dare on his own. When four couldn't do it, it took fifty.

She could nurture all the contempt she wanted, but she knew it could not change what had happened. Nate Champion was worth any number of these shameless cowards, yet they went on living, many of them in prosperity. That was all she had, knowing that he was a better man—that, and a little baby named Chance, and the determination that some day when her life was her own, she would go one more time to Blue Horse Mesa.

The Ones He Never Mentioned

Jeff Mariotte

Of all the wretched, low-down, no-account holes in which Wes Hardin had taken refuge over the years, this one counted among the lowest. He couldn't even be positive that he remained within the borders of his beloved Texas, since out in these dry desert wastelands no signs or markers existed to tell him so. The cabin in which he passed his days and nights was nothing more than a line shack for a cattle company, but years of drought had sapped all life from the brush-choked fields, leaving them yellow and brittle, of no use to cows or any other beast on God's earth with a brain larger than a walnut.

Except John Wesley Hardin, who—not for the first time, and likely not the last—found the need to locate himself someplace where no other human would have reason to be. The law claimed that a man could kill in self-defense, but just try it, he had learned, and see what happens. Since his teens he had been chased around the country by lawmen and others rabid to dispense their idea of justice. A week ago it had happened again—a man in Brackettville had drawn down on him in a saloon and Wes had been left with no choice but to put a window in the fellow's skull.

Fortunately, he had not been in Brackettville long enough to put down roots—nor, having seen the place, did he intend to. But at least the town had a hotel with private rooms, clean beds, and soft grub. No similar claims could be made of the line shack, which he shared with what seemed to be half of the insects in West Texas and a goodly portion of the rodents, reptiles, and smaller mammals. The shack smelled like their leavings, and like some of them had maybe teamed up to drag a dead buffalo in and bury him under the floor. The stove was busted, requiring him to do any cooking outside, where the other half of the insects waited for him. He had to climb a precarious cliff down to the nearest im-personation of a creek, and then when he had bathed or filled a pot or both, he had to climb back up again, cling-ing to the roots of trees that had long since given up and pitched themselves over the side.

He would give it another week, and then he would move on. The sidewinder in Brackettville had not, he thought, been such an important fellow that a posse would waste more time than that looking for his killer. If need be, Wes would ride into the New Mexico Territory for a spell (unless he already had) and return to Texas when things had calmed down again.

Thinking about that creek water, such as it was, caused Wes to shove himself out of his bedroll. The shack's floor was hard-packed earth and although Wes had not yet reached his twentieth year, sleeping on it night after night caused his back to ache like an old man's. Add to that the pressure on his bladder from waking up thinking about the long climb down to the creek, and he was a miserable wreck from the moment he gained his feet.

Standing outside the shack urinating onto the dried-out husk of a weed, he saw three riders coming toward him from out of the west. The one in front, atop a piebald mare, looked like a grown man, with two smaller men or maybe boys riding behind, one on a chestnut horse and the other on a gray mule. They might have been with the outfit that owned the shack, for all he could tell. If so, they might not appreciate his borrowing it. On the other hand, they might not care at all. They didn't look like a posse, that was the main thing, and they weren't coming from Brackettville way.

With his mind settled on that, he finished what he was doing, but decided to postpone his climb down to the creek until he had established for sure if the three were headed toward him or not. Instead, he went back into the cabin, tugged on a pair of trousers and a shirt, settled his hat on his head, and grabbed his .44-caliber lever-action Henry rifle. Well, one that had been his since he'd found it in a ranch house, the second day out of Brackettville. The weapon's owner had objected to its loss, but Wes needed a long gun and he'd had to leave Brackettville without one. Carrying it outside, he lowered himself to the dry, scratchy ground, rested the barrel on a flat chunk of rock, and sighted down its length toward the riders.

Wes set down his pen and picked up a glass of whiskey from a bottle that Hattie Morose had brought him. Its smoky, slightly woody aroma reminded him of a lifetime of saloons. He took a sip, felt the liquid burn the back of his throat, followed that with a longer swallow. A gas lamp glowed on the table beside his stack of papers. While Hattie plied her trade on the mattresses of El Paso, Wes had been working on his autobiography. His life's path had taken him from outlaw to convict to gentleman, a lawyer and a scholar, and he believed the world should know his version of the events that had shaped that path. He was, in many circles, somewhat of a celebrity. He had been accused of killing forty men over the last forty-two years. The book he wrote now would set the record straight on that—as straight as he wanted it set, at any rate. He had already decided he would own up to the forty, even though some of the killings that had attached themselves to his legend were ones he had not done. In some cases, the victims themselves had never existed.

For the sake of the book, though, he would invent details about those non-people. Still, that left about a half-dozen deaths he did not want to write about, at least unless he could change the circumstances he set down enough to make them unrecognizable. Some people bore long grudges, and Wes feared his gun hands weren't as fast as they had been when they got more regular use.

Although he had hung out his law shingle in El Paso, he spent most of his days wallowing in a stew of mescal and memory. Reliving his past had been a strange journey full of unexpected detours and surprising discoveries; patterns cropped up in places he would never have looked for them, like the delicate filigree of a leaf's veins after it has browned and fallen from the tree. The mental exercise kept him from working on the law (although, he allowed, the liquor might have had something to do with that), but in the long run he figured his fame would allow his book to sell well enough to earn him some money.

To finish the book, though, he would have to decide which incidents could be included and which left beneath history's faded rug. He took another sip, wiped whiskey from his mustache with two slender fingers, and determined to think this one over some more.

As the riders drew closer, Wes became more and more convinced that he had seen the man before. The fellow had a black beard that seemed to grow up out of his shirt like a murderous hand clutching his throat and chin. Dark eyes burned from beneath the brim of his dome-crowned hat with a righteous fire that Wes could make out even from a distance. His mouth was set into a scowl so practiced that Wes doubted a smile had ever crossed his face unchallenged. *I've seen that ugly face before,* Wes thought as he watched the man approach. He couldn't cipher out where it had been, but he knew the man.

Not so the two boys, though, for boys he saw they were. Judging by their faces—soft, rounded miniatures of the older man's—they had to be his sons. Even their clothes and hats were the same, as if their Maker had only the one mold but could cast people in different sizes.

The man held up his right hand and the two boys reined in their mounts. Alone, the man continued, inside Wes's range but not by far. He wore a hogleg on his hip and had a rifle shoved into a scabbard, but he held on to the reins with both hands. "You've had that rifle pointed our way a good long while," he called. "You plannin' to use it or should we keep comin'?"

"What's your business?" Wes asked.

"No business here," the man replied. "Passin' through is all. Been travelin' by moonlight so as to dodge the heat of the day, saw the shack and reckoned we'd bunk in there till sunset. If you ain't got the room or the inclination, why then, we'd as soon keep ridin'."

"Ain't my place," Wes said. The man's accent sounded local. "Y'all are Texans?"

"And proud of it," the man said. "John Junior and Anna there are born and bred, and I come here from Arkansas as a sprout."

That was all it took to remind Wes of where he had known the man. One phrase, and the way he said it. *I come here from Arkansas as a sprout.* It'd been years since he'd heard that, years and bodies gone past like river water in spring when the winter's snows melt and tear away at the banks.

* * *

"I come here from Arkansas as a sprout." The man held both his hands in the air, the left one trembling a little. His dark eyes betrayed no fear, though, and Wes felt as if he would wither before their glare like his mama's lilies in high summer. "I'm Texan through and through now. Listen to my voice, boy, then tell me you think I'm a Yankee."

Wes gripped the old cap-and-ball Colt with two hands, willing them not to shake although his heart hammered faster than a hummingbird's wings, and kept it pointed at the man's chest. The man had come up out of nowhere at the worst possible moment, and Wes's mind raced as he tried to lay out all the angles, the possibilities of what could happen.

Wes's father was a Methodist preacher who had named his son after John Wesley, the founder of his faith. Wes's family roots ran deep in Texas—one of his relatives even had a county named after him. Young Wes had always thought that his background and family placed a burden on his shoulders that they were ill prepared to bear. People thought he should *be* somebody someday, and didn't hesitate to tell him so. He tried to smile and nod when they did as if it was the most natural thing in the world. Inside, he seethed. Lately, it seemed the seething went on all the time, day and night, like he had swallowed a pot of boiling water and a cookstove and would boil over any moment.

He didn't know if he would *be* somebody or not. He knew only three things about himself for sure. He wanted people to tell him the truth, no matter what the truth might be (but his father instead recounted patently impossible stories from the Bible as if they were things that had happened to his kin just last week, which Wes found enraging). He wanted people to let him become whoever he would (but instead they tried to groom him to be who they wanted to see him become, whether it was a man of the cloth or a judge or a businessman). And while that pot of water in his gut simmered, the only way to keep it from exploding was to let little bits of rage out now and again, however he could. He knew it would blow one day anyway, and he would leave Bonham behind, never to return.

The only question remaining was whether he would leave a trail of blood and fire in his wake when he did, or not.

This particular day, things had come to a head early. His father had been on a tear, lecturing him virtually from the moment his feet hit the floor about what he called Wes's "slovenly and unchristian behavior" for remaining in bed past the rising of the sun. He punctuated his diatribe with blows; his fist struck Wes's temple, and with a spray of white lights like sparks from a farrier's anvil, Wes sprawled to the dirt outside their house. Like a dark angel, his father turned away and stalked back inside, muttering words that might have been prayers, curses, or both.

Wes wanted to retort that smacking his son to the ground for such a minor offense might also be considered less than Christlike, but he had gotten off without an actual whipping and hoped to keep it that way.

School beckoned, but instead of going there, Wes tucked his father's Colt in the waistband of his pants and lit off into the woods outside Bonham. He had hanged a dummy of the hated President Lincoln from the limb of an oak tree, and on days like this, when he thought his rage would swallow him whole, he liked to stand different distances away—sometimes with trees blocking the best angles—and shoot at it. Every time a ball struck the effigy, he imagined he could see Lincoln's blood fountaining from it. Wes both loved and hated John Wilkes

Booth—loved him for having the courage to assassinate the traitor Lincoln, hated him for doing it before Wes was old enough to do it himself.

He had fired five shots, missing twice, when he became aware of movement behind him. A cloud of bitter smoke hung in the still air. He didn't know if it was a sound that tipped him off, or the frenzied flight of flushed birds, but he stopped himself from pulling the trigger and spun around with the weapon still held in his hand. A man stepped into view from behind a tree trunk, light through the leaves glittering about his head like thrown gold coins. The man smiled and showed his empty palms. "You must hate that fellow," the man said. Wes knew at once that he came from the North; his accent and clothing made it as obvious as if he'd been carrying a carpetbag. A Reconstructionist, maybe even someone sent to arrest anyone shooting at their precious dead president.

"Who wouldn't?"

"Many people," the man said. He kept the grin glued to his face, but Wes could see it was as phony as anything. The man's long brown hair curled around his ears. He kept his chin clean-shaven. Wes hated him right from the start. "Some hold onto their hatred, but the war's been over for three years, son. You know that, right?"

"In the North maybe," Wes replied. "Not so much down here."

The man started forward, lowering his hands as he did. "I hate to see you bound by that feeling, boy."

"Don't you move!" Wes ordered.

The man froze, hands held chest-high. "Easy, there," he said. "Let's not do anything rash."

Rash, however, was exactly what Wes had in mind. All the anger and fear, the frustration, the unnamed and inexpressible emotions that stewed in his gut and made him want to run blindly across the landscape trampling everything and everyone in his path, bubbled up. The stranger represented the things he hated—the North, respectability, established authority, probably religion and government as well. *Rash? Nothing rash about it,* Wes decided, silently amending his earlier thought. *It had to come to this, sooner or later.*

The man took another hesitant step forward, his smile fading and then awkwardly returning, and Wes bit down on his lower lip and held his breath and squeezed the Colt's trigger.

For reasons he didn't understand, this shot sounded louder than the others, a thousand times louder. People must have heard it as far away as Austin, he believed. Stupidly, he wondered if it had hurt the man's ears, but then he realized that the man's throat had been torn away. Eyes wide with surprise, the man dropped to his knees, hands flailing uselessly, mouth falling open. Blood spattered the ground like water from a pump.

Panic gripped Wes. *What have I done?* he thought. *What do I do now? Why did he . . .*

But the man hadn't done anything. He had simply been, and now, flopping forward onto his face, blood burbling into the dirt, he no longer was.

Wes had imagined killing, had dreamed of it, sometimes longed to do it. Not like this, though. In his imagination it was always someone like Abraham Lincoln, an enemy of the South, or else some owlhoot bushwhacking him, and to save his own life or avenge his people he had to shoot. This man might have had a gun under his coat, but Wes hadn't seen one. He'd been mad at his father, mad at the world, and this unfortunate soul had simply walked into the wrong woods on the wrong day.

He made himself approach the man. He touched the man's shoulder, rolled him over. The blood didn't shoot out as far as it had before—reminding him of his imagined Lincoln wounds—but bubbled from the jagged pink wound like an underground spring emerging at the surface. His eyes remained open. He would never see anything again, never open his mouth to speak Yankee platitudes, never startle another innocent Southern boy in the woods. As he looked at him, the panic left Wes and a sensation of pride replaced it. Pride and power and well-being, as if the simmering cauldron in Wes's gut had been silenced for a spell.

The man wore a vest beneath his jacket, and a gold chain extended between two small pockets. Wes leaned closer, resting one hand casually on the corpse's chest, and tugged the watch free. A hunting scene decorated the case, looking like something out of England, Wes thought, with dogs and something up a tree that might have been a fox. He opened it with a low whistle, admiring its glow, the way it caught the sun's rays and threw them back like tiny daggers of light. He had never held anything so valuable. Tucking it in his pocket, he returned his attention to the problem of making sure no one ever found the body, or if they did, making it impossible to blame *him.*

Which was when the rustle of leaves and the snap of a dry branch alerted him to another intruder in his woods, no doubt this man's traveling companion. He brought the Colt up quickly, like a seasoned gunfighter. "Seems as if the woods're crawlin' with carpetbaggers today," he said, aiming the weapon at the dark-eyed, bearded man who emerged from the shadows. "You fixin' t'join your friend here?"

"You've got it wrong, boy," the newcomer said. "I'm no carpetbagger, but a Texan, same as you. I come here from Arkansas as a sprout."

Wes knew, when he heard those words again, that he was once more face-to-face with the man who had helped him bury the body of the first man he'd ever killed. No one knew about that victim, not his parents or the cousins whose ranch he'd been visiting when he'd fought Mage, the former slave who most people believed had been his first killing. He didn't think the man recognized him, certainly hadn't come here looking for him. Texas was a big state but not that crowded, after all. People ran into each other now and again. Wes had hoped never to see this man as long as he lived, because the man reminded him of that first murder—and murder it was, not self-defense, there was no way he could twist it into self-defense—and because the man knew a secret that Wes had hoped always to keep.

The man—he'd said his name was John as well, John Selman—had helped Wes bury the corpse. Wes had shown him the watch, and the man had searched the body until he'd found some coins, of which he gave Wes one and kept the rest for himself. He had only been passing through the area, he had said, when he'd heard the shot and come to investigate. After the body was buried, he shook Wes's hand as if they had become partners in some unholy enterprise, then continued on his way.

Wes realized he was staring at Selman, and the force of the man's gaze on him made him uncomfortable. He decided not to let on that he recognized the man. Five years had passed. He'd been the age of the man's children then (he'd thought both were boys until the man called one "Anna"), maybe just a little younger. Now he was a married man of twenty, hardened by life and responsibility. He knew his face had matured in the interim, filled out. His shoulders had broadened and he had grown into his height, no longer the gangly stripling he had been. Maybe the man had forgotten all about that day. Even if not, he might not connect Wes to the boy who had told him only that his name was John.

"Feel free to stay," Wes said, breaking the uncomfortable silence that had built. "Ain't much room inside, but I don't need it during the day. I been thinking maybe it's time to move on anyhow."

"Don't go on our account," the man said. "Soon's the sun sets we'll be out of your way."

"We'll see," Wes said. "Meantime, I reckon I'll be around today, so if it looks like someone's fixing to walk in on you I'll raise a warning."

The man touched the brim of his hat. "Appreciate that," he said. "I'm John Selman, by the way." He nodded toward the taller of the kids. "That's Anna, like I said. And John Junior."

"Pleased," Wes said, happy to have his hunch confirmed. "I'm Wes Hardin."

John Selman and his children tethered their mounts to a hitching post outside the cabin. Wes still had not made it down the cliff to the creek—if there was more than a spit's worth of water in it, he'd haul some up for the horses as well as for himself and the Selmans.

By the time the sun broke for California, Wes had scared up a couple of scrawny rabbits too stupid to move someplace where they could get their bellies filled, skinned them, and started them cooking on a makeshift spit. The rabbits wouldn't gorge anyone, but he'd be able to make a meal for four out of them, and then John Selman and his boy and his girl who looked like a boy would head on down the trail, leaving him alone. Which was the way he liked it, when on the run. He missed his wife Jane, wished he could lie with her again, but knew that would have to wait until the Brackettville law had stopped hunting him.

He sat back on his haunches to keep his face out of the greasy smoke, turning the rabbits to keep them cooking evenly. A boot scuffed the dry earth behind him—from the direction of the cabin—and he patted his ribs. He didn't wear a traditional rig, but kept his twin six-guns holstered inside his vest, where he could cross-draw with both hands and fire before most men could clear leather. He had left his vest in the cabin this morning, though, and hadn't gone back in because the Selmans were sleeping there. He had left the Henry in the dry grass, a couple of feet back from the fire.

"Mr. Hardin?"

The girl, what was her name? "You're Anna, right?" he said, remembering. He eyed her over his right shoulder. She carried her hat now, and he could see that she, or maybe John Selman himself, had cut her brown hair just like a boy's, and from the looks of her had used the dull edge of a bowie knife to do it. Since she had no curves to speak of and was wearing a boy's clothing, he wasn't surprised he'd mistaken her for one.

"That's right, sir."

"The menfolk still sleeping?"

"Like wore-out hounds. That's what menfolk do best," she said. "Not meanin' any offense."

Wes shrugged. In general, he didn't like men, with a few exceptions. But then he didn't care a lot for most women either. "None taken."

Anna walked around the fire, squatting on the other side. "Rabbit. Smells good."

"Can't promise that," Wes said. "But it'll fill your gut just the same."

"It's for us? I'm sure Pa didn't mean for you to feed us."

"This ain't exactly my place and I ain't exactly a host, but I gotta eat so you might's well do the same."

"Well, that's downright neighborly," Anna said. "You *are* a Southern gentleman."

"I'm a Southerner," Wes said. "That says it."

"Almost makes me feel bad I went rootin' through

your personals," Anna said. A ghost of a smile flitted across her face and for a moment she looked female after all. Wes stared at her. Even after the smile had fled, a mischievous glint lingered about her eyes.

"You did?"

A shrug. "I'm that way," she said, as if that excused it. "Southern, but no gentleman."

Anger filled Wes's lungs like smoke from the fire. "Your pa oughta whack some manners into you."

"Ought to," she said. "But me bein' a girl and all, I guess he just can't bring hisself." She dug in a pocket of her jacket and pulled out Wes's gold watch. "Anyhow, I found this. Funny thing too—Pa used to tell me a story about one just like it." She dangled it on its chain, letting it sway like a young tree in a stiff wind. "And he told me about the tall, blue-eyed, dark-haired boy who took it off a stranger he'd just murdered. A Texan, the boy was, and the dead man was a Northerner, so Pa didn't much mind, but he figured as how he could buy the boy a passel of trouble it ever crossed his mind to."

"Say I didn't take it from that boy," Wes said, wanting to see what the girl drove at. He felt a familiar rage well up from his gut, tried to bite it back. "What would that mean to you?"

"I ain't decided on that yet," Anna said. "I might want the watch. I might want the boy, especially if he'd growed up to be a handsome sort of man with big broad shoulders and strong hands. I may not look too girlish to you, Mr. Hardin, but that don't keep me from havin' a woman's thoughts and wants."

All Wes had ever desired from life was for people to be straight with him, to not tell him lies and feed him full of false hopes and promises, and not to threaten him. Trouble always came when people meant to cause him injury, and he had to act in his own defense. As he looked at this girl dangling his own watch like she was

some kind of mesmerist and he a willing victim, a red
scrim clouded his vision and the fury that always accompanied such moments returned in force. He pictured
her falling forward onto the fire with a hole between her
eyes, blood leaking from it and sizzling in the flames like
the rabbit grease.

His hand closed into a fist. "You ain't gonna hurt me,"
Anna said, not asking a question. "Not over somethin'
like this."

Wes glanced toward the cabin. John Selman and John
Junior hadn't shown themselves yet, but if he grabbed
the rifle and fired it they would. "Course not," he said.
He thought about reaching across the flames and just
snatching the watch, saw himself doing it, but as he
stood and actually leaned toward her, he caught the
amused light dancing in her brown eyes and he changed
his target. Instead of taking the watch, he closed his fist
and hit her in the head.

Anna fell over sideways, then sat up with a frown, rubbing her temple where he had struck her. "My pa ain't
gonna like that one little bit," she said.

"Your pa's never gonna know about it," Wes replied,
the rage having fully engulfed him now. He burned as
surely as the dry weeds would if a ring of rocks hadn't
contained his little cooking fire, if he'd kicked the sparks
in every direction. Anna saw something change in him
and tried to scurry away, moving like an injured crab,
but he caught her in two steps. The big strong hands she
had admired so recently closed on her throat. She tried
to scream, to fight, to kick. Wes preferred to kill with a
firearm, but her throat was slender and soft and squeezing it was just like squeezing butter. He lost track of time,
but it couldn't have been more than a minute or two
before she stopped fighting him, and then she gave a
shudder and stopped moving at all.

A panic similar to that which had overtaken Wes the

first time he had met John Selman came back to him. If Selman or the boy came looking for Anna, he would have to kill the two of them too. Someone might be waiting for them—for all he knew, Selman might be an important person now. This lousy, stinking line shack was supposed to be a hideout, not a killing ground.

He lifted the girl's body off the ground—she felt almost weightless somehow, like a bird—and turned in a slow circle, regarding his surroundings. The answer came to him almost at once. He carried her to the cliff and tossed her over, into the nearly dry creek. Climbing down, he caught her by the ankles, and dragged her to the base of the cliff, where it overhung slightly. From above no one could see her—looking down, you thought you could see the whole face of the cliff wall, and only by standing right here could you see the indentation.

He checked from above, just to be sure, and then ran toward the shack, screaming Selman's name. The man threw back the door and came out, John Junior crowding him from behind.

"What is it, Hardin?"

"It's your girl!" Wes said. His rage had left him the moment the girl died, and as soon as he'd tossed her empty husk off the cliff his near-panic had faded, but now he remembered both and the memory tightened his voice, lending veracity to his performance. "She shagged out! Made me promise not to say anything, but I just waited until she was out of sight. You can still catch her easy, with the horses."

"Shagged out?" Selman echoed. "Why would she do that?"

"I ain't her pa," Wes said. "How would I know? Kids are that way sometime, just can't wait to be shut of everyone and everything. We were talking by the fire a few minutes; then she said she had to light a shuck, made me swear to silence, and vamoosed."

Selman stared at him like he wanted to say something else. When nothing occurred to him, he swatted John Junior. "Saddle up," he said. "We've got to find that damn girl. Child was born on the prod and she ain't settled down yet."

While the boy did as his father said, Selman asked Wes a few more questions. Lies slipped easily from Wes's mouth and Selman's gaze burned holes in him. He didn't believe Wes, but didn't have any grounds to call him on it, and Wes began to believe that Anna had maybe run off a time or three before.

As the rabbits burned and the black smoke coiled into the sky, John Selman and John Junior rode off in the direction Wes had shown them, leading Anna's mule along with them. A short while later, Wes heard them calling her name.

He went back into the shack and packed his own few possessions. By the time Selman figured out he wouldn't find her, Wes would be miles in the other direction, riding fast.

Before he mounted up, he did two more things. He went back to the fire pit and found the watch where Anna had dropped it. Pocketing that, he kicked over the rocks that contained the blaze. If the flames spread, they would cover his tracks all the better, and smoke and darkness would screen him from Selman's eyes.

That done, he climbed up into the saddle. As he started off, he hoped that he would never encounter John Selman again as long as he lived.

Twice was plenty.

The front door squealed open and Wes heard the rustle of Hattie's skirts as she squeezed past its frame. A substantial woman, she swept toward him on an uneven course, pressed Wes's face into her deep décolletage, kissed the top of his head. He breathed in a noxious stew of her perfume and the stale sweat and cigar smoke of the men she had been with during the night.

"Martin came around again," she said when she released his head. "He wants to make trouble for us."

Martin Morose—her husband—had wanted to make trouble ever since Hattie had taken up with Wes. Wes had a plan to deal with it, and a meeting scheduled later this afternoon with the participants in that plan.

One of them was the town constable called Old John.

He would meet John Selman for the third time in his life. As before, he hoped the man didn't recognize him. If Selman did know him, then this might be the time, at long last, that Wes would have to add him to his list of victims.

Just the same, he decided, he would leave those two deaths out of his book.

No sense in tempting fate, he thought. *No sense to that at all.*

El Paso Courier-Gazette
August 20, 1895

"A scourge of all Texas was eliminated last night when El Paso Constable John Selman tracked killer John Wesley Hardin to the Acme Saloon and finished his career with two bullets to the head. Law-abiding citizens will sleep better knowing that Selman's quick hands and steady aim ended the gunman's life.

"Selman, who has sent many a hard man to an early grave, said of the nighttime encounter. . . ."

What Really Happened to Billy the Kid

John Duncklee

"Grab the sky, Bonney, and don't even think about goin' for your 'Thunderer'!"

I knew who it was as soon as he said my name because he always had pronounced it like the "o" was a "u," making it sound like "bunny." I thought he did that just for ridicule, but we never had time to discuss that matter. Finally, I figured out it was his natural accent because Patrick Floyd Jarvis Garrett had been born in Chambers County, Alabama.

I did as I was told and dropped the sack of money I was carrying after selling the herd of cows my friends and I rustled. Doggone, I had enough gold in that sack to retire. It was so heavy that I probably could have been clear of Fort Sumner if I had not been afoot. While I was counting out the coins, that fool horse I had stolen from the livery stable at the other end of town had snapped the reins from the hitch rack and taken off at a fast gallop. I saw him just as I was leaving the bank with the sack of money.

"All right, Mr. Garrett, I am reaching as high as I possibly can. Don't be getting in a hurry to yank that trigger."

"Just stand right like you are, Bonney, or I put enough

holes in you to ventilate all the air from here to Car-
rizo Springs."

I stood right still because I certainly had no desire to
become the home for Sheriff Pat Garrett's .44-caliber
slugs. I cannot say I blame him for being angry with me
because while he was holding me for hanging, I had
killed two of his guards and escaped from his jail. Mr.
Garrett hated to have prisoners escape from his jail.
What surprised me more than anything in my thus-far-
short, young life was what Mr. Garrett did next.

But before I tell you about that strange occurrence, I
must say that in spite of the fact that a lot of my activi-
ties were really against the law of the land, I had a passel
of really good friends. You have to understand that I am
essentially a very good person. I am calm, most of the
time. I speak softly without malice toward anyone. I seek
fairness and honor. Mr. Garrett is the first to back that
statement.

After he took my "Thunderer" and stuck it into his own
waistband, he told me to pick up the sack full of money
and we were going to his camp. I thought that quite
strange since Garrett's jail was fairly close by. But I did as
I was told because he still kept that carbine pointed
toward me in a very serious way. Having been around
firearms for a considerable part of my life, I can tell the
difference between a serious and a frivolous way of pointing a rifle. Mr. Garrett seemed essentially serious.

Garrett had made a camp just outside of town in a
grove of cottonwoods down by the Pecos River. It was not
much of a camp to my way of thinking. He had a fire
circle and a pot of coffee ready to heat. When we arrived,
he stirred the coals and put a few sticks of kindling on.
Then he took off his beaver hat and commenced waving
it to get a flame going. I suppose I could have jumped
him right then and there, but there was something in the

way he was acting that really got my curiosity going full speed.

"Take a seat on that cottonwood log, Bonney," Garrett said when the fire got going under the coffeepot. "We'll have some Arbuckle in a few minutes. I might just as well tell you right off what I have in mind to do with you."

"I expect you might be planning on shooting me right here and now since I escaped from that jail of yours."

"No, Bonney, what I have in mind is far from that. I am glad I caught up with you again, especially after you pulled off that rustlin' job without a hitch."

"That was easy, Mr. Garrett. The night guard didn't get his old Navy Colt out fast enough. I just shot him in the foot."

"Bonney, I've known you quite a spell and frankly I have seen your side to a lot of the trouble that you seem to attract. I know for a fact that you were abused when you were a youngster, and I reckon that has a bunch to do with why you are the way you are today."

"How do you know so much about me, Mr. Garrett? I was born in New York and my sickly mother brought me to Silver City. My father was a Civil War soldier who did not survive Confederate bullets."

"It don't matter how I know all this stuff about you. What does matter is I have a plan. I aim to send you east to a New England preparatory school so you can get into Dartmouth College."

"Mr. Garrett, pardon me, but have you lost your mind?"

"No, Bonney. I recognize your intelligence and think very strongly that you have a great deal more potential than bein' a gunslinger, even though you are the fastest and most accurate gun I have ever seen or heard tell of."

"All right, Mr. Garrett, so you see all this potential.

What I am curious about is why are you doing this for someone who just escaped from your jail while waiting there to be hanged?"

"Well, Bonney, you and I used to be friends. Good friends. Now I'm callin' you Bonney and you're referrin' to me as Mr. Garrett. There's somethin' wrong about that."

"All right, Pat, tell me what you have in mind."

"Until I got appointed sheriff in this Lincoln County, I always felt kind of like your big brother. I hated to see you gettin' into trouble and involved with so many killin's. I always thought that with an education you'd amount to somethin'. What I aim to do is take this cow money you stole and use it to get you an education."

"That is sort of against your oath of office as sheriff, isn't it?" I inquired.

"I expect it is, but that doesn't seem to bother me like it should," Garrett said, and chuckled. "Remember when you told me about the mischief you got into over in Bonita, Arizona? They tossed you into jail and you escaped after killin' two guards. You told me that Bonita is real close by Arivaipa Canyon, where that citizens' committee from Tucson went and killed and raped all those Apache women and children. The citizens' committee were found innocent by the jury."

"I remember telling you about that and how I thought there was little justice dealt me when they tossed me in jail for just a prank that did not hurt anybody," I said.

"I remember all that. I agreed with you before as I do now. About this school. I had a great-uncle, or some such relative, who started the Garrett School outside Bellows Falls, Vermont. It's a private boarding school that mainly prepares boys for Dartmouth College up there in New Hampshire."

I liked the way he pronounced Vermont with the

accent on the "Ver" and how, for New Hampshire, the "New" got all the emphasis.

"Tell me more about this Garrett School."

"I don't know any more to tell except I can get you in there and I have enough of this cow money to pay your way. However, if you hanker to go on to college later on, you had better find some way to pay for it yourself."

"How easy for robbing are the farms back there?" I asked, making myself sound serious.

"I assume you are joking, Billy."

"I suppose I might as well accept your offer, Pat. The other alternative does not appeal to me at all."

And so it was done. Pat went into town and bought me some new traveling clothes, including a brand-new silver-belly Stetson beaver hat, at the Lincoln Mercantile, rented a good stout sorrel gelding at the livery stable, and came back to the camp with his purchases. We finished what beef and beans Pat had at camp, and by dusk we saddled up and headed for Santa Rosa to catch the eastbound train. We did not say much during that forty-mile ride.

As the train chugged into the station, I could see that I was the only passenger on the platform. Pat and I said our good-byes and he wished me good luck at the Garrett School. We had talked all that out at supper. I was to lie about my age because there was no way that the headmaster would allow a twenty-two-year-old to enter the junior class. Pat had faked my credits in a letter he had written to Ethan Everett, the admissions officer. I had no worries about telling them my phony age because I was small and rather scrawny as it was. My beard had never amounted to much either. Pat had changed my name before writing the letters to the Garrett School. We decided that Patrick Henry McCarty was as good a name to go by as any. I decided to sign it as P. Henry McCarty because it looked more distinguished.

I wondered why Pat had given me back my "Thunderer." I could have gotten off the train at Tucumcari and gone back to stealing livestock. I reckon he knew I was curious as all get-out about going to the Garrett School in Vermont. After I got settled in my seat aboard the train, I felt a twinge of homesickness even though I didn't really have a home since my mother took up with Antrim. That Lincoln County War, when Old Man Tunstall got himself killed, put me into a situation that kept building every time there was any trouble. When Pat Garrett told me that I was being held responsible for twenty-some-odd killings, I laughed out loud. "If you believe all that, Mr. Sheriff," I said, "you probably believe Mexicans do not eat chili."

I have no idea how long after I dozed off that the sudden stop occurred. It almost jolted me off the seat and onto the floor of the railroad car. I saw out the window that dusk had nearly settled in. Glancing around at the other passengers, I noticed them looking around as if they might discover the reason for the slamming stop. It occurred to me that the engineer may have halted the train to take on water as he had before. I had not long to wait for the answer.

Through the forward door to the car, a gunman suddenly entered waving a .44-caliber Remington revolver in the air. Another man busted through the rear door, and the first one ordered everyone to toss their money and valuables into the canvas sack the second man was carrying with both hands. I took note of that by glancing quickly to the rear of the car. I eased my "Thunderer" from its holster, cocking it as the man waving his gun blabbed on about nobody making a move. The fellow was a rank amateur. First of all, he should have made everyone in the car raise both hands. Not only a novice train robber, but a durned fool to boot.

I jumped up and fired a .41 slug into his heart before he knew I had jumped up. Then, spinning around, I fired another round into the poor sucker holding the canvas sack with both hands. Two rank amateurs. Both would-be robbers slumped to the floor of the railroad car dead and harmless, blood staining their shirts. I slipped the "Thunderer" back in its holster, sat back down in my seat, exhaled with relief, and again looked outside through the grimy window.

I reckon the sudden episode took every passenger by complete surprise because there was an awesome silence throughout the car until a woman toward the rear screamed. I glanced around and saw that the robber who had been holding the canvas sack had fallen so that his head rested on the woman's feet.

Just as the conductor walked in, two of the passengers approached him, turned to point back toward me, and told him that I had saved all their lives. The conductor made sure the gun-waver was dead, and then came down the aisle and stopped by my seat. "Well, young feller, it looks like you're a hero today. What's your name?"

"P. Henry McCarty," I answered, wishing the man would go about his business.

"There's a reward for you from the railroad, young feller. Give me your address and I'll make sure the reward gets to you."

"I am a student at the Garrett School in Spring River, Vermont."

The conductor wrote down all the information in his small notebook, shook my hand, and said, "It's my pleasure meeting a brave young man, P. Henry McCarty. Have you traveled this railroad much? Your face seems familiar."

"This is my first trip, sir," I said, and tried to look away so he would not eventually recognize me from some wanted poster.

"Well, on behalf of the railroad, I want to thank you for your bravery and what looks like damn fine marksmanship."

I nodded and looked out the window at the darkness that had enveloped the land. I didn't care about any reward. All I wanted was to be left alone to finish the trip to Vermont without anyone recognizing that I was many times a worse threat than any train robber they might encounter from here to Chicago. Then I happened to think of the biggest joke of all. If I was appointed a sheriff because of this so-called bravery, then Pat Garrett and I would be on equal ground.

Chicago was a big temptation for me. I had an entire day to wait for the train to New York City. I found a restaurant that had ice-cold sarsaparilla, and I drank three delicious glasses of it before my stomach filled up and I felt as bloated as a desert cow suddenly put out on green feed. I looked around here and there for a monte game, but there was no action anywhere I went. I ambled back to the railroad station and sat down in the waiting room so I wouldn't forget where I was and miss the train to New York. As I sat there, it suddenly occurred to me that there would probably be no Mexican girls in Vermont. I was surprised I had not thought of that before Garrett and I started riding to Santa Rosa. I reckon I just got caught up with the idea of going to the Garrett School and forgot about how much I loved Mexican women and how much they seemed to love me. I thought about the time I spent in Chihuahua learning Spanish and loving every minute in the arms of so many señoritas I lost track of their names.

New York City teemed with people and all kinds of horse-drawn carts, carriages, and buggies. The streets smelled like a New Mexico horse corral that hadn't been cleaned in five years and a rainstorm had just passed through. I found a restaurant close to the railroad station and ordered a plate of bacon and eggs with biscuits. The coffee tasted lots weaker than I was used to. Mexicans made coffee that would make a teaspoon stand up in the cup without touching the sides. I noticed that the waitress gave me some funny looks, as did some of the customers. When she came over to fill my coffee cup, I asked her what was so funny. Her face turned reddish pink with embarrassment. "It's your hat, sir. I have never seen one so big."

"I reckon you have never been out West."

"No, I have never even been to New Jersey. Are you a cowboy?"

"I sure am. What is your name?" I asked, thinking she might invite me home.

"Sadie," she replied.

I kept her in conversation for a few minutes until her boss yelled at her to get to work. So much for a chance at some female companionship, even though Sadie was not Mexican.

I looked through the window of the railroad car and saw forests and farms along the way. We crossed several rivers as the train moved steadily north, first to Connecticut, then through Massachusetts and into Vermont. There was still plenty of daylight left when the train stopped at Bellows Falls. I jumped down to the platform and made my way over to the stationmaster's office, where I inquired about transportation to Spring River. The man at the desk told me about a stage that would be by in a half hour, so I sat down in the small waiting room. I was glad he did not inquire about why I wanted to go to Spring River.

When the stage finally pulled in, I asked the driver what the fare was to Spring River. He looked me up and

down and asked if I was going to the Garrett School as
a student. I told him that I was to be a student there if I
ever got there.

"Well, sonny," he said. "If you're a Garrett boy there's
no charge. I collect from the school office every month
with the passenger count."

I was delighted that the stage was free. I still had a
bunch of double eagles, but I wanted to make sure I had
enough to get back to New Mexico Territory in case the
Garrett School gave me the willies.

The stage driver let me off at the entrance to the
main building. A sign told me that the red-brick structure, three stories high, was where I could find the
headmaster. I must say that when I walked into Mr.
Haroldson's office, I nearly turned around to leave. He
had received Garrett's letter and tuition money, but he
sounded like he cared little about my arrival. I wondered if he had ever been to the West. Somehow, it
seemed to me that coming such a distance to attend his
school should have made the man appreciate my presence more than he sounded. I was soon to learn that
Haroldson considered himself so far above anyone else
at the Garrett School that it wouldn't have made any difference if I had come in from China. He gave me a cold
welcoming talk about what was expected of me, and
then gave me directions to the office of Jacob Logan,
the master who would assign me a room in one of the
two dormitories and tell me what my schedule of classes
would be.

They assigned me a room on the second floor of Jackson Hall because I was entering as a junior classman.
Logan asked if I would prefer a single room or have a
roommate. I didn't hesitate to tell him I would much
rather live alone. He said that ordinarily there would be
no choice, but there was a dearth of students enrolled
for the year. I didn't have any idea what he meant by

dearth, but I wanted to remember the word when I found a dictionary.

The bed had a thin mattress with no blankets or even a pillow. Logan noticed that I had little in my war bag and asked if I had bedding.

"I figured you would have all that," I said, not knowing what to say.

"Come with me and I will see that you are provided with bedding. It gets quite cold here winters and you will need at least three blankets."

Logan found some blankets, and gave them to me after I signed a paper promising to return them at the end of the school year. When the settling in got accomplished, I went to the dining hall for supper. That was what almost made me flee from the Garrett School. There were round tables. Each table had a master and his wife except when the master was single. There were six students at each table. I got stuck at a table where the master's wife kept talking to her husband during the entire meal. He just nodded his head occasionally or grunted. The food was all right, but the experience awful.

There were other things that were objectionable as far as I was concerned. Living with the sound of a bell telling everyone what to do and when was enough to drive me off balance. Just too much routine for one used to freedom.

The first Sunday, I took off into the surrounding hills with my "Thunderer" under my coat. When I was a good distance away, I put in a little target practice. Pleased that I had not forgotten how to shoot, I strolled back to the campus to put the revolver away and talk to some of the other students I had met during the week. Just as I entered my room on the second floor of Jackson Hall, Mr. Logan followed me in without warning. Surprised, I whirled around and drew down on the poor soul, forgetting where I was. Luckily, I didn't put a bullet in his heart.

I could see the poor devil was scared out of his wits. "Sorry to scare you. Mr. Logan," I said. "But you should not sneak into my room behind me like you did."

"McCarty, I came in here to have a talk about you having a weapon on campus. It is strictly against the rules at the Garrett School."

"Well, Mr. Logan," I said. "If you think I will surrender my 'Thunderer' because of some silly rule, you might just as well start walking."

"You are forcing me to report this matter to the headmaster."

"Now, Mr. Logan, I would not do that if I were you. In fact, if you insist on saying anything about me and my 'Thunderer' to the headmaster, I will empty 'Thunderer' into your heart."

I felt sorry for the man because I gave him no choice. He left my room, and for the next two years he never came by. I kept "Thunderer" under my mattress except when I took off into the woods for target practice.

The classes at the Garrett School were interesting and I enjoyed being on the headmaster's honor roll. I particularly liked my senior English class. The master taught us all he knew about English literature, and that was considerable. I was at the top of my class, graduating summa cum laude. I spent the summer between graduation from the Garrett School and the start of my freshman year at Dartmouth working as a busboy in a hotel on the coast of New Hampshire. I made good tips and with the full scholarship I received from Dartmouth, my financial worries did not amount to anything and I did not have to think about stealing horses or rustling cattle. Robbing livestock was more of a challenge because all I had to do in the dining room of the hotel was smile and the tips began filling my pockets.

Like Pat Garrett once told me, "Your buck teeth don't matter a damn as long as there's a smile around 'em."

Pat Garrett and I exchanged letters occasionally. He expressed how proud he was of my academic accomplishments and that he did not care a bit that I never did much in the athletic program at the Garrett School. "You can dance to Mexican *baile* music faster than those Eastern fellers can run," he wrote.

Dartmouth was quite different in many ways from the Garrett School. The classes were more interesting. I nearly got booted out before the first class convened when a group of upperclassmen began harassing me. They later told me it was "hazing."

When I arrived at Dartmouth, I had no idea what to expect, so I kept "Thunderer" under my coat. So when these snobby upperclassmen started shoving me around, I opened my coat, drew "Thunderer," and scared them crazy by shooting a couple of shots near their feet. After that, the dean of men summoned me. I walked into his office and the bushy-haired, ruddy-complected man did not invite me to sit down. I knew I had to do some fast thinking and talking.

"McCarty, I understand you found it necessary to shoot a weapon at a group of upperclassmen. Is that correct?"

"Yessir. Where I come from in New Mexico Territory, I would not have shot at their feet for shoving me around."

"Well, McCarty, this is not New Mexico Territory and all those upperclassmen were doing was having their turn at hazing lower classmen. What you did was un-called for."

"I understand all that now, Dean. However, when the incident occurred, I reacted in the only way I knew how. Like I said, if the same thing happened around home, those upperclassmen would not be breathing right now."

"I am forced to place you on probation, McCarty," the dean said. "I also want you to surrender that revolver of yours."

"Well, Dean, I am afraid I cannot surrender 'Thunderer.' Wherever I go, 'Thunderer' goes. I will not take it into class or other functions while I am here, but I cannot surrender 'Thunderer' to anyone. You seem to be forcing me to leave Dartmouth and I am happy here."

We talked back and forth for a while, and I finally convinced the dean that I would not surrender my weapon under any circumstance. He was concerned because my reputation as a scholar had arrived from the Garrett School and the dean did not want to be responsible for my departure from his precious Dartmouth. "Thunderer" remained hidden under my mattress until graduation, except for the times I went deep into the forests of northern New Hampshire for target practice. Most of the college boys found recreation in drinking. Mine was in shooting "Thunderer."

Again, I graduated summa cum laude from Dartmouth in three years. The department of literature at Harvard offered me a job as an instructor while I was working on my doctorate. They were waiving the master's-degree requirement because of my academic accomplishments as an undergraduate at Dartmouth. Pat Garrett was beside himself with pride. He apologized for having no money to send because a couple of his business deals had not turned out to be profitable.

But I was dubious about studying toward a doctorate. I had not been to New Mexico Territory in five years. I had not spoken Spanish to any sweet Mexican señorita in just as long a time. I had not danced a *baile* nor eaten a bowl of *chile verde* in so long, I had almost forgotten what they were like. I still remembered what the señoritas were so expert at. I suppose it might have helped if

I could have gone out and spent a drunken weekend, but I never drank.

I was still anxious to complete the degree and get back to New Mexico. I knew there would be little I could do for employment in English literature in the territory, but at least I could spend a little vacation time with the señoritas and see my friends around Lincoln and Silver City.

My committee seemed surprised when I handed them copies of my dissertation. One professor exclaimed, "I say, McCarty, this is highly out of the ordinary. You have only been in residence two years."

"I realize that, sir. However, I am anxious to find a position at a good institution."

"Your rush to finish certainly takes me by surprise. I had thought you might help on my book on Shakespeare."

Inside, I had to laugh, but I kept my face as somber as possible. The professors were all alike. They depended on their graduate students for research so that they could publish more books. I was determined never to use students for researching the topics I was interested in. Research was what I found most enjoyable about the entire business of scholarship.

In spite of their ruffled feathers, my committee allowed me to graduate with the doctorate. The hood seemed strange as I went by the chancellor at graduation. Since I had been offered a position as a professor of English literature at Yale, my committee at Harvard was very impressed with my prospects.

I decided that I would buy a rail ticket to Las Cruces and take the coach up to Silver. I would like to see Garrett, but that could come later after I had a *baile* or two and seen some of those beautiful Mexicanas.

Remembering the amateurish train robbers on the

trip east, I had "Thunderer" ready to pull out if another such occasion arose, but the trip was uneventful.

I had written to Pat Garrett, announcing my arrival time in Las Cruces, so I was not in the least surprised to see him on the platform standing as tall as ever, waiting for the train to come to a stop. He looked older, but I could see the sparkle in his eyes through the grimy railroad car window.

"Well, Dr. McCarty," he said smiling as he walked over to greet me. "It certainly is good to see you after all these years."

"It is a pleasure for me as well, Pat. It is nice to be back in New Mexico."

"I hope you don't mind, but I found you some work."

"What in the world are you talking about?" I asked.

"There's an outfit here in Cruces that likes plays and drama, so I got you booked to read Shakespeare at their next meeting. They are all excited since you are a famous Yale professor of litrachure."

"I am not famous, Pat Garrett. I might have been famous in Lincoln County a while back, but not for my knowledge and appreciation of literature."

"After I got through talkin' to all those people last week, you are now famous for your knowledge and appreciation of litrachure. They agreed to pay you two hundred dollars for an evening reading to them. Did you bring any books of Shakespeare?"

"Two hundred dollars? Pat Garrett, you are something. I can use the two hundred, and I did bring a book or two. Let me know when and where your drama crowd is having their reading. For two hundred dollars, I will read all night! *Madre de Dios.* Two hundred dollars, just to read part of a book. It sure beats rustling cows."

Pat had a cab waiting to take us to the Sierra Blanca Hotel. After a good, long soaking in a big copper tub of hot water, I put on some clean clothes and we had supper in Restaurante Clara. I did not have to look at the menu because I had been thinking and dreaming about green chili for seven years.

We had a great time talking. Pat warned me to keep introducing myself as Dr. McCarty because he was sure there were still warrants out for my arrest. It was not as bad here in Doña Ana County as it was up north around Lincoln and Fort Sumner. It was Thursday. He told me that the reading would be held in the evening of the coming Saturday at the Opera House starting at 7:30 P.M. Pat told me not to worry because he was planning on being there to introduce me.

Garrett had some business to take care of on Friday, so I took a walk around town looking for a monte game. I found one in La Cantina del Río. I had won close to twenty dollars when I noticed a man of medium height with a long, reddish handlebar mustache and wearing a dirty black Stetson. He first looked at my hands, and then began to look me up and down as if he knew me. As far as I knew, I had never seen the man before.

Satisfied with my winnings, I started for the door. The man in the dirty Stetson stepped in my way. "You seem familiar, sir. What's yer name?"

Following Pat's advice, I said, "I am Dr. P. Henry McCarty, professor of English literature at Yale University."

"Hmm, you sure look familiar. Have you ever lived around these parts?"

"I am sorry, but I must ask you to step out of my way. I have an appointment to keep."

As he stepped back, I had a thought. "What is your name, sir?"

"I'm Jackson Slocum," he said.

"Well, Mr. Slocum, it has been a pleasure making your acquaintance."

I touched my silver-belly beaver hat brim and walked as casually as I could through the door. As I looked around town, I saw a poster tacked to a wall by a hardware supply store. It announced the reading on Saturday evening by none other than Dr. P. Henry McCarty of Yale University. Just after sunset, I met Pat for supper.

I asked him if he knew anyone by the name of Jackson Slocum.

"Damned bounty hunter. The worst kind. He rarely goes out after a quarry unless the reward is for dead or alive. He seems to be very good at shooting wanted men in the back."

We finished supper and I retired to my hotel room to read. At breakfast the following morning, Pat promised to come by the hotel at least an hour before the reading was to begin. He had some kind of cattle deal he was trying to put together. He seemed bothered by the business and said he wished he had never bought a cow ranch.

As he promised, Pat showed up at the hotel five minutes before six, ready to take me to the Opera House. He said that some of the folks would be early in order to chat before the regular meeting.

We arrived a half an hour early after a cup of coffee. Pat introduced me to the people he knew and the rest introduced themselves to me. They all seemed impressed that I was a professor, and especially from Yale. I tried to keep conversation interesting, but for some reason all I really wanted to do was get the reading finished so I could meet Jaquelina, a beautiful Mexicana whom I had met that afternoon. I had only talked to her for ten minutes, but she had made up my mind for me. I wanted to take her back to Connecticut.

Promptly at seven-thirty, the president of the Las Cruces Opera Society stood up behind the podium and rapped his gavel on the hardwood pad. He first introduced Pat, and then he went into a long presentation about Shakespeare, and then he came to me. There was little else to say except about my present position at Yale. He made one statement about my occupation not always being in academia, which caused me a slight amount of concern. However, with the lawman Pat Garrett sitting next to me, I forgot the worry.

When the president had finished, I stood up and carried my book to the podium. Opening it to Hamlet's soliloquy, I said, "It is a great pleasure to be with you kind people this evening."

I started to say something about Hamlet and Shakespeare when I saw Jackson Slocum come in the door and walk down the aisle toward me. I was just about to reach inside my coat for "Thunderer" when he stopped and pulled a folded piece of paper out of the breast pocket of his shirt. He took the tattered edges and unfolded it. As he waved the yellowed paper in the air, I recognized it as an old wanted poster with my picture on it in black.

"You may be Dr. Whoever-you-are at Yale, but you are Billy the Kid out here in New Mexico."

Everyone in the audience gasped and looked at the man, who now brandished a "Peacemaker."

"I am puttin' you under arrest, Bonney. Don't even think about escaping this time."

I knew I could get "Thunderer" out and shoot him dead before he could get his brain moving fast enough to pull the trigger on his "Peacemaker." But I didn't need to. The audience stood up and swarmed around the bounty hunter. I heard his revolver hit the wooden floor and saw the people pounce on him. Just as Pat Garrett holstered his weapon, I saw bits of torn-up yellowed paper tossed up into the air.

"To be or not to be, that *is* the question." *Or, it certainly is nice to know one has friends,* I thought as I paused after the first line. I never enjoyed that soliloquy more than I did that evening. When I finished and got done palaverin' with all the people in the Las Cruces Opera Society, I stepped outside where Pat Garrett waited for me.

"Shall we go find some good tequila?" he asked.

"No, thanks, Pat. I believe I'll find a pretty gal named Jaquelina and see if there's a *baile* somewhere in town."

"You may have a bunch of letters after your name, but you haven't changed any, Billy."

"I sure hope not," I replied

The Tombstone Run

John Helfers
and Kerrie Hughes

Dear Lord, I may never walk properly again, Nancy Smith
thought.

It wasn't the attention of a well-dressed gentleman
that caused her face to flush, although her trim figure
and attractive features had already drawn admiring
glances that day. Nor was it the imminent threat of
danger from some nefarious criminal—something she
had faced more than once during her career with the
Pinkerton's National Detective Agency—that made her
stomach turn and roil as she swayed back and forth.
Since she had faced both train and bank robbers during
her time with the famous law enforcement company, it
would have taken more than a few thieves or petty criminals to unnerve her now.

No, the circumstances that made her modest dark
blue long-sleeved dress feel like a constrictive prison
were nothing so exciting. Rather, the source of Nancy's
discomfort was the rocking, bouncing, jouncing stagecoach that she was traveling in. She tried in vain to find
an accommodating position on the narrow, hard-backed
seat sandwiched between two men and facing another
woman and pair of men across from her as the vehicle

shuddered south on the rough trail from Tucson to Tombstone. The newest of the silver boomtowns had exploded near the border between Mexico and the Arizona Territory, and attracted criminals like a herd of buffalo draws scavengers hoping to feast on the unwary.

The Pinkerton Agency had been hired by both Wells Fargo and the Sonora Exploring and Mining Company to solve several payroll thefts that had occurred on the Tombstone stagecoach. With her previous successes at foiling train robbers near Dodge City, Kansas, and bank robbers in Houston, Texas, Nancy was a perfect choice for this job. After several hours on the trail, however, she was starting to doubt the wisdom of accepting this assignment.

They had started the eleven-hour trip early that morning, when it was cold enough to see her breath in the crisp February air. After the sun had risen, the interior of the coach was warmer than she would have thought for winter in the desert. Conversation was practically impossible due to the clamor of the six galloping horses towing the stage from one way station to the next. At each stop, there was just enough time for Nancy and the other passengers to disembark, stretch their legs, and maybe get a drink of water before the next team was hitched up and they were off again.

This certainly makes me long for the relative comfort of the train to Tucson, Nancy mused. But she had been assigned to bring the perpetrators behind these crimes to justice, and she had never failed in an assignment yet.

Although if I were them, I certainly would not want to risk tangling with the guard on this run, she thought. She had only caught glimpses of the lean man in a long canvas duster, but she had immediately noticed his alert blue eyes and ready demeanor. He was also unfailingly polite, tipping his hat to her when she had boarded and suggesting that she take the seat nearest to the driver, so she wouldn't be jostled as much by the motion of the coach as they traveled. *Of course, if this is less jostled, I would hate to be sitting in the rearmost seat,* she thought. Nancy had thought about requesting to ride on top of the stage, as she knew that was allowed, but since she was traveling undercover, she didn't want to do anything that would draw attention to herself.

As she always did wherever she was, Nancy had taken a moment to examine her surroundings, and found the situation not exactly to her liking. The canvas curtains were drawn to try and keep the dust down, but the only thing they blocked was her view outside. Nancy could catch only occasional glimpses of the stark desert landscape through the slim crack between the shade and the window frame. Of course, this also meant she couldn't see if anyone was approaching.

The rest of the passengers kept to themselves, usually napping in the stifling compartment during each stage of the trip, apparently lulled by the rocking motion. Only the other woman, a stern-faced matron wearing wire-rimmed spectacles and clutching what looked like a well-worn, leather-bound Bible, remained awake, her eyes darting around the compartment as if she expected to be accosted at any second. Nancy didn't smile at the sight; she remembered all too well her first impressions of the West: the seemingly endless wide-open spaces, the dirty, ramshackle cow towns and mining towns, and the often less-than-genteel men and women that she had met in her travels. She had made her peace with this land and accepted it on its own terms, but she wondered if the woman across from her would be able to do the same.

She heard a loud "Whoa!" and felt the rocking motion of the stagecoach lessen as it slowed. Nancy heard the whicker and snort of the team outside, and she peeked out the window on one side, then the other, trying to ascertain exactly where they were.

As she looked, the frock-coated man next to her awakened with a yawn, stretching his gangly limbs and pushing his bowler hat back on his head. "Are we at the next stop already?"

"I don't think so, sir, as I see only desert to our right, and some kind of cliff wall to our left." As Nancy finished speaking, everyone awake in the compartment heard a rap from up top, followed by the driver's voice.

"Ladies and gentlemen, there is a small rock slide ahead, which will take a few minutes to clear. Since we're in pretty rough country, I would appreciate it if you would all stay in the passenger compartment, and we will be moving along shortly."

The driver's announcement did little to assuage Nancy's concerns, and she reached into her purse and grasped the handle of her Colt Lightning .38 double-action revolver, just in case. She heard muttered conversation from the driver's box; then the stagecoach leaned to one side as someone got off and began rummaging around on the underside of the coach.

At the same time, a rifle shot cracked out and the motion outside the coach stopped immediately. This was followed by the sound of several horses' hooves as riders approached at a gallop. *Damn, it's happening right now!* Nancy drew her pistol as she rose, crouching in the confines of the passenger compartment.

The black-dressed matron regarded Nancy with wide eyes, looking at her as if she had just sprouted wings and announced that she intended to fly the rest of the way to Tombstone. "Madam, what do you think you are—"

"Shh, I'm a detective." Nancy grabbed the handle of the door on her left and pushed it open. She was about to step out when the rifle boomed again, and a puff of dust erupted right in front of her. At the same time, an arm curled around her waist and hauled her back.

"Beggin' your pardon, ma'am, but you are likely to

get shot if you go out there," the lanky youth said behind her.

Before Nancy could retort, everyone heard another voice outside. "Everyone in the stage stay inside for your own safety!" It was the shotgun guard, his last words almost drowned out by the pounding of the approaching horses and a loud voice issuing commands.

"Drop your weapon or my rifleman will be forced to perforate you! You there, reinsman, stand and deliver!"

Even as she tried to formulate a plan, Nancy frowned as she heard the bandit's voice. *That doesn't sound like any criminal I have ever heard.*

She wasn't the only one confused by his demand, as she heard the driver also ask, "What?"

"He means give up the box, gents, and no funny business," another voice said.

Nancy disentangled herself from the youth and used the barrel of her pistol to move the window shade aside just enough to peek out. Three mounted men with flourbag masks on their heads pointed pistols at the top of the stagecoach, while the man in the middle kept talking.

"To all ladies and gentlemen inside this carriage, kindly remain where you are, and no harm shall come to you. We are simply here for the strongbox conveyed by this contraption, and once it is in our grasp, we shall depart and leave you to continue on your way unmolested."

Nancy exchanged puzzled glances with the other occupants. *Last I heard, Black Bart was still robbing stages in California. Has he decided to move east to richer pastures?*

The vehicle shifted as the two men moved around up top. One of the bandits nudged his horse close to the stagecoach to take the strongbox, positioning himself near the passenger compartment as he reached up for the prize.

Nancy couldn't reach him, but there was another option. As the man grunted with the weight of the iron strongbox, she stuck her pistol under the window shade and pulled the trigger, shooting at the ground. As she had hoped, the sudden noise and smoke spooked his horse, which launched itself and its rider into the air with a startled neigh. Although just as surprised, the rider managed to keep one hand on the heavy box across his saddle, the other hand on the reins, and his feet in the stirrups as his mount danced away from the stagecoach. Nancy pushed the shade aside and scanned the area for another target.

"They're shootin' from inside!" the bandit shouted as he tried to regain control of his jittering steed. One of the other masked men, dressed in a ruffled white shirt and string tie, swung his pistol toward her just before two shots sounded. His shirt puffed when the bullets hit him, and he sagged in the saddle before toppling off his horse.

"Let's get out of here!" the man with the strongbox shouted, spurring his horse into a gallop.

"Lord have mercy, you are going to get us all killed!" the matron said as she wedged herself between the two seats onto the floor. Nancy fumbled with the outside door handle as more rifle shots sounded from above, one punching a hole through the stagecoach's roof and the place where she had been sitting a moment ago.

"Everyone out on this side!" she called, ushering the unarmed passengers to the ground, right next to the driver and the guard, who had his pistol out and a frown on his face as he saw the men tumbling out of the coach.

"Get down!" he said, pushing them to the ground while tracking one of the fleeing riders with his own revolver. He squeezed off a shot, but missed, just as another fusillade of shots sounded from above. With a fearful whinny, the lead horses reared in their traces and lurched forward, sending the stage into motion again and Nancy falling against the seat as she was trying to pry the last passenger—the other woman—from the floor.

"What the—?" Nancy cried as the stagecoach tipped precariously to one side, sending her sprawling back against the seat.

"What's happening?" the bespectacled woman shouted.

"I think the team's left the road!" Nancy called back. Indeed, the ride had gotten much worse, with the stagecoach bouncing along, and actually seeming to leave the ground in a few instances. Stowing her pistol, Nancy contemplated trying to climb through the window to the box to reach the reins, but her first grab at the window ledge nearly sent her flying from the coach as the front wheels jounced over a rut, sending her airborne for a moment and making her see stars as her head cracked against the doorjamb.

Nancy fell back inside as the unguided stagecoach rumbled across the desert. The matron dressed in black was praying loudly, her grating voice scraping across Nancy's already frayed nerves, but she didn't say anything. *As long as she's out of the way,* Nancy thought. *But that still leaves the problem of what I'm going to do.*

A shadow fell across the window, and Nancy looked up to see the shotgun guard leaning over the neck of a running horse as he pulled up alongside the coach. The horse veered away to avoid something on the desert floor; then he deftly brought it back and urged it closer.

Oh, my God, he's not going to do— Even as she formed the thought, the guard grabbed the top metal rail of the coach and swung off his saddle, pulling himself up enough to get his boot onto the windowsill of the door. Just then, the stage hit another rut that sent it and those inside into the air, coming down in a crash of wood and bruises. Nancy had lost sight of the guard for a moment, and when she raised herself up to look outside, he was nowhere to be seen.

Oh, no! Nancy thought, glancing behind the stage expecting to see the guard's lifeless body skidding to a stop on the ground. But then the stage began to slow, and she heard a powerful voice cry, "Whoa! Whoa there!" The team responded to the command, and slowed from a full run to a gallop to a trot, finally coming to a stop in the middle of the hardpan.

Taking a deep breath, Nancy opened the door and stepped out on unsteady legs just as the guard jumped down from the driver's seat and strode over to her, his blue eyes flashing. "Are you all right, ma'am?"

Nancy gingerly explored her scalp with a gloved hand, and was relieved to find just a bump rising where she had impacted the door, but no blood. "Yes, sir, thanks mainly to your timely assistance. That was quite a feat."

The guard accepted the compliment with a tip of his flat-brimmed hat. "I've driven these coaches as well as guarded them, so it wasn't really anything at all."

The murmur of mumbled prayers reached both their ears, and Nancy looked back to see the woman still crouched on the floor of the stagecoach, still clutching her Bible and praying fervently. Nancy winced and tried to ignore her. "As if I didn't have enough of a headache already."

"By God, ma'am, a headache should be the least of your worries. You're either the luckiest or craziest woman I ever saw, and I've met my share of both. You're most lucky you don't have a hole in your head or elsewhere after you frightened that horse. What I can't figure out is why you did that in the first place."

Nancy frowned. "Why, sir, would you think I was the one who shot that pistol?"

The guard pointed at her gloved hand. "I've carried a gun for more than a few years, ma'am, and I know powder marks when I see them."

Nancy smiled. "Well spoken. Perhaps we could discuss this further on the way back to the road."

The guard nodded, his professional expression not changing one iota. "Now that's the best idea I've heard all day."

He checked the stage and team, making sure nothing had broken and no horses had lamed themselves during the wild chase, then swung up into the driver's box and extended a hand to Nancy. "Perhaps we should leave the madam to her own devices below?"

Hiding her grin, Nancy clambered up to the seat beside him and settled in as he got the team moving forward with a practiced flick of the reins. "Forgive me for not introducing myself. I'm Nancy Smith."

"Pleasure to make your acquaintance, Miss Smith, my name is Wyatt Earp," the guard replied.

"Wyatt Earp—*the* Wyatt Earp? The marshal of Dodge City and Wichita?"

"Actually, I was just a peace officer in Wichita, but the other sounds about right."

Nancy was dumbfounded. "Pardon my inquiry, but what is a well-known gentleman like yourself doing serving as a shotgun guard on a stagecoach?"

Wyatt turned to regard her with a wry smile. "You might call me a jack-of-all-trades, master of none, Miss Smith. The folks at Wells Fargo offered me a lift from Cheyenne to Leadville if I'd guard the coach along the way, and I took them up on it. When they were looking for someone to handle the run from Tombstone to Tucson, I offered my services again, and I'm headed back that way to rejoin my brothers in town."

Nancy breathed a sigh of relief as she fished her Pinkerton's badge out of her purse and held it up in the sunlight. "Sir, am I ever glad I made your acquaintance." She quickly filled him in on the case she had been assigned to, and the rash of thefts that had occurred on this run. "Obviously, that was why I had tried to spook that horse, in the hope that the rider would drop the lockbox."

"Wouldn't it have just been easier to shoot the man instead? After all, he was in the middle of robbing the stage, and his comrades certainly were breaking a few laws as well."

Nancy's eyes narrowed. "I prefer to use violence as a last resort, not as an automatic response."

Wyatt nodded. "That's a decent enough philosophy, ma'am, but I haven't found the criminals to be so accommodating."

Nancy cleared her throat and put her handkerchief up to her mouth to cut some of the dust as she continued. "Needless to say, the men at both Wells Fargo and Sonoma Exploration and Mining are quite worried about the effect these crimes could have on their business. I would be much obliged if you wouldn't mind assisting in bringing these men to justice."

Wyatt's features turned thoughtful. "Am I to assume that you will continue pursuing this matter with or without me?"

Nancy summoned her sternest expression before replying. "I am quite capable of handling this on my own; Mr. Earp. However, your assistance would be welcomed."

The guard shot her another sidelong glance. "I thought you might say something like that. Assuming that we'll be able to track these thieves down, it certainly wouldn't hurt to solve a case like this when I arrive in Tombstone." He nodded. "Once we get back to the rest of the folks, we'll try and find a mount for you and see what we can see."

"I would appreciate that. Also, I'd appreciate if you didn't let on to the rest that I'm a Pinkerton agent. We're still not sure if the jobs are being orchestrated by someone on the inside, and I would rather not tip anyone off as to who I am."

"My lips are sealed, Miss Smith."

The trip back was uneventful; Nancy even spotted the horse Wyatt had used to chase the stage down, and they tied him to the back of the stage and brought him back as well. When they reached the road, they soon found that the others had cleared the small rockfall away and taken care of the dead bandit by covering him with a blanket.

Wyatt brought the team to a halt and helped Nancy down, then handed the reins over to the driver. "Careful, Bill, it looks like the brake handle's been shot away."

"Shoot, so that's why the team took off." The driver shoved his battered, shapeless hat back on his head and frowned. "I'll have to rig a new one before we get moving again. Shouldn't take too long, though."

"That's good, since the able Miss Smith and I have some unfinished business to take care of—speaking of which, Miss Smith, what exactly are you doing there?"

Nancy stood over the blanket-covered body on the ground. "The rest of you may wish to take a few steps back while I take a look at this man." She saw Wyatt and the driver exchange glances; then she knelt and drew the blanket back to reveal the bandit's face. The floursack mask still covered his face, and she untied it and pulled it off, careful not to reveal any of his body, especially the wounds that had ended his life.

The man's handsome face was unfamiliar, but she noticed that his black mustache was waxed and his hair smelled of a popular pomade that could be purchased in any town with a general store. Nancy lifted up the sides of the blanket, patting down his pockets for any identifying items, but came up with nothing. She spotted laundry marks on the inside of his shirt collar, but it would take far too long to trace them. Fingering the material, she discovered it was made of high-quality cotton, not the rough linen or homespun shirt she expected to find. Peeking at his legs, she saw that his pants were of the same fine quality. *A gentleman robber, out here?*

A shadow fell over her, and she looked up to see Wyatt standing over her, a strange look on his face. "Is something wrong, Mr. Earp?"

"I'd certainly say so. I've seen this man before."

"Well, given the nature of his profession, I'm not surprised."

Wyatt shook his head. "No no, he wasn't a criminal—at least, not when I saw him last. I saw him on the stage in Dodge City about a year ago, give or take. Carstairs—Carter—Carson Bramley, that was his name. Did a pretty good Macbeth, as I recall."

Nancy rearranged the blanket before she stood. "You're saying that this man was an actor?"

"I am."

"Then what is he doing robbing a stagecoach in the middle of nowhere? Although that would certainly explain his choice of language."

"Agreed, but your question is the puzzler." Wyatt trotted a few yards into the desert and examined the ground. "We can follow the tracks of the rest, especially the one carrying the strongbox." He walked back to the stage and recovered his short-barreled shotgun. "Bill, I'm going to need to borrow one of the team for a bit, but I expect those bandits haven't gone too far."

The driver stopped in the middle of lashing a new brake handle onto the broken shaft. "You ain't planning to go after them?"

"Sure, their leader is gone, so they'll be demoralized, and they'll need to hole up and figure out what to do next. Besides, it's the last thing they'll expect."

"Here now, what about us?" one of the passengers, a stocky man with a florid face, asked.

"If I recall, the next way station is only a few miles down the road. If you want to start walking, I'm sure Bill will pick you up on the way."

Nancy kept only one ear on the conversation, more occupied with ensuring that she was well supplied with bullets for both her pistols, then mounted the dead bandit's horse.

Leaving the rest of the passengers to argue about moving on with the driver, she watched as Wyatt unhitched one of the team horses and accepted the offer of a saddle from another one of the other passengers who had been taking it with him to Tombstone. Wyatt saddled the horse, then mounted and nudged his mount over to her. "Let's get moving."

Nancy heeled her own mount into a trot and followed Wyatt as he set out into the desert, following the hoofprints, and soon leaving the stagecoach and its increasingly irate passengers behind.

The desert around them seemed possessed of two things in abundance—dirt and silence, both of which were marred only slightly by their passing. She studied Wyatt as they followed the bandits' trail, which was so easily marked that Nancy could have tracked them with little difficulty herself. Wyatt looked to be relatively average on the outside, but she sensed in him a resolute ability, even fearlessness, that almost seemed to be larger than the man himself. Now that she thought about it, his name had come up at the Pinkerton offices in their voluminous files on both criminals and lawmen alike, since Allan had always liked to know who he might be dealing with in an area. Mr. Earp had once been charged with horse stealing in his youth, but had skipped town before being summoned to court. He had gone on to make his reputation in Dodge City, although there had also been rumors of illicit behavior, including his keeping of tax payments that he collected, resulting in the city abruptly canceling his appointment. *Which is most likely why he came south,* she thought.

After several more minutes, Wyatt slowed his horse, waiting for her to bring her mount alongside. "They've slowed to a trot—the horses are tired after all that running. Let's keep going, slowly, and we should come upon them soon enough."

Nancy nodded, and they slowed their horses to a walk. After another mile, the sound of a gunshot broke the silent air. "Up ahead, and fairly close, wouldn't you say?"

"That I would. We should be cautious now, especially if they posted that rifleman somewhere high up."

They were coming to another butte, and it was obvious that the hoofprints curved around the rock outcropping, and suddenly, carrying clearly to them in the chill winter air, came the sound of an aggrieved voice, answered by another.

"That sounds like them, all right." Wyatt reined in his horse and secured the reins to a nearby madrone plant, with Nancy doing the same. "If we can hear them, then they'll be able to hear the horses, so we'll go in on foot from here." He hefted the double-barreled shotgun, and Nancy drew her .38. "Pardon my forwardness, ma'am, but I assume by the way you handle that pistol that you know how to shoot."

"You assume correctly, Mr. Earp. Shall we?" Nancy picked her way across the uneven ground toward the voices, pistol at the ready, with Wyatt right beside her.

As they approached, the sounds of an argument grew louder, although the voices seemed to be echoing so much that Nancy couldn't pick out the words. But then she heard something else that was even more curious— a galloping horse approaching from the opposite direction.

"Another bandit?" she whispered.

Wyatt was no less intent on the unfolding scene before

them, but he was just as puzzled as she. "Maybe, but then why wasn't he at the stage?"

"Perhaps he was the rifleman, or they thought they had enough men to get the job done, and the real leader stayed behind. Either way, there's only way to find out." Nancy crept up to the red rock wall of the butte and, using it as cover, began moving closer to the talking.

With two large strides, Wyatt stepped in front of her. "No offense, ma'am, but the scattergun will do a better job of making them duck if necessary." Without waiting for an answer, he walked forward noiselessly, with Nancy following right behind.

By now they were so close that they could make out actual words, and they also realized why the voices were echoing—the bandits had holed up in a concave depression on the bluff that provided a good bit of shelter. In the lee of the rocks, Nancy and Wyatt eavesdropped, trying to get a sense of what was going on.

"Yeah, what the hell is going on? Carson's dead, and the damn lockbox is full of rocks, not the payroll like you claimed."

"You said we'd be paid well for this job, and that there wouldn't be any killing involved. Now I don't see Carson, 'cause he's lying back there on the ground, and I certainly don't see any money here either!"

"All right, just relax, gentlemen," said a third voice. "I agree that Carson's demise was a regrettable accident, but from your story, it seems that the guard was faster on the draw than you gave him credit for."

"Guard nothing!" the first voice exclaimed. "There was a shooter inside the coach! Someone lit off a pistol, and my horse nearly broke her leg getting away from it. That was when the whole plan went straight to hell!"

"Not to mention that we risked our lives for a box of worthless rocks! Now what are you going to do about that?"

"After I'm through, there won't be any need for me to do anything more."

While the third man had been speaking, Nancy poked her head around the rock wall in an effort to get a glimpse of who was speaking. What she saw made her raise her pistol and step out from the rock, calling, "Pinkerton agent, nobody move!"

Wyatt, his eyes widening in surprise, slipped around the corner as well, trying to cover everyone at once with the shotgun.

The scene that greeted them was right out of a dime novel. The three bandits that had gotten away stood in a loose semicircle around the open strongbox, in which could be seen ordinary rocks. A few paces away from them stood another man dressed in a suit, with a bowler hat and spectacles, and a pistol he had just drawn to cover the three men.

At the sound of Nancy's voice, he half-turned, and the pistol swung in her direction. Without hesitation she aimed her own pistol at him, calling out, "Henry Stanton, you are under arrest for embezzlement!"

The bespectacled man's face first registered shock, then anger, and his pistol, which had dipped a few inches in his surprise, came up toward her. Nancy didn't warn him again, but squeezed the trigger of her Lightning twice. Her aim was true, and both bullets hit the natty gunman. He staggered, but didn't fall until Wyatt's shotgun roared, and a spray of buckshot crashed into him, dropping him to the ground in a lifeless heap.

Nancy immediately turned on the three men, all of whom were in the act of going for their own weapons. "I said nobody move!"

"Best listen to her, boys. I've got one barrel left that says I can take down any two of you in one shot."

Nancy guessed it was the cold, matter-of-fact tone in Wyatt's voice more than anything that decided the issue for the rest of the bandits. Each of the trio froze, then slowly raised their hands. "Been too much damn killing already, I guess," one of the men said.

"You got that right, and Mr. Stanton there was about to add your dead bodies to his list of crimes." Nancy kept her pistol on the three, and she was relieved to see that Wyatt's shotgun didn't waver from them in the slightest. "All right, all of you take two steps forward, and we'll secure you for the ride to Tombstone."

Nancy kept them covered while Wyatt made sure each one was disarmed, then collected their various weapons together, bound their hands in front of them with rope from one of the men's saddles, and loaded up the strongbox, along with Stanton's blanket-wrapped body, on Stanton's horse. They had each man lead his horse back to theirs; then everyone mounted up and they all proceeded back to the stagecoach.

Once there, Wyatt posted the man who had loaned him the saddle as a rooftop guard to keep an eye on the prisoners. He took his customary position next to the driver in the box, and they continued on their way to Tombstone without further incident.

In town, they turned over the bandits—all of whom were actually members of Carson Bramley's former acting troupe—to the town marshal, a kindly-faced man named Fred White.

Nancy was finishing her arrangements with the marshal to testify at the actors' trial in Tucson when she heard steps on the sidewalk outside, and glanced behind her to see Wyatt walk into the marshal's office.

"The stagecoach has been taken care of, and the folks at Wells Fargo in Tucson have been alerted as to Stanton's crimes. I expect they'll find the money he stole soon enough. What I'm not sure of is how those actors fit into all of this."

Nancy signed a copy of her statement and passed it over

to the marshal. "Remember when I said this was an inside job? Apparently Stanton, the accountant at the Sonoma company, must have caught on that we were getting close to catching him, so he decided to have the stage robbed to throw us off the trail. Too cautious to trust real bandits, he hired those actors—including the rifleman, a former buffalo hunter—to heist the empty strongbox."

"Empty because he had already removed the money before the stage set out." Wyatt nodded. "Then he was going to kill the robbers and make it look like they had shot each other over the strongbox, and the money would have disappeared with the survivor, who, coincidentally, also wouldn't have shown up for work at the Sonoma company the next day."

Nancy smiled. "Not bad, Mr. Earp. You know, you'd make a pretty good detective yourself."

"Funny you should mention that, Miss Smith, as I'm about to get out of the stage-guarding business, and into something a bit more lucrative. A deputy sheriff's position has just opened up, and I'm heading over to the town hall right now to put my name in."

"I'm sure the town of Tombstone will be grateful for your services, just as I am." Nancy nodded to the tall man, who tipped his hat to her and walked on out of the office, joining a group of three other men, two of whom looked as if they could have been related to Wyatt, and a slender third man with black hair and a handlebar mustache that rivaled Wyatt's own.

"I assume those are Mr. Earp's brothers?" she asked the marshal, who looked at the group with an odd expression on his face and a sigh.

"The two flanking him are Virgil and Morgan Earp. The fourth one is Doc Holliday, currently Tombstone's most notorious shootist and gambler. One thing's for certain, this town is going to be even more interesting with them around."

Nancy watched the four men walk down the bustling main street until they had faded into the distance. "Yes, I imagine it certainly will be."

Authors' note: Although the accounts of Wyatt Earp's life are varied in their accuracy, it is known that he had been both a stagecoach guard and driver for Wells Fargo as well as a city policeman, professional gambler, and later a saloon owner, deputy sheriff, and assistant marshal to his brother Virgil in Tombstone before the gunfight in 1881 that would make his name synonymous with the American West.

The Wild-Eyed Witness

Lori Van Pelt

Rustling noises startled him awake. They sounded like those he had heard in the dream. But that vision had a more rushed quality, the sound of leaves crunching beneath boots, as if a person were running from something, and he recalled catching a glimpse of a blue shirt flashing among the pine boughs.

He reached for his pistols. The familiar ivory-handled weapons were not at his waist. He felt of his pockets but the guns were not on his person. Frantic now, he flung off the wool blanket that had covered him. He felt a tug against the sleeve of his frock coat.

"You lost, mister?" The child's voice rang high and thin in his ears. He raised his heavy head, blinked, and focused his attention on a grubby youngster kneeling next to him. The boy peered at him through eyes the color of spring bluebells. One of those beautiful irises veered to the left and made him feel a little queasy. He let his head fall back, but the boy was not easily dissuaded. "Wake up!" He felt another tug on his sleeve and opened his eyes again, squinting against the painful bright sunlight.

"My mama's so scared. She says that Ramsey Kinkaid is a no-account thief and murderer. You ain't with him, are you?" He again pulled at the cloth coat covering the man's elbow. "She says you ain't, but I said I weren't so sure. You lost, mister?"

When no response was forthcoming, he drew a hawk feather across the man's cheek. The tip of the feather tickled the sensitive skin beneath his nose. The disoriented man wriggled his mouth and heard a deep giggle.

"Your mustache looks funny when you do that. Do it again!"

He did, and the boy, laughing hard now, collapsed into a ball. His mirthful chortling carried and echoed across the hill. The squirrels commenced their chatter atop the pines.

The man struggled to sit up and get his bearings. His mouth was dry. The child appeared to be a boy of about seven or eight. They sat on the ground on the edge of a rutted road atop a ridge fringed with lodgepole pines. A creek burbled nearby. He blinked, but his eyes remained blurry. He squinted against the injurious sunlight, ruffling through his vest pocket for his dark glasses. They, at least, were intact. Putting them on brought some relief, but he knew he would soon need something stronger to calm the incessant thumping in his head.

The boy crawled near and once again stared at him. "Those sure are fancy." He sat back on his heels. "Are they magic speck tackles?"

"They make my eyes feel better."

"Would they make my eye see straight?"

A dust devil twirled along the two-track road, spiraling and throwing dirt as it moved forward along the deep rut of the grass-choked, rocky trail. The twisting wind sped toward them with a faint whistling sound, and almost as quickly as it had come upon them, the whirlwind dissolved.

"Reckon not." A spiderweb dangled from the branches of the nearby pine tree. The delicate threads formed concentric circles, bearing the force of the sudden spinning wind with sturdy grace. The heat of the heavy air intensified the sappy pine smell.

"Oh. I still say you must be lost. I ain't seen you round here."

"What's your name, son?" The words came hard through his parched throat. He reached inside his jacket for his flask, but when he held it to his lips, he drank only dry air.

"Joey. What's yours?"

He hesitated a moment, then extended a hand toward the boy. "James," he said. "What are you doing here?"

"I live here," the youngster said proudly. "What about you?"

"I came to stake a claim," James replied. He must have been doing that. But the truth was he could not remember how he got here. Memories of women, raucous laughter, and a creaking, rickety wagon merged in his clouded brain.

"Gonna say you're lost?"

"I came to stake my claim," James repeated, struggling to stand. The movement made him dizzy. He put hands on his knees and bent, his face even with Joey's.

"This ain't your claim. It's my pa's."

"Who's your pa?" He rose, putting a hand at his back for support.

"Oliver Hemming."

James brushed the dust from his blue velvet coat. One sleeve was torn. His shirtsleeve had been ripped as well. He winced when he touched his elbow. Dried blood and dirt covered a nasty cut. "Well, then, I guess this ain't my claim. So I s'pose I'd better admit I'm lost or you won't be helping me none, will you?"

Joey smiled. "My pa's claim has the stream coming through it. We'll have gold enough to live like kings one day."

"What'd he name it?"

"The Deadwood Dancer."

"In honor of your ma?"

The child giggled again, holding his sides this time. "She don't dance."

"Joey! You get away from there!"

They both turned to see a slight woman wielding a Winchester. "You get over here with me."

"But Mama, this man ain't with Ramsey. His name's James."

"That's fine, then. You get over here."

"Obey your ma," James said. He raised his hands. "I don't mean you any harm, ma'am."

"He's lost, Ma," Joey interceded.

"I see," she said. "Well, maybe he'd best be lost somewhere else."

"Ain't you gonna give back his guns?"

Her cheeks turned the color of wild roses. "Joey!" The tone of her voice indicated her deep displeasure. "How did you know about the guns?"

"You put 'em up on top of the china cupboard. I climbed up on the chair to look. That's where you always put things you want me to stay away from."

Despite this disturbing revelation, she did not waver in her aim with the weapon.

"I'd be much obliged for the return of my pistols, ma'am."

"They're right purty," Joey remarked. "White handles. Just like Wild Bill's in the story we're readin'."

The two adults exchanged a knowing look. Joey's mother said, "Yes, just like Wild Bill's." She examined James a moment longer, and then relented. "I see you've hurt your arm. Best come inside and let me tend it. Then I'll give you your guns and you can be on your way."

The log cabin was dark and cool. James removed his sunglasses. The throbbing in his head made thinking difficult. He sat in the chair she offered and gratefully drank water from the tin cup she placed before him. "Thank you, ma'am." He leaned his forehead on the palm of his hand.

"You're in a bad way this morning."

"Been worse."

She brought a water-soaked cloth, instructing Joey to bring her another. The first she placed on James's forehead. The cool, damp rag provided momentary bliss, and he relaxed. "Don't mind my asking, what brought you up here?"

The boy came with the second rag. They helped James remove his jacket and shirt. With a gentle touch, she cleaned the cuts on his elbow.

"I staked a claim up here," he answered.

She worked quickly, then applied a bitter-smelling salve and wrapped gauze around his arm. She noticed his trembling and the jerky tracking of his eyes, and calmly said, "Joey, I believe that James would like a nap while I mend his jacket. Help me."

James felt grateful for even the slight support of her dainty shoulder and for the tiny hand the boy offered. Together they led him to a back room, where a bed stood by a window. As he sank into the pleasing comfort of the straw mattress and luxuriated in the feel of the cool pillow cradling his sore head, he thought he told them of his appreciation.

By the lamplight, she looked younger and less fearful. "I don't know your name," he said.

She started, but continued sewing. "Delia Hemming."

The cabin was furnished sparsely. A table and chairs stood near a wood stove with a single cupboard hung above and beside it to make the kitchen and living area. The china cupboard stood against one wall. She saw his gaze fall on the fine crystal goblets and platters inside.

"I wanted to have my things," she admitted. "They belonged to my parents. I—I feel closer to them this way."

"No need to explain," he said, taking the chair next to her. "Your home's your own."

The bedroom where he had slept had a window and was separated from the front room by a couple of pieces of muslin hung from the rafters. Another muslin partition at that room's edge made a place for the boy's straw bed. The child's steady breathing brought a peculiar comfort and false sense of safety to him.

"I've mended your clothes, Mr. Hickok," she said, motioning to the jacket and shirt folded neatly atop her sewing basket. She held up a small sock. "I can hardly keep Joey in socks."

"I'm sorry to cause you trouble, Mrs. Hemming. And please, call me James."

"Joey thinks you hung the moon, you know." She reached over to a table and picked up a magazine. She handed it to him. He recognized the *Harper's New Monthly* that had first featured him. The artwork showed Wild Bill Hickok's mare, Black Nell, standing atop a pool table. The amazing pistoleer, long hair cascading down his back, stood, his arm outstretched as if issuing commands to the horse. "He especially likes Black Nell," Delia continued. "He's wanted a horse of his own since I don't know when, but it—" She cleared her throat. "We can't right now." She laid the mended sock on top of her sewing basket. "His pa loves Wild Bill. That's one of his pa's favorite stories. I should be using better stories, but this is easier because he likes it. I want him to learn to read. To love to read." She stood, brushing threads from her brown calico skirt. "If he can read, he'll always be free." She turned her attention to him. "Are you hungry now?"

He was, but he said, "I've bothered you enough,

ma'am. I'll just take my clothes and go ahead back to Deadwood."

She shook her head. "No." Her tone was sharper than necessary. She moved toward the stove. "There's an outlaw afoot out here somewhere. I can't send you off on your own in the dark. You're welcome to stay with us tonight. There's a wagon going back down in the morning."

"That's right nice, but Mrs. Hemming, I can take care of myself."

She smiled. "Ah. But you don't have Black Nell, do you?"

He chuckled, glad to find this serious-seeming woman had a sense of humor. "No. Fact is I used to have a pretty good mule. That mare's a legend for sure."

She set about frying some bacon and warming beans. She brought him a steaming cup of coffee. Almost as an afterthought, she reached into the top of the cupboard and retrieved a bottle. She sat the bottle on the table before him. "It's not much, but in your condition, it may help. I don't drink it myself."

He poured a swig of whiskey into his coffee and took a sip. He watched her in silence for a few minutes, letting the liquor seep into his long-deprived system. "If you don't mind my asking, won't your husband be concerned if a strange man stays with you?"

She concentrated on her task so long that he thought she was ignoring him. But finally she said, "My husband's not come home. Yet." She handed him a plate heaped with the bacon and beans as well as a thick slice of bread and honey. "Fact is, I'd feel better this night if you would stay with us." Despite the heat of the stove and her cheeks being rosy from having prepared the meal, she shivered. Her expression revealed her loneliness and fear. "Ramsey Kinkaid is on the loose again. I don't know where Oliver's gone to—and—there was bad blood between them. And you are a lawman, aren't you?"

Before he could answer, Joey came from the back room, rubbing his eyes. "Do you feel better now, James?" His voice was thick with sleep.

Delia put her hands on his delicate shoulders. "Yes, dear, James feels much better. He's going to stay here with us tonight. Now you just go right back to sleep." She kissed the top of his head and ruffled his blond hair. "Sweet dreams."

"Will you read me another story about Wild Bill?"

"Not tonight, honey."

The cockeyed child focused his one good eye on the man at the table. "He's my hero," he said. "He can do anything. And he never misses a shot. I want to shoot like him."

"You shouldn't believe all you read," James said. "That man's made up. Someone who exists only in another person's imagination."

He looked at his mother, puzzled.

"Pretend," she said.

"Make believe?"

"Yes," James said. "You have a far better hero right here. You should follow your ma. Look at how hard she works. Help her, Joey. Leave those guns to other folks. If you must use one, only aim at something if you mean to shoot it. And only shoot if you mean to kill. Otherwise, don't aim the gun at all."

The child nodded and rubbed his eyes. "Are you gonna look for my pa?"

"No, he's not," Delia said. "It's time you were in bed."

"But he gave me something and maybe you can find him before that Ramsey gets him." He handed James a pocket watch.

"Where did you get that?" Delia's face turned as pale as her muslin apron.

"I saw him in the woods yesterday and he gave this to me and told me to hang onto it."

The adults fell silent, stunned at the admission. Delia, her voice barely a whisper, said, "The watch belonged to Oliver's father. He always carried it with him. If he gave it to Joey, he must have known—" She let the rest of the sentence remain unspoken. She turned toward the stove and sliced another piece of bread. "Why didn't you tell me before?"

"You didn't ask me."

"Weren't you scared?" James asked.

"Not till I found you, mister." He accepted the slice of bread and honey that his mother handed to him. "But I'm not scared of you no more." He took a bite and chewed intently. "Will it help you find him? Will you find my pa?"

The plaintive request touched James to the core. "I'll do the best I can, Joey. But I think maybe we'll all do better if we go down to Deadwood tomorrow. You just get some sleep now. Your ma and I will have a little talk."

She took Joey back to bed, waited for him to finish the snack, then tucked him in and returned to James.

"More coffee?"

He nodded. "Maybe you'd best be telling me about why you're so afraid of this Kinkaid fellow."

Then, the story tumbled out of her, words spilling from her as if a waterfall had been released from the granite hillside itself. Kinkaid, she said, was her husband's cousin. He had cut a man in Cheyenne but escaped from the lawmen there. When he found the Hemmingses, he insisted that their claim was his.

As James sipped his liquor-laced coffee, he listened, watching the woman's expression as the flickering light from the coal-oil lamp made shadows leap and tremble across her face. Her eyes—blue as her son's but set straight in their sockets—appeared sincere. And yet, when she spoke of this Kinkaid, there was a strangeness in them, a terror that spoke of a fiercer fear than that of someone insisting on taking a mining claim.

"Oliver said he'd be back to check on us in a few days," she said. "He was taking Ramsey to town to put him in jail." She fell silent.

"He didn't come back?"

She bit back tears and shook her head. "It's been several days."

"Have you asked around?"

"I've done as much as I can," she said. "I didn't want to frighten Joey. He thinks his father has gone for extra supplies."

"And Kinkaid?"

"He'd do anything to get back at Oliver, especially since Oliver took him to jail." She rose and refilled his cup. "But things were bad before that anyway."

"Do you think that Kinkaid has murdered your husband?"

She shrugged. "Maybe. I don't know what to think anymore."

"You're afraid he'd cause you and Joey harm now? Then why not leave?"

"I can't desert our claim. Too many others around here would take it as their own. And Nugget Creek runs through it. Oliver always said that would be our fortune— in that silly creek water. One man found a bunch of nuggets there big enough to set him up for the rest of his life. And what if he does come back? He might be out there right now. He'd be ashamed of me for leaving."

"It's worth the risk to stay, then?"

"Almost always, Ollie used to say."

He motioned around the cabin. "You know how to take care of yourself." In that trait she reminded him of his Agnes, who had stayed behind with her folks in Ohio until he could get a claim staked and make a new start. He'd done one helluva fine job at that all right. Here he sat, in the home of another strong woman, being taken care of instead of taking care of things himself. "Things will look brighter in the morning," he said aloud, although the remark was directed more at himself than at her.

"I do hope you're right."

The food settled his stomach and made him feel human again. He had the curious feeling she wasn't telling him everything. But then, he often felt that way when he had conversations with women. He never knew the whole story. And he almost always felt uncertain about them.

He stood, but he was still unsteady on his feet.

"You rest," she said. "I'll sit up a while. I can sleep out here." She motioned to a blanket. When he hesitated, she said, "Go on, now, get to bed."

Thunder boomed across the sky. Lightning flashed across the room and faded. The darkness thickened as the clouds gathered above and stirred the heavy air. The coal-oil lamp in the front room gave off a sweet thick smell, its flame low and throwing just enough light through the muslin and into the bedroom to give definition to shapes and create fluttery, queer shadows on the walls. The curtain flapped against the oilcloth window and a hoot owl called, its voice throaty and deep.

A hand seized his shoulder. Hickok rolled with a practiced swiftness, tensing his muscles to spring at the first opportunity.

"Now that's more like it, Delia," a deep, masculine voice said. The intruder moved closer, took Hickok's other shoulder, pulled him close, and kissed him square on the lips. He tasted mustache, then spit and spluttered and cried, "What the hell?"

Hickok jumped up and pushed the surprised intruder

against the wall, using his arm as a brace against the man's neck. "Who in hell are you?"

"Who's asking?"

"Name's Hickok."

The man choked and sputtered against the weight of the arm pressed to his throat. "Where's Delia?"

Hickok applied heavier pressure. The man coughed.

"I'm right here, Ramsey. Me and my loyal old Winchester." Delia pushed through the muslin, rifle barrel first.

The distraction caused James to loosen his grip just enough that Kinkaid wriggled free and leaped toward the woman. She moved to get away and fired a stray shot. The bullet thudded into the log roof. Bits of bark and dust sifted down from the ceiling. Kinkaid had fallen across the bed, and Hickok caught his ankle as he wriggled to get free, kicking and cursing. He bumped Hickok's injured arm, causing him to release his grasp. The outlaw ran toward Delia, who by this time had recovered and aimed the rifle straight at his chest. She was shaking.

"You'll never do it, Delia," he said.

"Stay away from me, Ramsey." She held fast. "Stay away."

Ramsey laughed almost maniacally. It was so loud a guffaw that it rattled Delia's crystal in the china cupboard. He nodded toward Hickok. "Does Oliver know you're keeping company tonight?"

She steadied herself, but her voice came in terse bursts, like a handsaw being pulled back and forth across a thick and knotty pine tree. "Where is he? What have you done with him?"

He was near enough to grab the gun, but the hulking presence behind him apparently gave him pause. "Oh, your precious Oliver. Well, Ollie was in on it from the git-go. He got scared and wanted to stop. But it was too late. He knew all about that killing. He was in on it. Christ, woman, love is blind. He was always in on it."

"You killed him." She uttered the words, her voice firm and quiet, as if she had always known what had happened.

"You were a true prize, Delia. He didn't need a gold mine. Someone who believed him to be pure as the Savior himself. What a treasure!"

"And you thought you deserved a piece of that pie," Hickok chimed in. He caught Delia's eye as he moved toward the chair where his mended frock coat lay.

Ramsey's eyes glittered. He raked them over Delia, slim and attractive, even in her worn cotton wrapper. "Ah, now. You wanted it. Just as much as I did. Maybe more."

"No," she said.

"Ollie didn't believe it of you, Delia. But I told him all about us." The words came fast, the man's tone as sinister as his meaning. "He died defending your honor. Tried to kill me for those words. But I cut him afore he could move. He died quicklike."

She dropped her eyes, and he lunged. She gasped as he grabbed the rifle barrel. They struggled. She pulled the trigger. Nothing happened. The rifle had jammed. Again, Ramsey's maniacal laughter filled the room. He pushed forward against the gun, pinning her against the wall.

A piercing cry startled them all.

"You ain't gonna hurt my mama no more!" Joey pointed the ivory-handled pistol square at Kinkaid's back.

"Joey," Hickok said. "Remember what I told you, son. Don't aim—"

"'Less you're killin'," the boy finished.

"You don't want to kill him. Save your bullets for the squirrels." Who knew where the youngster's eyes were tracking?—especially in the murky half-light flickering through the room.

"But he hurt my mama. I saw him do it."

"But don't you make it worse now. If you kill him, you'll hurt your mama, too."

The boy wavered, looking first toward Hickok and then at his mother, whose face shone with tears. Hickok pushed forward and spun Kinkaid around. He gave him a solid punch in the jaw. The man reeled from the devastating blow and fell at Delia's feet. Joey, lips quivering, let the pistol drop. His own face crumpled with bitter tears. He ran to his mother, who knelt and accepted his embrace, and then wiped his tears away. "You are my big man now, Joey," she said. "That was very, very brave."

Hickok took the pistol, placing it in his waistband. "Just like Wild Bill," he said. He winked at Delia. The words hung in the air like gun smoke for a moment.

"Yes, just like Wild Bill."

She held her son apart from her embrace. "You got that from the cabinet." He nodded. She scolded him for disobeying her.

Hickok examined the Winchester. "It's not jammed," he said. "No ammunition."

"But I loaded it—" She looked at Joey. He looked away.

"I've already been squirrel hunting."

"Oh, Joey." Because she felt distraught and relieved all at the same time, she hugged him. "Don't ever do that again. You tell me before you get an inkling to do such a thing."

Hickok used his belt to tie Kinkaid's hands behind his back. Delia herded Joey back to the kitchen and made him sit in a chair. She retrieved a length of rope that Oliver had bought for his mining chores and helped Hickok tie the outlaw's ankles together.

"If he had to kiss one of us," she said, serious as could be, "I'd just as soon it was you."

He had to laugh because she was such a sober sort that the way she said it sounded comical. His glee spurred her own. She giggled like a little girl, with high-pitched, musical cheeps.

"I used to play dead and scare one of my little girl cousins near to death," he said. "I got such a tickle out of her. She never could just leave me. She always had just enough fear of death that she tried to come to my rescue, and she'd always jump and be mad when I sat up and spoke to her."

"Good thing you've changed." She said it with a straight face.

He laughed again, and his mirth was contagious. But then she held her arm across her face as if laughter was not an allowable joy.

In the morning, Hickok gave Joey a lesson in reloading and let him shoot one of his pistols. Despite the uneven track of his eye, the boy was a remarkably straight shot. He and the escaped jailbird had slept during the short night. Delia and Hickok both feared the man would awaken and bolt, so they took turns holding Hickok's pistols on him.

As promised, the neighbor, Martin Daley, came with his wagon, ready for his weekly sojourn out of the hills and into town for supplies. When Delia explained the situation, he said, "Well, I'll be switched." His gaze fell on Hickok, and he began to speak, but Delia gave a curt nod toward her son and quickly introduced Hickok as her friend, James.

"Pleasure," said Daley, and he winked at her so she knew their secret would be safe.

Hickok had convinced her to ride back to Deadwood, and promised he would make arrangements with his friend, Charlie Utter, to make sure "The Deadwood Dancer" would be properly recorded and that Delia and

Joey would receive the proceeds from the diggings, with a small percentage paid to Charlie for his assistance.

When they arrived in town, she asked, "Where will you go now?"

"Oh, I'll be around," he said. "I'll be back to check on you in a few days."

Someone across the street hollered to him about a poker game brewing at the Number 10. "Glad you're back. We didn't think you'd stay long, but you were on such a winning streak, we didn't know how else to cool that off."

He lifted Delia from the wagon. "Thanks for straightening me out, Jeb. Sure appreciate your help. Next time you might leave a horse."

Jeb slapped his knee and chortled. "You're the one what likes those practical jokes, eh? Gotcha good, didn't we?"

"You did, and I'll tan your hide at the table for it." His tone was good-natured, but he sighed heavily as he held Delia steady. To her, he said, "That settles that. Now we know why I landed on your doorstep in such a world of hurt."

"You're a gambler, then?"

"All my life, ma'am."

"Is it worth the risk?"

"Almost always."

She returned his smile. "I don't know how to thank you."

"Well, I believe since you nursed and fed me, we'll just call honors even. No thanks necessary. Just you and Joey take care of yourselves. He's a good little man."

"We might never see you again."

"Oh, I'll check on you in a few days."

She reached into her bag and drew out a small, silver thimble. "A memento of your day with us," she said. Accepting the gift, he closed his hand on her smaller one, rough from overwork. He became aware of how smooth his own hands had gotten as a result of not enough work. They stood there, caught in the moment, their friendship thickening like the chokecherry juice his mother used to make into jelly. He was reluctant to leave her.

The boy watched them and said, "Was it a surprise?"

"Yes," James said, his eyes still on hers. He put the thimble in the inside pocket of his frock coat. "The best kind of surprise. I'll keep it near my heart." He shook Joey's hand. "You're a man now. And I am always in your debt."

"James?" Delia Hemming's voice came soft. He turned to her, and she said, "Watch your back."

"You too, Delia." Her cheeks colored at the use of her first name, the first time he had called her by her given name. He handed her a card. It named Dr. Joshua Thorne, an eye specialist from Kansas City, Missouri, and gave an address. "This might help Joey," he said. "Maybe one day they can make some magic 'specktackles' for him."

A dust devil turned up the dirt in the street, whirled along the boardwalk past Goldberg's Grocery, and twirled beside Delia's skirts. The twister stopped at the wagon. They parted there. She and her son headed to the boardinghouse, and he and Martin Daley took the frustrated Kinkaid to the deputy. Despite himself, he couldn't help but turn back and watch the handsome woman and the brave little boy walking hand in hand down the street.

After midnight, he took a walk around town, a habit he had acquired way back when he had been in charge of the law in Abilene. Laughter and tinny music and all sorts of ruckuses spilled from the saloons. The sounds and smells touched his senses in a different way now that he had finally been sated with a dose of opium. He felt as if his feet barely touched the boards, but the hollow ringing of his footfalls echoed long in his mind like the tapping of pickaxes against granite. He wouldn't be doing any of that mining after all, he decided. His gold would have to be found in the cards. Inside his canvas tent at the edge of town, he lit his coal-oil lamp. He planned to write a letter to Agnes, but his eyes burned. There would be time in the morning to tend to such details. He trimmed the wick. Sweet darkness soothed his aching eyes. He fell asleep to the questioning call of a nearby hoot owl.

The Gift of Cochise

Louis L'Amour

Tense, and white to the lips, Angie Lowe stood in the door of her cabin with a double-barreled shotgun in her hands. Besides the door was a Winchester '73, and on the table inside the house were two Walker Colts.

Facing the cabin were twelve Apaches on ragged calico ponies, and one of the Indians had lifted his hand palm outward. The Apache sitting on the white-splashed bay pony was Cochise.

Beside Angie were her seven-year-old son Jimmy and her five-year-old daughter Jane.

Cochise sat his pony in silence; his black, unreadable eyes studied the woman, the children, the cabin, and the small garden. He looked at the two ponies in the corral and the three cows. His eyes strayed to the small stack of hay cut from the meadow, and to the few steers farther up the canyon.

Three times the warriors of Cochise had attacked this solitary cabin, and three times they had been turned back. In all, they had lost seven men, and three had been wounded. Four ponies had been killed. His braves reported that there was no man in the house, only a woman and two children, so Cochise had come to see for himself this woman who was so certain a shot with a rifle and who killed his fighting men.

These were some of the same fighting men who had outfought, outguessed, and outrun the finest American army on record, an army outnumbering the Apaches by a hundred to one. Yet a lone woman with two small children had fought them off, and the woman was scarcely more than a girl. And she was prepared to fight now. There was a glint of admiration in the old eyes that appraised her. The Apache was a fighting man, and he respected fighting blood.

"Where is your man?"

"He has gone to El Paso." Angie's voice was steady, but she was frightened as she had never been before. She recognized Cochise from descriptions, and she knew that if he decided to kill or capture her, it would be done. Until now, the sporadic attacks she had fought off had been those of casual bands of warriors who raided her in passing.

"He has been gone a long time. How long?"

Angie hesitated, but it was not in her to lie. "He has been gone four months."

Cochise considered that. No one but a fool would leave such a woman, or such fine children. Only one thing could have prevented his return. "Your man is dead," he said.

Angie waited, her heart pounding with heavy, measured beats. She had guessed long ago that Ed had been killed, but the way Cochise spoke did not imply that Apaches had killed him, only that he must be dead or he would have returned.

"You fight well," Cochise said. "You have killed my young men."

"Your young men attacked me." She hesitated, then added, "They stole my horses."

"Your man is gone. Why do you not leave?"

Angie looked at him with surprise. "Leave? Why, this is my home. This land is mine. This spring is mine. I shall not leave."

"This is an Apache spring," Cochise reminded her reasonably.

"The Apache lives in the mountains," Angie replied. "He does not need this spring. I have two children, and I do need it."

"But when the Apache comes this way, where shall he drink? His throat is dry and you keep him from water."

The very fact that Cochise was willing to talk raised her hopes. There had been a time when the Apache made no war on the white man. "Cochise speaks with a forked tongue," she said. "There is water yonder." She gestured toward the hills, where Ed had told her there were springs. "But if the people of Cochise come in peace, they may drink at this spring."

The Apache leader smiled faintly. Such a woman would rear a nation of warriors. He nodded at Jimmy. "The small one—does he also shoot?"

"He does," Angie said proudly, "and well too!" She pointed at an upthrust leaf of prickly pear. "Show them, Jimmy."

The prickly pear was an easy two hundred yards away, and the Winchester was long and heavy, but he lifted it eagerly and steadied it against the doorjamb as his father had taught him, held his sight an instant, then fired. The bud on top of the prickly pear disintegrated.

There were grunts of appreciation from the dark-haired warriors. Cochise chuckled.

"The little warrior shoots well. It is well you have no

man. You might raise an army of little warriors to fight my people."

"I have no wish to fight your people," Angie said quietly. "Your people have your ways, and I have mine. I live in peace when I am left in peace. I did not think," she added with dignity, "that the great Cochise made war on women!"

The Apache looked at her, then turned his pony away. "My people will trouble you no longer," he said. "You are the mother of a strong son."

"What about my two ponies?" she called after him. "Your young men took them from me."

Cochise did not turn or look back, and the little cavalcade of riders followed him away. Angie stepped back into the cabin and closed the door. Then she sat down abruptly, her face white, the muscles in her legs trembling.

When morning came, she went cautiously to the spring for water. Her ponies were back in the corral. They had been returned during the night.

Slowly, the days drew on. Angie broke a small piece of the meadow and planted it. Alone, she cut hay in the meadow and built another stack. She saw Indians several times, but they did not bother her. One morning, when she opened the door, a quarter of an antelope lay on the step, but no Indian was in sight. Several times, during the weeks that followed, she saw moccasin tracks near the spring.

Once, going out at daybreak, she saw an Indian girl dipping water from the spring. Angie called to her, and the girl turned quickly, facing her. Angie walked toward her, offering a bright red silk ribbon. Pleased at the gift, the Apache girl left.

And the following morning there was another quarter of an antelope on her step—but she saw no Indian.

Ed Lowe had built the cabin in West Dog Canyon in

the spring of 1871, but it was Angie who chose the spot, not Ed. In Santa Fe they would have told you that Ed Lowe was good-looking, shiftless, and agreeable. He was also, unfortunately, handy with a pistol.

Angie's father had come from County Mayo to New York and from New York to the Mississippi, where he became a tough, brawling river boatman. In New Orleans, he met a beautiful Cajun girl and married her. Together, they started west for Santa Fe, and Angie was born en route. Both parents died of cholera when Angie was fourteen. She lived with an Irish family for the following three years, then married Ed Lowe when she was seventeen.

Santa Fe was not good for Ed, and Angie kept after him until they started south. It was Apache country, but they kept on until they reached the old Spanish ruin in West Dog. Here there were grass, water, and shelter from the wind. There was fuel, and there were piñons and game. And Angie, with an Irish eye for the land, saw that it would grow crops.

The house itself was built on the ruins of the old Spanish building, using the thick walls and the floor. The location had been admirably chosen for defense. The house was built in a corner of the cliff, under the sheltering overhang, so that approach was possible from only two directions, both covered by an easy field of fire from the door and windows.

For seven months, Ed worked hard and steadily. He put in the first crop, he built the house, and proved himself a handy man with tools. He repaired the old plow they had bought, cleaned out the spring, and paved and walled it with slabs of stone. If he was lonely for the carefree companions of Santa Fe, he gave no indication of it. Provisions were low, and when he finally started off to the south, Angie watched him go with an ache in her heart.

She did not know whether she loved Ed. The first flush of enthusiasm had passed, and Ed Lowe had proved something less than she had believed. But he had tried, she admitted. And it had not been easy for him. He was an amiable soul, given to whittling and idle talk, all of which he missed in the loneliness of the Apache country. And when he rode away, she had no idea whether she would ever see him again. She never did.

Santa Fe was far and away to the north, but the growing village of El Paso was less than a hundred miles to the west, and it was there Ed Lowe rode for supplies and seed.

He had several drinks—his first in months—in one of the saloons. As the liquor warmed his stomach, Ed Lowe looked around agreeably. For a moment, his eyes clouded with worry as he thought of his wife and children back in Apache country, but it was not in Ed Lowe to worry for long. He had another drink and leaned on the bar, talking to the bartender. All Ed had ever asked of life was enough to eat, a horse to ride, an occasional drink, and companions to talk with. Not that he had anything important to say. He just liked to talk.

Suddenly a chair grated on the floor, and Ed turned. A lean, powerful man with a shock of uncut black hair and a torn, weather-faded shirt stood at bay. Facing him across the table were three hard-faced young men, obviously brothers.

Ches Lane did not notice Ed Lowe watching from the bar. He had eyes only for the men facing him. "You done that deliberate!" The statement was a challenge.

The broad-chested man on the left grinned through

broken teeth. "That's right, Ches. I done it deliberate. You killed Dan Tolliver on the Brazos."

"He made the quarrel." Comprehension came to Ches. He was boxed, and by three of the fighting, blood-hungry Tollivers.

"Don't make no difference," the broad-chested Tolliver said. "'Who sheds a Tolliver's blood, by a Tolliver's hand must die!'"

Ed Lowe moved suddenly from the bar. "Three to one is long odds," he said, his voice low and friendly. "If the gent in the corner is willin', I'll side him."

Two Tollivers turned toward him. Ed Lowe was smiling easily, his hand hovering near his gun. "You stay out of this!" one of the brothers said harshly.

"I'm in," Ed replied. "Why don't you boys light a shuck?"

"No, by—!" The man's hand dropped for his gun, and the room thundered with sound.

Ed was smiling easily, unworried as always. His gun flashed up. He felt it leap in his hand, saw the nearest Tolliver smashed back, and he shot him again as he dropped. He had only time to see Ches Lane with two guns out and another Tolliver down when something struck him through the stomach and he stepped back against the bar, suddenly sick.

The sound stopped, and the room was quiet, and there was the acrid smell of powder smoke. Three Tollivers were down and dead, and Ed Lowe was dying. Ches Lane crossed to him.

"We got 'em," Ed said, "we sure did. But they got me."

Suddenly his face changed. "Oh, Lord in heaven, what'll Angie do?" And then he crumpled over on the floor and lay still, the blood staining his shirt and mingling with the sawdust.

Stiff-faced, Ches looked up. "Who was Angie?" he asked.

"His wife," the bartender told him. "She's up northeast somewhere, in Apache country. He was tellin' me about her. Two kids too."

Ches Lane stared down at the crumpled, used-up body of Ed Lowe. The man had saved his life.

One he could have beaten, two he might have beaten, three would have killed him. Ed Lowe, stepping in when he did, had saved the life of Ches Lane.

"He didn't say where?"

"No."

Ches Lane shoved his hat back on his head. "What's northeast of here?"

The bartender rested his hands on the bar. "Cochise," he said.

For more than three months, whenever he could rustle the grub, Ches Lane quartered the country over and back. The trouble was, he had no lead to the location of Ed Lowe's homestead. An examination of Ed's horse revealed nothing. Lowe had bought seed and ammunition, and the seed indicated a good water supply, and the ammunition implied trouble.

But in the country there was always trouble.

A man had died to save his life, and Ches Lane had a deep sense of obligation. Somewhere that wife waited, if she was still alive, and it was up to him to find her and look out for her. He rode northeast, cutting for sign, but found none. Sandstorms had wiped out any hope of back-trailing Lowe. Actually, West Dog Canyon was more east than north, but this he had no way of knowing.

North he went, skirting the rugged San Andreas

Mountains. Heat baked him hot, dry winds parched his skin. His hair grew dry and stiff and alkali-whitened. He rode north, and soon the Apaches knew of him. He fought them at a lonely water hole, and he fought them on the run. They killed his horse, and he switched his saddle to the spare and rode on. They cornered him in the rocks, and he killed two of them and escaped by night.

They trailed him through the White Sands, and he left two more for dead. He fought fiercely and bitterly, and would not be turned from his quest. He turned east through the lava beds and still more east to the Pecos. He saw only two white men, and neither knew of a white woman.

The bearded man laughed harshly. "A woman alone? She wouldn't last a month! By now the Apaches got her, or she's dead. Don't be a fool! Leave this country before you die here."

Lean, wind-whipped, and savage, Ches Lane pushed on. Mescaleros cornered him in Rawhide Draw and he fought them to a standstill. Grimly, the Apaches clung to his trail.

The sheer determination of the man fascinated them. Bred and born in a rugged and lonely land, the Apaches knew the difficulties of survival; knew how a man could live, how he must live. Even as they tried to kill the man, they loved him, for he was one of their own.

Lane's jeans grew ragged. Two bullet holes were added to the old black hat. The slicker was torn; the saddle, so carefully kept until now, was scratched by gravel and brush. At night he cleaned his guns and by day he scouted the trails. Three times he found lonely ranch houses burned to the ground, the buzzard- and coyote-stripped bones of their owners lying nearby.

Once he found a covered wagon, its canvas flopping

in the wind, a man lying sprawled on the seat with a pistol near his hand. He was dead and his wife was dead, and their canteens rattled like empty skulls.

Leaner every day, Ches Lane pushed on. He camped one night in a canyon near some white oaks. He heard a hoof click on stone and he backed away from his tiny fire, gun in hand.

The riders were white men, and there were two of them. Joe Tompkins and Wiley Lynn were headed west, and Ches Lane could have guessed why. They were men he had known before, and he told them what he was doing.

Lynn chuckled. He was a thin-faced man with lank yellow hair and dirty fingers. "Seems a mighty strange way to get a woman. There's some as comes easier."

"This ain't for fun," Ches replied shortly. "I got to find her."

Tompkins stared at him. "Ches, you're crazy! That gent declared himself in of his own wish and desire. Far's that goes, the gal's dead. No woman could last this long in Apache country."

At daylight, the two men headed west, and Ches Lane turned south.

Antelope and deer are curious creatures, often led to their death by curiosity. The longhorn, soon going wild on the plains, acquires the same characteristic. He is essentially curious. Any new thing or strange action will bring his head up and his ears alert. Often a longhorn, like a deer, can be lured within a stone's throw by some queer antic, by a handkerchief waving, by a man under a hide, by a man on foot.

This character of the wild things holds true of the Indian. The lonely rider who fought so desperately and knew the desert so well soon became a subject of gossip among the Apaches. Over the fires of many a rancheria they discussed this strange rider who seemed to be going nowhere, but always riding, like a lean wolf dog on a trail. He rode across the mesas and down the canyons; he studied signs at every water hole; he looked long from every ridge. It was obvious to the Indians that he searched for something—but what?

Cochise had come again to the cabin in West Dog Canyon. "Little warrior too small," he said, "too small for hunt. You join my people. Take Apache for man."

"No." Angie shook her head. "Apache ways are good for the Apache, and the white man's ways are good for white men—and women."

The Apache rode away and said no more, but that night, as she had on many other nights after the children were asleep, Angie cried. She wept silently, her head pillowed on her arms. She was as pretty as ever, but her face was thin, showing the worry and struggle of the months gone by, the weeks and months without hope.

The crops were small but good. Little Jimmy worked beside her. At night, Angie sat alone on the steps and watched the shadows gather down the long canyon, listening to the coyotes yapping from the rim of the Guadalupes, hearing the horses blowing in the corral. She watched, still hopeful, but now she knew that Cochise was right: Ed would not return.

But even if she had been ready to give this up, the first home she had known, there could be no escape. Here she was protected by Cochise. Other Apaches from other tribes would not so willingly grant her peace.

At daylight she was up. The morning air was bright and balmy, but soon it would be hot again. Jimmy went to the spring for water, and when breakfast was over, the children played while Angie sat in the shade of a huge old cottonwood and sewed. It was a Sunday, warm and lovely. From time to time, she lifted her eyes to look down the canyon, half smiling at her own foolishness.

The hard-packed earth of the yard was swept clean of dust; the pans hanging on the kitchen wall were neat and shining. The children's hair had been clipped, and there was a small bouquet on the kitchen table.

After a while, Angie put aside her sewing and changed her dress. She did her hair carefully, and then, looking in her mirror, she reflected with sudden pain that she *was* pretty, and that she was only a girl.

Resolutely, she turned from the mirror and, taking up her Bible, went back to the seat under the cottonwood. The children left their playing and came to her, for this was a Sunday ritual, their only one. Opening the Bible, she read slowly.

" . . . though I walk through the valley of the shadow of death. I will fear no evil; for thou art with me; thy rod and thy staff, they comfort me. Thou preparest a table before me in the presence of mine enemies: thou . . ."

"Mommy." Jimmy tugged at her sleeve. "Look!"

Ches Lane had reached a narrow canyon by mid-afternoon and decided to make camp. There was a small possibility he would find another such spot, and he was dead tired, his muscles sodden with fatigue. The canyon was one of those unexpected gashes in the caprock that gave no indication of its presence until you came right on it. After some searching, Ches found a route to the bottom and made camp under a wind-hollowed over-hang. There was water, and there was a small patch of grass.

After his horse had a drink and a roll on the ground,

it began cropping eagerly at the rich, green grass, and Ches built a smokeless fire of some ancient driftwood in the canyon bottom. It was his first hot meal in days, and when he had finished he put out his fire, rolled a smoke, and leaned back contentedly.

Before darkness settled, he climbed to the rim and looked over the country. The sun had gone down, and the shadows were growing long. After a half hour of study, he decided there was no living thing within miles, except for the usual desert life. Returning to the bottom, he moved his horse to fresh grass, then rolled in his blanket. For the first time in a month, he slept without fear.

He woke up suddenly in the broad daylight. The horse was listening to something, his head up. Swiftly, Ches went to the horse and led it back under the overhang. Then he drew on his boots, rolled his blankets, and saddled the horse. Still he heard no sound.

Climbing the rim again, he studied the desert and found nothing. Returning to his horse, he mounted up and rode down the canyon toward the flatland beyond. Coming out of the canyon mouth, he rode right into the middle of a war party of more than twenty Apaches—invisible until suddenly they stood up behind rocks, their rifles leveled. And he didn't have a chance.

Swiftly, they bound his wrists to the saddle horn and tied his feet. Only then did he see the man who led the party. It was Cochise.

He was a lean, wiry Indian of past fifty, his black hair streaked with gray, his features strong and clean-cut. He stared at Lane, and there was nothing in his face to reveal what he might be thinking.

Several of the younger warriors pushed forward, talking excitedly and waving their arms. Ches Lane understood some of it, but he sat straight in the saddle, his head up, waiting. Then Cochise spoke and the party turned and, leading his horse, they rode away.

The miles grew long and the sun was hot. He was offered no water and he asked for none. The Indians ignored him. Once a young brave rode near and struck him viciously. Lane made no sound, gave no indication of pain. When they finally stopped, it was beside a huge anthill swarming with big, red desert ants.

Roughly, they quickly untied him and jerked him from his horse. He dug in his heels and shouted at them in Spanish. "The Apaches are women! They tie me to the ants because they are afraid to fight me!"

An Indian struck him, and Ches glared at the man. If he must die, he would show them how it should be done. Yet he knew the unpredictable nature of the Indian, of his great respect for courage. "Give me a knife, and I'll kill any of your warriors!" They stared at him, and one powerfully built Apache angrily ordered them to get on with it. Cochise spoke, and the big warrior replied angrily.

Ches Lane nodded at the anthill. "Is this the death for a fighting man? I have fought your strong men and beaten them. I have left no trail for them to follow, and for months I have lived among you, and now only by accident have you captured me. Give me a knife," he added grimly, "and I will fight *him*!" He indicated the big, black-faced Apache.

The warrior's cruel mouth hardened, and he struck Ches across the face.

The white man tasted blood and fury. "Woman!" Ches said. "Coyote! You are afraid!" Ches turned on Cochise, as the Indians stood irresolute. "Free my hands and let me fight!" he demanded. "If I win, let me go free."

Cochise said something to the big Indian. Instantly, there was stillness. Then an Apache sprang forward and, with a slash of his knife, freed Lane's hands. Shaking loose the thongs, Ches Lane chafed his wrists to bring back the circulation. An Indian threw a knife at his feet. It was his own bowie knife.

Ches took off his riding boots. In sock feet, his knife gripped low in his hand, its cutting edge up, he looked at the big warrior.

"I promise you nothing," Cochise said in Spanish, "but an honorable death."

The big warrior came at him on cat feet. Warily, Ches circled. He had not only to defeat this Apache but to escape. He permitted himself a glance toward his horse. It stood alone. No Indian held it.

The Apache closed swiftly, thrusting wickedly with the knife. Ches, who'd learned knife-fighting in the bayou country of Louisiana, turned his hip sharply, and the blade slid past him. He struck swiftly, but the Apache's forward movement deflected the blade, and it failed to penetrate. However, as it swept up between the Indian's body and arm, it cut a deep gash in the warrior's left armpit.

The Indian sprang again, like a clawing cat, streaming blood. Ches moved aside, but a backhand sweep nicked him, and he felt the sharp bite of the blade. Turning, he paused on the balls of his feet.

He had had no water in hours. His lips were cracked. Yet he sweated now, and the salt of it stung his eyes. He stared into the malevolent eyes of the Apache, then moved to meet him. The Indian lunged, and Ches sidestepped like a boxer and spun on the ball of his foot.

The sudden side step threw the Indian past him, but Ches failed to drive the knife into the Apache's kidney when his foot rolled on a stone. The point left a thin red line across the Indian's back. The Indian was quick.

Before Ches could recover his balance, he grasped the white man's knife wrist. Desperately, Ches grabbed for the Indian's knife hand and got the wrist, and they stood there straining, chest to chest.

Seeing his chance, Ches suddenly let his knees buckle, then brought up his knee and fell back, throwing the Apache over his head to the sand. Instantly, he whirled and was on his feet, standing over the Apache. The warrior had lost his knife, and he lay there, staring up, his eyes black with hatred.

Coolly, Ches stepped back, picked up the Indian's knife, and tossed it to him contemptuously. There was a grunt from the watching Indians, and then his antagonist rushed. But loss of blood had weakened the warrior, and Ches stepped in swiftly, struck the blade aside, then thrust the point of his blade hard against the Indian's belly.

Black eyes glared into his without yielding. A thrust, and the man would be disemboweled, but Ches stepped back. "He is a strong man," Ches said in Spanish. "It is enough that I have won."

Deliberately, he walked to his horse and swung into the saddle He looked around, and every rifle covered him.

So he had gained nothing. He had hoped that mercy might lead to mercy, that the Apaches' respect for a fighting man would win his freedom. He had failed. Again they bound him to his horse, but they did not take his knife from him.

When they camped at last, he was given food and drink. He was bound again, and a blanket was thrown over him. At daylight they were again in the saddle. In Spanish he asked where they were taking him, but they gave no indication of hearing. When they stopped again, it was beside a pole corral, near a stone cabin.

* * *

When Jimmy spoke, Angie got quickly to her feet. She recognized Cochise with a start of relief, but she saw instantly that this was a war party. And then she saw the prisoner.

Their eyes met and she felt a distinct shock. He was a white man, a big, unshaven man who badly needed both a bath and a haircut, his clothes ragged and bloody. Cochise gestured at the prisoner.

"No take Apache man, you take white man. This man good for hunt, good for fight. He strong warrior. You take 'em."

Flushed and startled, Angie stared at the prisoner and caught a faint glint of humor in his dark eyes.

"Is this here the fate worse than death I hear tell of?" he inquired gently.

"Who are you?" she asked, and was immediately conscious that it was an extremely silly question.

The Apaches had drawn back and were watching curiously. She could do nothing for the present but accept the situation. Obviously they intended to do her a kindness, and it would not do to offend them. If they had not brought this man to her, he might have been killed.

"Name's Ches Lane, ma'am," he said. "Will you untie me? I'd feel a lot safer."

"Of course." Still flustered, she went to him and untied his hands. One Indian said something, and the others chuckled; then, with a whoop, they swung their horses and galloped off down the canyon.

Their departure left her suddenly helpless, the shadowy globe of her loneliness shattered by this utterly strange man standing before her, this big, bearded man brought to her out of the desert.

She smoothed her apron, suddenly pale as she realized what his delivery to her implied. What must he think of her? She turned away quickly. "There's hot water," she said hastily, to prevent his speaking. "Dinner is almost ready."

She walked quickly into the house and stopped before the stove, her mind a blank. She looked around her as if she had suddenly woken up in a strange place. She heard water being poured into the basin by the door, and heard him take Ed's razor. She had never moved the box. To have moved it would—

"Sight of work done here, ma'am."

She hesitated, then turned with determination and stepped into the doorway. "Yes, Ed—"

"You're Angie Lowe."

Surprised, she turned toward him, and recognized his own startled awareness of her. As he shaved, he told her about Ed, and what had happened that day in the saloon.

"He—Ed was like that. He never considered consequences until it was too late."

"Lucky for me he didn't."

He was younger-looking with his beard gone. There was a certain quiet dignity in his face. She went back inside and began putting plates on the table. She was conscious that he had moved to the door and was watching her.

"You don't have to stay," she said. "You owe me nothing. Whatever Ed did, he did because he was that kind of person. You aren't responsible."

He did not answer, and when she turned again to the stove, she glanced swiftly at him. He was looking across the valley.

There was a studied deference about him when he moved to a place at the table. The children stared, wide-eyed and silent; it had been so long since a man sat at this table.

Angie could not remember when she had felt like this. She was awkwardly conscious of her hands, which never seemed to be in the right place or doing the right things. She scarcely tasted her food, nor did the children.

Ches Lane had no such inhibitions. For the first time, he realized how hungry he was. After the half-cooked meat of lonely, trailside fires, this was tender and flavored. Hot biscuits, desert honey . . . suddenly he looked up, embarrassed at his appetite.

"You were really hungry," she said.

"Man can't fix much, out on the trail."

Later, after he'd got his bedroll from his saddle and unrolled it on the hay in the barn, he walked back to the house and sat on the lowest step. The sun was gone, and they watched the cliffs stretch their red shadows across the valley. A quail called plaintively, a mellow sound of twilight.

"You needn't worry about Cochise," she said. "He'll soon be crossing into Mexico."

"I wasn't thinking about Cochise."

That left her with nothing to say, and she listened again to the quail and watched a lone bright star in the sky.

"A man could get to like it here," he said quietly.

Younger and Faster

Mike Thompson

Sheriff Seth Bullock finished polishing the lenses of his wire-rimmed glasses, hooked the earpieces over his ears, thumbed them back up his long thin nose, and glanced at the clock. It was almost two o'clock. Decision time. Should he take a nap? It had been a long poker game last night and the town was quiet. These days life for the sheriff in Belle Fourche, South Dakota, was, for the most part, sedentary. Now, should he lock the door and lean back in his chair, with his feet up on his desk, or go in back and stretch out on a bunk in a jail cell? Before he could make up his mind, the doorknob rattled and the door was tentatively pushed open.

A small freckled face, topped by a shock of red hair, peeked in through the opening and flashed a large gap-toothed smile at the sheriff. Bullock waved the boy into the office, but the boy's smile quickly vanished as he stepped into the room.

"Sheriff Bullock, sir, my pa says he needs you over to his saloon quick!" the boy blurted out.

"What's the problem, Danny, and why aren't you in school?"

"'Cause it's Saturday, Sheriff, and my pa says you better hurry over to his place!"

"Why didn't he just phone . . . ?"

Before the sheriff could finish his question, the boy started backing out the door. "Pa says I gotta go do my chores!" He spun and disappeared, slamming the door behind him.

Seth Bullock looked up at a calendar, thumbed his great walrus mustache, and slowly rose to his feet. His eyes searched the calendar. "Well, I'll be damned, it is Saturday, 19 September 1908," he told himself as he pushed his chair back and lifted his coat from a nearby hook. "Losing track of the days, I guess." He shrugged into his coat, tugged on a nondescript, old black hat, took a small pistol out of a drawer, and dropped it into a pocket. *You never can tell.*

Sheriff Bullock stepped out onto the sidewalk, adjusted his hat, and pulled the door shut behind him. As was his custom, his eyes slowly surveyed the main street. He noted four automobiles parked along the muddy street. Not very long ago these spaces were only used by horses and wagons. *Times sure are changing.* He looked up at the electrical and telephone wires hanging from poles and running from building to building. He heard the phone behind the closed door of his office begin to ring and shook his head. *Probably Jensen calling to see what's taking me so long. I wonder what's so damned important this early on a Saturday afternoon.* He shrugged and strode down the board sidewalk toward Milo Jensen's Buffalo Bull Saloon.

In passing he admired two spotless automobiles. Saturday, and even though the bank wasn't open, Burnell Finney, the owner, had his black Maxwell parked in front to show it off. The long blue Packard told him Finney's long-time crony, R. C. Gardner, was with him.

I still can't figure how those two keep their cars so clean with all this mud on the roads. Finney must have one of his employees polish his every day.

The sheriff stopped and rattled the knob on the bank door, then put his hands up beside his face and leaned to the glass to see if he could see anything inside. The bank was dark, but there was a dim light showing in the window of the bank president's office in the back.

Gardner and Finney are probably lying to each other about who has the best car, like the rest of us do about horses. I suppose they're drinking expensive whiskey, smoking good cigars, and figuring out ways to make more money. I'm glad I took some from him in that game last night.

He pushed away from the door and looked at the two other cars as he passed them. He didn't recognize either of them, but noted the topless black Ford was heavily encrusted with mud, inside and out. *Now that's what a car should look like when it's been driven on rough roads. That one's come a ways to get here.*

Bullock sighed. *Yes, indeedie, things sure are different.* He turned and continued his walk to the Buffalo Bull Saloon. He paused on the sidewalk in front and looked over the tops of the batwing doors into the dimly lit interior of the saloon.

Milo Jensen, the owner and daytime bartender, leaned against the far end of the bar.

A nattily dressed young man with a mud-spattered derby cocked down over one eye sat at a table using a cloth to wipe at the mud on his shoes. He took a drink from a mug of beer, said something to Jensen, and continued to work on his shoes.

Annie, a young woman who waited tables and worked as a part-time bartender, sat at a nearby table, a handkerchief held to her face, obviously crying. *Annie must be part of the problem.*

Another man sat slouched at a table, his head resting on his arm. He appeared to be asleep. A muddy derby lay beside him on the table and two mud-spattered duster coats were draped over empty chairs.

There's not much doubt about who was riding in that muddy car. Best get in and see what's happening. Bullock squared his shoulders, patted the gun in his pocket, and took a deep breath as he pushed in through the doors and stopped at the near end of the bar.

Milo Jensen said something to the man who was working on his dirty shoes and walked down to where Bullock stood. "Coffee, Sheriff?" he asked loudly. "What took you so long?" he whispered and rolled his eyes over his shoulder. "That dude back there cleaning his shoes is making me damned nervous. He and Annie had a hell of a shouting match a few minutes ago."

Bullock shook his head. "No, Milo, give me a mug of beer," he said, loud enough for the other man to hear.

"Isn't it a bit early for a beer, *Sheriff*?" Jensen asked, putting emphasis on the word "sheriff."

"You don't look like my mother, Milo, so don't be talking like her," Bullock admonished.

Jensen nodded. "One mug of beer coming up, Sheriff."

"Hey, Sheriff!" the man in the dirty derby shouted, looking up from the work on his shoes.

Bullock slowly turned his head and looked at the man. He had a thin, sallow face and a narrow brown mustache that reminded Bullock of a caterpillar. "Yes?"

"Did you know that Annie here was once my girl?" he asked, hooking a thumb at the woman who was now glaring at him.

Bullock shook his head. "No, can't say that I did."

"Back in Minneapolis, it was."

Annie muttered something and wiped at her eyes.

"Shut up or I'll give you a taste of my hand!" the man shouted, and swung his hand in the general direction of the scowling young woman.

Bullock started to speak, but decided to wait and see

what would happen. He didn't know anything about Annie's background and to him she was a young woman with an honest job.

Jensen set a mug of beer in front of him. "That'll be a nickel, Sheriff."

Bullock dropped a handful of coins on the bar. "Would you or your friend care for a drink?" he called to the man wiping at his shoes.

"I think Leroy's had enough, but I'll take a shot of whiskey as long as you're buying."

Jensen nodded, brought up a shot glass, filled it from a nearby bottle, and carried it over to the table where the man was buffing the toes of his shoes. He returned to the bar and selected a coin from the bar in front of the sheriff. "Two bits."

"Your friend's name is Leroy, but I didn't catch yours." Bullock said, and took a sip of beer.

"That's because I haven't given it," the man answered, and downed the shot of whiskey.

"So you haven't," Bullock agreed. "What brings you boys way out here?"

"We were in Deadwood and someone told me Annie was working here. Since we were going to pass this way, I decided to pay her a visit. Us having been betrothed and all."

Bullock nodded. "I see. Would you care for another shot of whiskey?"

The man smiled slightly as he stood, gave each shoe a final buff on the back of his pant legs, walked to the bar, and slid his glass to the center of it. "I'm told you're the man who cleaned up Deadwood back in the seventies, Sheriff Bullock. Story is that you were one hell of a lawman."

Bullock nodded. "It seems you know my name, but I still don't know yours." He made a motion for Jensen to refill the man's glass.

"What difference does my name make?"

"When I'm talking to a man and buying him whiskey, I like to call him by name."

"You think if you keep buying me whiskey, you'll be able to get me in the same condition as Leroy over there? It'd make your job a lot easier, wouldn't it?"

Bullock smiled, shrugged, and pretended to take a sip of beer. "You're a smart one, you are."

The man returned his smile, lifted the shot glass in a toast, and drank his whiskey down.

"I would surmise from the mud spattered on your fine shoes and derby hat that you'd be the gentlemen driving the mud-covered Ford automobile down the street a bit." Bullock took a slow sip of beer and studied the other man over the rim of the mug.

The man nodded. "The top's broken and won't stay up, so we did get a little muddy." He looked down, admired the shine on his shoes, and gave them another buff on the back of his pants legs. "Most of the mud on my shoes came from your damned street out there. They're cleaned up pretty good, though."

"Are you all right, Annie?" Sheriff Bullock asked.

"That's nothing for you to be concerned about, Sheriff," the man in the derby answered.

Bullock heard a noise, and turned to see the man at the table sitting up and grinning drunkenly at him. He was red-faced, with heavy, oiled black hair parted down the middle and long pointed sideburns. His well-waxed mustache was bent downward on one side from being slept on.

"The sheriff wants to buy you a drink, Leroy," his friend announced.

"Wunnerful," the man muttered as he jammed his derby on his head and pushed himself partway to his feet. He waved his arms for balance and crashed over his chair to a heap on the floor. He lay silent and unmoving until he started to giggle. Finally, he got his hands under himself, pushed up to his knees, managed to stand, and straightened his jacket. "Damn, it's drunk out, Gordon," he slurred, and began to giggle again as he worked to put the chair back on its legs.

"Would you be having another drink, *Gordon?*" Bullock asked with a slight smile.

"So, now you know my name, Sheriff," Gordon said, glaring at Leroy.

"Give these lads a shot of whiskey, Milo," Bullock said, pushing at the coins on the bar. He watched Leroy in the mirror behind the bar as he stood looking around the room as if trying to decide what to do. "Leroy, why don't you come over here to the bar and have a drink?"

Leroy cocked his head as he looked at the sheriff and then smiled drunkenly. "You buyin'?"

"Yes, I am," Bullock answered, motioning him over. "Belly up to the bar."

Leroy walked several unsteady steps to the bar and leaned his elbows on it.

"Pour, Milo," Bullock instructed, pushing at the coins again.

Milo Jensen poured two shot glasses full of whiskey and slid them across the bar.

Leroy quickly downed his, but Gordon looked down at the glass in front of him and then back up at Sheriff Bullock. "I don't want to get in the same condition as Leroy here."

"Suit yourself," Bullock answered and pretended to take a sip of beer.

The telephone on the wall at the end of the bar began to clang in a series of long and short rings. "That's my ring," Milo stated, and lifted the receiver to his ear. "Buffalo Bull Saloon."

Leroy pushed back from the bar, shuffled over to his table, and flopped in a chair. "Damn, it's drunk out," he mumbled, put his head on his arm on the table, and appeared to fall asleep.

"Sheriff, the phone's for you," Milo Jensen announced, setting the receiver on the bar. "Sounds like it's long distance."

"Looks like Leroy's a bit worse for wear," Bullock told Gordon as he walked past him. He lifted the receiver to his ear. "This is Bullock."

"Seth, this is John Mason, over in Fort Pierre," the voice from the wire announced.

"How are you, John, and how'd you know you'd find me here?"

"The operator rang a few places for me. It is Saturday and the town isn't all that big."

"What can I do for you?"

"I called to ask you to be on the lookout for a couple of hard cases that broke out of jail up in Dickinson two days ago. They were locked up for a bank robbery over in Montana. Jumped the deputy and escaped. Beat him up pretty bad. They're men not to be fooled with. Looks like they stole a car here sometime last night and lit out in your direction."

"Interesting," Bullock answered, glancing at Gordon, who was watching him intently. "Tell me, John, how much are those two critters going for today?" He put his hand up loosely over the mouthpiece. "Man's trying to sell me a couple of horses. Been dealing for over a week now."

Gordon nodded and turned his attention to the girl sitting at the table glaring at him.

"What's your best offer, John?" Bullock asked, into the telephone mouthpiece.

"You got somebody there, Seth?" the phone voice asked.

"Yep, both of them."

"Those two I was just talking about?" Concern showed in Mason's voice.

"Correct, both of them. Won't deal on just one. Two or nothing."

"Watch out for the skinny one. He's got a thirty-eight-caliber automatic pistol. Fancy silver thing with pearl handles. They took it away from him when they arrested them, but the safe wasn't locked and they cleaned it out when they escaped. They've got at least six handguns!"

"That's an interesting point."

"Can you talk at all? Is there anybody in town I can call to help you?"

Hell, I can't tell him anything. "Not right now."

"I can be there in two hours. I'll bring a couple of deputies. Don't do anything foolish. Just stall 'em. Understand?"

"That'd be fine and I'll look forward to it."

"I'm on my way." The phone line went dead.

"I won't go more than my original offer." Bullock hung up the receiver. "Damn fool must think I'm an idiot when it comes to buying horses," he muttered loud enough for Gordon to hear.

Gordon seemed to be centering his attention on Annie as Bullock returned to his beer.

"What line of work are you men in?" Bullock asked, pretending to take another drink of beer.

"What difference does that make?" Gordon answered, looking over at the sheriff.

"Well, with those fancy shoes and clothes, I didn't figure you to be men who worked with your hands. You look more like salesmen. I mean, what the hell, you've even got a car."

Gordon laughed. "Gimme a beer," he ordered.

"Sure you don't want another shot?" Bullock asked.

"No, I don't want another damned shot!" Gordon

shouted. "I may be younger than you, Old Man, but I sure as hell ain't stupid!"

Careful, the boy's getting testy.

Jensen quickly poured a mug of beer and slid it in front of Gordon.

"The sheriff's buying this one," Gordon said, lifting the beer and taking a drink. "Are you wearing a gun, Old Man?"

Bullock shook his head and slowly spread his coat open. "Don't need one in a quiet town like this. Are you wearing one, Gordon?"

Gordon ignored him as he took another drink of his beer and leered at Annie. "Now that you mention it, Old Man, I do have a pistol," he answered, lowering his beer and smiling smugly. He opened his coat, revealing the pearl handle of a silver automatic pistol sticking up from the waistband of his pants. "Eight shots as fast as I can pull the trigger," Gordon stated proudly, patting the handle of the pistol. "And I'm good with it too!"

"Never fired one of those automatic pistols," Bullock said. "How about we go out behind the building and you can show me how fast it shoots?"

Gordon looked at him blankly and broke into wild laughter. "You're funny, Old Man! Really funny! Just how damned stupid do you think I am?"

Bullock shrugged, smiled, and took a drink from his beer. *This man is not to be fooled with.* "You must sell something awfully valuable if you have to be that well armed."

The smile left Gordon's face as he tipped his head and studied Bullock through narrowed eyes. "What do you think we sell, Old Man?"

"Why is it you're calling me Old Man now?" Bullock asked. "What happened to Sheriff?"

"How do I know you're the sheriff? I haven't seen your badge. How do I know he's not just calling you sheriff?"

Bullock pulled back his coat, patted his vest pockets, drew out a badge, and slid it down the bar toward Gordon. "There, how's that?"

Gordon took a drink from his beer, lifted the silver-circled star from the bar, and looked at it closely. "It says United States Marshal. I thought you were the sheriff."

"I'm the sheriff, but I'm also a United States marshal for the state of South Dakota," Bullock replied. "I was appointed by my friend, President Theodore Roosevelt. Federal marshal is higher than town sheriff, so I carry that badge."

"How can you be both?" Gordon asked.

"I'm only the temporary sheriff until they have an election for a new lawman."

Gordon studied the badge and dropped it into a pocket. "It doesn't make any difference. It's my badge now."

Bullock took a deep breath. *That wasn't very smart to give him the badge, old hoss.* "It'll save you a lot of trouble if you'll just slide the badge back down the bar."

Gordon shrugged. "You can come and try to take it away from me, *Old Man.*"

"You don't want me to do that," Bullock stated.

"Here's how it is," Gordon answered and laughed hysterically. "You're an old man and I'm a young man. I'm younger and faster. I've got an automatic pistol and you're not wearing a gun."

Bullock's eyes narrowed and he nodded in agreement.

Gordon motioned with his hands. "Come and try to take *my* badge, *Old Man!*"

Bullock shook his head. *I've seen a lot of your kind in my fifty-nine years. I'm still around and most of them aren't.* He heard a chair screech behind him and glanced in the mirror to see Leroy stand and stretch.

"A man can't hardly get a decent nap with all the talking going on," Leroy stated in a sober voice. "Let's do what we came to do, Gordon, and get the hell out of here."

"I'll be damned," Gordon said, and laughed. "Looks like Leroy ain't as drunk as we thought. He used to be a stage actor, you know. Guess he was just pretending to be drunk."

"All right, what are you here for?" Bullock asked.

"We need traveling money," Gordon answered. "And we figure you're as good as anybody to get the banker to come in and open up for a quick Saturday withdrawal."

They must not know Finney's in town, Bullock told himself as he glanced quickly in the mirror to check on Leroy's location. *I don't like him behind me.* He lifted his mug of beer, turned, and leaned his elbows back on the bar. *Now I can at least see both of them.*

"Bartender, what's the banker's name?" Leroy asked.

Jenkins looked at Bullock, who shook his head ever so slightly.

"Ah, we got a man who comes over from Deadwood a couple of days a week to open the bank," Jenkins answered. "He won't be here again till Monday. Not much bank business in a town this size. Especially on Saturday."

Gordon's hand flipped his coat open, grabbed the fancy pistol, and in one smooth move fired a shot into the bar mirror. "I don't like being lied to!" he screamed.

Jenkins ducked behind the bar, Annie covered her face with her hands and Bullock cringed at the fast action and noise. *He's getting worse. I've got to try to calm him.*

Gordon started to laugh and waved the pistol at them.

Bullock glanced over his shoulder at the spider-webbed hole in the mirror. It was centered on the reflection of his face. *He's either lucky or a damned good shot!*

"Easy, easy," he soothed, raising his hands. "Put the gun away, Gordon. Let's talk this over without the gun."

"You're giving a lot of orders for an old man who ain't got a gun."

Leroy stepped in front of Bullock. "My partner here has a tendency to get a little crazy at times. It's best not to provoke him."

Bullock nodded. "I can see that. Any chance you can talk some sense into him?"

Leroy shook his head. "Probably not. He gets stuck on something, he's kinda like a dog on a rat. Like I said, he gets a little crazy at times!"

Gordon turned his gun toward Annie. "What's the banker's name, darlin'?"

She looked at him and shook her head.

Gordon took three quick steps and slapped her face. "I asked you a question!"

"Don't hit her!" Leroy ordered. "I warned you about hitting women!"

Gordon's face hardened and he pointed the gun at Leroy. "Don't you be giving me orders!"

Leroy's eyes narrowed and he slowly unbuttoned his coat. "I warned you a long time ago about pointing a gun at me!" he hissed through clenched teeth.

"You ain't gonna get your gun out fast enough," Gordon warned. "Don't be stupid."

Leroy's eyes moved from Gordon to the sheriff and back to Gordon waving the pistol. "You aren't going to shoot me, Gordon," he stated softly. "I'm the only friend you still got. I'm the only person left in the world you can trust."

Gordon began to giggle, broke into loud laughter, and fired two quick shots into the floor on either side of Leroy, who slowly raised his hands.

"You shouldn't have done that!" Leroy said. "I've warned you for the last time!"

That man is crazy! Bullock told himself as he slowly slid his hand into his gun pocket.

Gordon swung the pistol to point at Bullock. "Put your hands up, Sheriff!"

Bullock quickly raised his hands. "Easy there."

Gordon turned the pistol back to Leroy. "Put your gun on the bar," he ordered. "I don't trust you anymore."

Leroy's face was expressionless and he didn't move.

The gun in Gordon's hand fired and a slug tore into the floor in front of Leroy.

Leroy's face hardened and he flexed his fingers.

Bullock's eyes moved quickly back and forth between the two men and then over to Jensen, who took a small step to his right behind the bar. *I hope he's not going to be stupid and try for that short shotgun he keeps under the bar!*

"I'm going to tell you one more time to put that gun down, Gordon," Leroy said.

"What're you gonna do if I don't?" Gordon asked.

Bullock saw Jenkins was continuing his slow trip behind the bar. *Damnit! Don't be stupid, Milo. He'll shoot you down if you try for the shotgun.*

"If I have to, I'll take that gun away from you," Leroy threatened. "We came to this town to rob the bank, not fight between us. Now, put the damned gun down and we'll talk this out."

Out of the corner of his eye Gordon saw Jenkins reach down under the bar and start to raise a shotgun. He turned and fired two quick shots at him.

Jenkins cried out in pain. The shotgun in his hands discharged, blowing a hole in the front of the bar. He bounced against the back bar, tipping a rack of bottles and toppling to the floor, a bloody tear in the shoulder of his shirt.

Gordon instantly swung the gun back and fired two fast shots at Leroy, who was fumbling inside his coat for a gun.

Leroy staggered backward, looked down at the fresh holes in the front of his shirt, and tried to say something before he collapsed, tipping a table and crumpling to the floor.

The air was still and full of gun smoke.

Annie's eyes were wide, her hand held over her mouth.

Gordon held the pistol steady at Bullock, who was standing with his hands raised.

If my count's right, that gun isn't loaded anymore.

Gordon laughed, dropped the automatic pistol on the bar, and pulled a short-barreled revolver from a coat pocket. "Countin', weren't you, Sheriff?"

This man's on a blood run and dangerous as a fresh-shed rattler! "No, I wasn't," Bullock lied, shaking his head and raising his hands higher. *He's just shot two people, so another one won't make any difference. I've got to try to calm him down.* "Can I get a drink?" he asked, putting his hand to his chest. "I'm getting some terrible pains in my chest and the doc warned me about my heart and too much excitement."

Gordon laughed. "This is too much excitement, *Old Man?*"

Bullock nodded and rubbed on his chest. "Just one shot of whiskey."

Gordon motioned him to the bar. "Go ahead and help yourself."

Bullock's hand was shaking as he poured himself a shot of whiskey and downed it.

Gordon stepped to the bar and poured himself a shot of whiskey. He toyed with the glass, but didn't drink it. "That was some pretty fancy shootin', wasn't it? I'm young and fast and good!"

"Some of the fanciest gun work I've ever seen," Bullock agreed, looking at Leroy's body on the floor. "You are the best and the fastest. There's no doubt about that." *Keep talking nice.*

Milo Jensen moaned from behind the bar.

Gordon pointed to Annie. "Go take a look at him."

She nodded, slipped behind the bar, and knelt beside the wounded man. "It's his shoulder," she stated, grabbing a towel from the bar and gently pressing it to his wound. "He's awake."

"I could've killed him, you know," Gordon stated, laughed, and downed the shot of whiskey.

"Now, seems to me we was talking about a banker, Sheriff."

"Let me think a minute on how to get him over here on a Saturday," Bullock said slowly. "Can I get myself a beer?"

Gordon nodded and motioned for him to help himself.

Bullock leaned over the bar, glanced at the wounded man, and put a mug under the tap. He pulled down the handle, watched the beer level rise, pushed up the handle, lifted the beer, took a drink, and thumbed the foam from his mustache. "You want one?"

"Quit your damned stalling!" Gordon shouted, wagging the gun for emphasis.

"All right, all right," Bullock said.

Gordon stepped closer and tapped the pistol barrel on the sheriff's chest. "Your time is about up, *Old Man*. What if I shoot the bartender again to help speed up your memory?"

"No, no," Bullock pleaded. "I've got an idea." He put his foot under the rim of the spittoon beside Gordon's feet and tipped it over, spilling the contents on Gordon's shoes.

Gordon looked down and leaped back. "What the. . . ."

The beer from the mug in Bullock's hand made a lopsided halo when it collided with the side of Gordon's head and he toppled to the floor.

Sheriff Seth Bullock bent down and took the pistol

from Gordon's limp hand. He patted the man's pocket, pulled his badge from it, and hooked it on to the front of his own coat as he straightened. He looked down at the unconscious man on the floor and nudged him with his boot. "You're under arrest for murder, stealing a car, and a few other things, you demented bastard. Oh, yeah, one more thing. You may be younger and faster than me, but I'm older and wiser and a helluva lot more devious!"

The Cody War

Johnny D. Boggs

January 10, 1917
Denver, Colorado

Shock slaps her like the brutal wind, and she quickly
looks away, focusing on a frosted pane of glass, anywhere
but the bed. She can picture Boy Scouts on the porch,
freezing but determined to help the old man and his
family. Can visualize reporters on the death watch, can
almost smell their cigar smoke and whiskcy-laced coffee.
Can see Harry Tammen, that heartless lout, rubbing his
gloved hands, joking with ink-spillers, pretending to be
friend, philanthropist, when ruination is what he sows for
others to reap.

Sobs sound behind her, a moan from her sister-in-law,
and whispers, but she can't make out any words, which
sound as if they are coming from the bottom of an Arizona well. From behind, the priest's hand squeezes her
shoulder, while Cody Boal kneels beside her, kisses her
cheek. "Grandma?" he mouths.

She shakes her head. At least, she thinks she does.
Maybe she can't move.

Low voices finally reach her. *He's gone. . . . An era has passed.*

Her head jerks toward the men as they test their quotes for reporters—speechifyin', Will would have called it—and she snaps, "Why don't you just say 'now he belongs to the ages,' you damned fools?"

Silence. They stare at her, before quietly filing out to the parlor and kitchen. A door closes; she's alone.

She finds him again, and is chilled by the sight. Tentatively, she forces her heavy body out of the chair, weaves to the bedside, takes his cold hand in her own, and remembers the last time he shocked her so.

July 28, 1910
North Platte, Nebraska

"What the blazes are we doin' here?"

"Aunt Irma said to bring you," his grandson answers, setting the brake and jumping from the spring wagon to help the honorable Colonel William F. Cody down. Though only fourteen, Cody Boal's old enough to understand his grandfather is well in his cups, sure to fall face-first into the dirt without a steadying hand.

"Welcome Wigwam," the old man says. "That's what I called it. Well, she sure didn't make me feel welcome last time I was here."

"I know."

He stumbles against the child, pushes back to lean against the wagon.

"Locked herself in her room, she did. Not a word, not even a good cussin' would she give me. I went up and begged her to at least open the door. Three times I done it, and Buffalo Bill ain't a beggin' man. Not a word. Not one damn word."

"Aunt Irma said to bring you."

"Irma." His breath stinks of rye, and it's not ten in the morn. "She's a good daughter. So was your ma, God rest her soul." Grandfather runs fingers through grandson's hair. "And you're a top hand."

"Thank you, sir." He leads the old scout up the steps, opens the door, guides him inside.

Irma stands in the parlor, wringing her hands, biting her lip.

"Papa," she says, her voice quiet, and gives him a peck on the cheek.

"Thought I was goin' to the ranch," he says. "I could use a rest."

"Yes," his daughter says, "but . . ." She sighs.

He straightens. "Lulu? Has something happened to your ma?"

Her head shakes nervously. "She's . . . come inside." Taking him by the hand, she leads him to the family parlor, where he bristles at the sight of his wife, sitting on the oak divan, reading the *Telegraph,* and he bellows, his words too slurred for either Irma or her nephew to understand.

Seeing him, Louisa Frederici Cody tosses the paper aside, bolts out of her chair. "What's he doing here?" she demands.

"You two need to talk things out." Irma has found her voice—surprisingly forceful. "And don't come out until you've done it." With that, she is gone, leading her sister's son to the porch. Once the door slams, husband and wife stare at one another from across the room.

"You're drunk," she says.

"I've had my mornin' bracer." He looks across the room, finds the brandy decanter. *And I'd like to have another.* He starts to remove his hat, but when she barks at him, asking if he has a head cold, he leaves it on. *That'll show that ol' witch.*

"Well, why are you here?" Lulu asks. "To torment me

more? Shame me? Why aren't you at your lovely Scout's Rest Ranch with all those friends of yours?" Contempt laces her voice.

"Weren't my idea, woman. 'Specially after the welcome I got in March."

"What did you expect, you old fool? You were in your cups the whole time. And it was you who tried to divorce me! My parents . . ."

He rolls his eyes. He has heard that before. *They're spin-nin' in their graves.* Sounds like that melodramatic Buntline at a temperance lecture when she speaks of that shame, that agony, heartbreak. Criminy, he had been trying to do her a favor. This wasn't a marriage. Hadn't been for some time, and he would have been shuck of her except for that judge. Wouldn't grant the divorce, nor would the court agree to a new trial. That had cost him, damn near broken him, and it had been, what, four years ago? Tormented her? Shamed her? What about him?

He glares at her, a stout—hell, *fat* is the word—woman, short and stooped, with gray hair put up in a bun, clad in an ill-fitting dress and sandals in boot country. A hard-rock woman with a cast-iron heart. Sure not that charming, beautiful girl he had wooed back in St. Louis all those years ago.

"Well, you got your wish, Lulu."

"It wasn't my wish, Will."

He turns to go, but sags at the parlor entrance. He'd have to walk past his grandson and Irma, waiting outside. Be like runnin' from a fight, and Buffalo Bill never retreats, if you believe the dime novels or his Wild West show.

So he whirls, waving a finger at her. "You ain't been a wife for years, woman."

"And what kind of husband have you been? Consorting with strumpets!"

"What? You mean them actresses?"

"Whores!" she hisses.

That had been a disaster from the get-go. *Get-go?* she thinks. *Now I sound like the fool.*

It had been Buntline's idea. Ned Buntline, or Edward Zane Carroll Judson. Take Buffalo Bill, King of the Bordermen, transform him from scout to thespian. "You don't know the difference between a theater cue and a billiard cue," she told him, but he wouldn't listen. He never listened. "You'll make a fool of yourself, Will."

"I'll make us rich," he answered.

So they went to Chicago in the winter of '72, and he had played the fool, a mighty big one, stumbling over his lines when he didn't forget them. Critics panned the play, rightfully so, but performance after performance sold out. People couldn't get enough of the West back East. Chicago . . . St. Louis . . . Cincinnati . . . Philadelphia . . . Boston . . . Washington City . . . New York. Scouts became celebrities on stage and off. The reaction struck her dumb.

Of course, he had to bring his friends along. Buffalo Bill had to share the glory with his drunken troupe of bitter merry men. First Texas Jack Omohundro, then that man-killing Hickok, later Captain Jack Crawford. Yet Will had made the family, if not rich, at least comfortable, and he had gotten them out of that hellhole frontier to civilization, with homes in West Chester and Rochester. Nice homes . . . until the . . . tragedy.

"Criminy," he's saying, "that was nigh forty years ago."

"You embarrassed me," she tells him.

She starts to stand, to head upstairs to her room. She'll lock herself inside again, until that walking whiskey vat takes his leave. She sinks back, however, her legs suddenly weak. She can't . . . not break Irma's heart, not her grandson's. *They're all I have left.*

The fool's speaking again. She looks at him, rolls her eyes.

"If you mean that time I called you out from the balcony . . ."

She hasn't forgotten that, although she can't remember the city.

He had just killed about twenty "supes," the low-paid actors pretending to be savage Indians, and, for the umpteenth time, couldn't remember his lines. Usually, when that happened, he'd just start slaughtering Indians again, but they were all scattered about stage left and stage right, playing dead, and when he looked up, his face frightened, he found her in the balcony. "Mama," he cried out, "what a horrible actor I am!"

The audience loved it, clapping, whistling, cheering, then forcing her to come on stage and take a bow. "Say a few words, Mizzus Cody!" they demanded when she stood beside the show's star at center stage, but she found herself speechless, terrified, and he pulled her close, telling the crowd, but mostly her, "You see what hard work I do to support my family."

Strength returning to her legs, she pushes herself out of the divan, waves a finger in his face. *Talk things out, Irma says. Well, I'll tell that old mule a thing or two.*

"That's not what I mean, and you know it. I saw you kissing those women . . . in our hotel! With me there, with your children there. I would not be shamed so. That's why I left you, wouldn't travel with you anymore!"

"I was rehearsin', Lulu."

"Horseshit."

A long finger jabs back at her. "There. You lied! Proof you lied in court. You said you never used profane language. Your friends said you never used profane language, but you do, Lulu. You do!"

"You'd drive anyone to it. That or the bottle. Or both. You and that sorry lot you call friends. Anybody with a sad story or not a cent to his name. All he had to do was say, 'We scouted together.' Or 'We freighted together.' Or 'I was in the Army with Carr.' Or, by jingo, 'We met on a stage once.' Maybe even 'I just read one of your stories!'"

"Man who'd turn his back on a friend ain't a man," he says.

"And you'd never turn your back on a bottle, Will Cody!"

"Well, all I did was kiss actresses, either rehearsin' or celebratin' a performance. Ain't like I was ever untrue to you. And I ain't gonna say I'm sorry for bein' kind to stranger or friend, 'specially one in need."

"Even Hickok!"

He looks dismayed. "You liked Jim."

"I tolerated him. Like I tolerated all those drunken sots you brought to our home."

He hadn't known her when he first met Hickok. He was just a kid of twelve, freighting for Majors and Russell, barely knowing one end of an ox from another, fetching anything for that bear of a man with Lew Simpson's train until the brute pushed him too far.

"Fetch that corncob, boy, and come with me to wipe my arse."

"I'll do no such." He braced himself for the whipping sure to come.

"You'll do what I say, or I'll leave welts on your back and arse. I'll make you bleed, boy, bleed and hurt."

When he looked for help, finding no friendly eyes, the

skinner—he had long forgotten the villain's name—
knocked him off his seat on the ox yoke, stood, and
kicked at him. Will scrambled to the fire ring, found a cup
of coffee, flung the hot liquid into the man's face.

The teamster screamed, but only briefly. Wiping his
eyes, he charged, a maddened bear. Will figured he'd be
killed certain-sure, when towering Jim Hickok stepped in
and slammed the attacker to the ground. "Lay a hand on
that boy again, and I'll put a pounding on you that'll take
a month of Sundays to get over."

He eyes the brandy, runs his tongue over his lips, and
glares back at Lulu. "I won't apologize for havin' Jim
Hickok for a pard. Not ever."

"Pard? He quit on you when he was trying to be an
actor in your Combination. And how many times did you
have to go his bail, or give him spending money because
he was broke? Money you were supposed to send to us.
Your family."

"I ain't gonna apologize for havin' Jim Hickok for a
pard," he says. "He saved my bacon, more times than
once. Freightin'. Ridin' for the Pony."

"Pony! You never rode for the Express, Will, unless you
count being a messenger boy for Majors. And neither did
that assassin. All he did was muck stalls before he murdered those men at Rock Creek."

"Freightin'. Ridin' for the Pony," he repeats, ignoring
her slander. "And fightin' redskins."

Laughing, she falls back on the divan. "Indians? My
Lord, Will, you killed more Indians on your Wild West
than on the Plains. How many did you bury in Europe?"
Her cackle slices him to the quick. "There didn't have to
be a Wounded Knee, Will. General Miles should have just
sent all the Sioux off with you. They'd all be good Indians,

then. Dead of rot and consumption and infection. Probably embarrassment."

He moves to the bottle. "There wouldn't have been no need for that fracas at Wounded Knee had they allowed me to arrest Sittin' Bull," he says. His hands stop short of the bottle. Her words stop him.

"You were too drunk. Remember? A good thing too, or you both would have died, you and that heathen, and what fun the newspapers would have had with that."

"I could have saved him." His eyes shut, and he sees the old Sioux again, sees him babying Annie Oakley as if she were one of his grandchildren. He sees the trained horse he had given Sitting Bull when he left the Wild West, pictures the fine stallion rearing while the gunshots fired by Metal Shirts kill the great holy man. "Could have stopped all that bloodshed. At Sittin' Bull's camp at least. He was a friend."

"The problem with you, Will, is that you believe all your managers tell you. First Buntline, then John Burke. Salisbury. Cooper. Ingraham. Biggest liars ever, next to you."

"Maybe if you had ever believed in me, woman."

That silences her.

She had believed in him once, hadn't she?

Here was this dashing young soldier, quite handsome, with dark eyes that shone so bright. They met in St. Louis, shortly after the end of the Rebellion. Their courtship began as a joke. A cousin brought Trooper Will Cody to her house, and they began talking. Uncouth, but charming—quite a horseman, they said—and then he had suggested a joke. A suitor was calling on her that evening, and Louisa really did not want to accompany that cad to the symphony, so when he knocked on the door, she had introduced William F. Cody as her betrothed.

She never saw the suitor again, but Will Cody became a

fixture on her doorstep, and when he asked her father for her hand, she felt excited. They married on March 6, 1866. He was twenty; she almost two years older, and had never been outside of St. Louis and all its splendor.

Immediately afterward, she stepped into hell.

Two days out of St. Louis on the Missouri River steamer, she fainted in his arms when some rough men threatened to kill her husband for being a Jayhawker. When they reached Salt Creek, Kansas, he showed her the hotel he planned on running, as decrepit a building as she could ever imagine, not fit for a wharf rat. He proved a mighty poor businessman, always would, so he left to scout for the Army. He wasn't there when Arta was born that December. He wasn't there when any of the babies came, and barely around before or after. Long enough to plant his seed and say good-bye. She spent more time in St. Louis with her parents than in Kansas or Nebraska with her husband. Soon, she preferred it that way.

In 1867, Goddard Brothers Company hired Will to provide twelve buffalo a day for the Kansas Pacific crews. It paid $500 a month, if he lived, and she saw him even less. He mailed some money home, spent more on whiskey, gave plenty to his lowly friends, and invested whatever he had left. Those investments never paid off. Will had better luck betting on horses than on land, and he had little luck with horses, and none at cards or dice, certainly none at choosing business partners. He did have success with the Army, scouting, especially after killing the Cheyenne leader Tall Bull at Summit Springs. That's how he had met up with Buntline, and the writer had made Buffalo Bill Cody a man of legend, even if those early stories had their roots in Hickok's depravity rather than her husband's.

* * *

"And I killed Indians." He sounds childish, but that's what he really is. A child. "Killed me aplenty. But I made a bunch of friends with the red man too."

"Yeah," she says, mocking him. "You killed plenty, Will. You shot Tall Bull from ambush."

"Got a damn fine horse too."

"And then . . ." Well, she can't speak of that other one.

"Then what?" he demands, not understanding. "What? I was out riskin' my hair, woman, riskin' it for you and our country. And afterward, after I became Colonel William F. Cody . . . Good Lord, woman. I've met heads of state. You see this diamond stickpin?" He points, but it's missing. Probably lost it, or gave it to some saloon beggar. Or he's so drunk he has forgotten he's clad in buckskins and not a fancy broadcloth suit. "I had Queen Victoria ride in the Deadwood stage. All these years with my Wild West, you could have come with me. You could have seen the world. You—"

"Maybe by then I was just used to being left alone!"

"I done it all for you. You and the little ones."

"You did it for yourself, and your own vainglory!"

His hands grasp the decanter. She thinks he might hurl it at her, but he releases it and whirls, ripping off his hat, tossing it to the floor. His horsehair wig falls with it.

She almost laughs.

He looks like the old fool he truly is, his once-flowing locks reduced to sweaty remnants resembling something on a mangy cur—though mustache and goatee remain thick and white—dressed in absurd boots up to his thighs and buckskins with so much beadwork the outfit must weigh more than a knight's suit of armor. It's an improvement, she thinks, mayhap over that hideous velvet suit of the vaquero. She closes her eyes to dam the tears, wishing she had never thought of that costume.

"I never wanted to be away!" he's telling her. "I done it all for you and the little ones. It broke my heart, you know, broke my heart when Kit died. Soon as I got word, I left the show, took the train home, only to have my son die in my arms."

There. It's finally out.

"*Our* son, damn you! He was *our* son. And he died in *my* arms, not yours!"

"Mine . . . I got home—"

"You weren't there, Will! Till after Kitty died!"

He grips the mantel for support, glances at his hat and hairpiece, and staggers to the divan. Suddenly she's afraid, but she sees the tears welling in his eyes, and he collapses beside her, trying to remember, to sort it out.

It was spring, April 1876. The Combination had opened in Springfield, Massachusetts, performing *Life on the Border* with Jack Crawford when the telegram arrived. Joe Arlington, an actor with the Combination for years, handed him the telegram during the first act.

KITTY HAS SCARLET FEVER STOP
DESPERATE STOP COME HOME QUICK
STOP LOUISA

That image remains engraved in his brain forever. Over thirty-four years, not one day has gone by that he hasn't seen it.

She tells him, her voice a hoarse whisper. "You just listened to Burke and those others until you finally convinced yourself you were there."

"No." He shakes his head. *No. But . . .*

"Go on, Will," Major Burke said, but Will stubbornly shook his head. "After the first act." Somehow, Will made it through, then raced out of the opera house, still in his vaquero suit, ran to the depot. Old Moses met him at the Rochester station, driving him home without a word. Kit died on April 20, five years old, apple of his eye, his only son. Kit Carson Cody.

Yet he can't see himself holding the boy in his arms. He looks at Lulu for help, but her face is blank, unblinking eyes boring holes into the wall. He thinks back to that horrible night, hearing the clock's chimes, remembers writing the letter to Julia after Kit was called to Glory, remembers checking on Lulu and the other little ones, all sick, all heartbroken.

Why Kit? he wrote his sister, wiping tears as he sat alone in the library. He tried to make himself believe Kit had crossed the Jordan, was waiting for them on that better shore, but he wasn't sure he believed it. Wasn't sure what he believed anymore.

"You weren't there," Lulu snaps beside him. "You weren't here when Orra died either. Or with Arta when she . . . Well, at least you were decent enough to see your son planted. Then you went back to your actresses. And you left me, and your daughters, to grieve alone. You couldn't help us, just yourself, your career. So you went back to tread the boards, and then avenge Custer!"

It had been a bad year. First Kit. Then Custer. Later Hickok. All dead. He had left too, after the season ended in June, but not to avenge Custer. Will wouldn't learn of the Little Bighorn until he was scouting in Nebraska. When Wesley Merritt read him the report, he passed the news on to the troops. "Custer and five companies of the Seventh wiped out of existence."

But why had he taken the train West to join the Indian fight in the first place, to put down the Sioux and Cheyenne? Why had he not changed out of that vaquero suit of black velvet with silver buttons he had worn on stage in Wilmington, Delaware, and elsewhere during the season?

"This is what I do," he told a newspaper editor, "when not actin'. I'm a scout. And the Fifth Cavalry needs their chief of scouts."

Duty? Or was he running, running from Lulu and poor Kit Carson Cody? Running from his breaking heart? Somehow discovering who he really was?

The fight came up quickly but, by thunder, he didn't kill Yellow Hair from ambush, not the way he had shot Tall Bull back in '69. He wasn't the first to see the Army couriers, but he did detect the Dog Soldiers pursuing them. "God have mercy," General Merritt said. "Those poor bastards don't know the savages are after them."

So Merritt ordered him and eight troopers to rescue the white men. Spurring his rangy gelding, whipping the Winchester from its scabbard, he soon outdistanced the soldiers.

He spotted the Dog Soldier—Yellow Hair he would learn—raised his own rifle as soldiers and Cheyenne, now yipping like coyotes, charged. Reins in his teeth, he lifted his Winchester, found his target. Their weapons spoke at once, and his horse stumbled, pitching him into the sand.

He rolled, levering the rifle, seeing that his shot had killed the Cheyenne's horse. Yellow Hair had already recovered, but his second shot flew wild. He took his time, let out a breath—the way Jim Hickok had taught him—and shot the Indian in the head. Then he was running, screaming curses, unsheathing his knife. He slid beside the dead Dog Soldier, gripping the greasy black hair. He didn't know why he said it, didn't plan it, but he worked the knife and raised the gory trophy, yelling triumphantly as troopers galloped past in vain pursuit of the fleeing Cheyenne.

"The first scalp for Custer!"

"You just had to leave me," Lulu says softly.

"I reckon." His words come out more as a sigh.

She buries her face in her hands and wails. When her head lifts, she turns to him. "And then you had to mail your . . ." She shudders. "Mailed it home, Will? For the love of God."

"I wrote you a letter."

"The box showed up first. I opened it and saw the scalp. The flies, crusted blood. I fainted, Will."

Yet she's laughing now, and he sniggers a bit too.

"Reckon it was dumb of me."

Their laughter fades.

"I miss our children," she blurts out, and the dam bursts once more. "Kitty . . . Orra . . . Arta. Irma's all we have left."

"I miss 'em too." He starts to reach for her hand, but pulls away.

The ache is leaving him. Perhaps he's just sobering up.

"It's the leavin'?" he says, his voice suddenly sympathetic. "Is that what hurt you so?"

"And your drinking."

She makes her tears stop. She has always been strong, well, stronger than he would expect for a spoiled rich girl from St. Louis who had married some wild, fatherless boy who came of age in the wilds of Kansas.

He offers her a handkerchief. To his surprise, she takes it.

"I can stop the drinkin'," he says.

"You cannot," she barks sharply.

"Hell I can't," he retorts. "I'm Buffalo Bill."

Besides, them old pill-rollers have been hammering at me for years

*now that the John Barleycorn would kill me. Maybe I should cork the
jug. God knows, I've spilt more whiskey than most men ever seen.*

"I guess I ain't been much of a husband, Lulu. Probably was never cut out to be one, way I grew up. Guess I just
liked the notion of bein' hitched."

"You said as much during our . . . our divorce proceedings." The bitterness has returned, but he'll parry it.

"Yeah, and I'm sorry for that, and all the torment I put
you through. But I can't stop the leavin'. Owe it. I owe too
many folks."

"I know that. The Wild West. Buffalo Bill's Wild West. I
never understood the fascination."

"Me neither."

Although he had, and he had learned. By the winter of
1876, he was performing on stage again, *Red Right Hand,*
or *Buffalo Bill's First Scalp for Custer,* wearing that vaquero
costume again and displaying Yellow Hair's scalp and
other spoils of war in opera halls across the East. He had
become the showman. Westerner at heart. Showman by
nature. He discovered that about himself along Warbonnet Creek.

So he had returned East, and later ventured across the
world. He envisioned, not a play, but an outdoor spectacle of the West. Since '83, when he lost little Orra, his traveling exhibition—now Buffalo Bill's Wild West and
Pawnee Bill's Far East—had made Buffalo Bill Cody's
name recognized across the globe. Ironically, Lulu had
fled West, back to the frontier she had loathed, to the
North Platte to bring up their family, later to hold Orra's
hand as she died at age eleven, to become the recluse,
hating him whenever he stopped in for a visit at the Welcome Wigwam—his stupid name—or Scout's Rest Ranch.

* * *

"I got my faults."

"You're generous, Will Cody, kindhearted to strangers, children, dogs, horses, old people, even those red savages. Maybe I shouldn't see that as a fault, but I do. Maybe I'm selfish."

"You brought our kids up right. Orra, Arta, Kit . . ."

When his voice breaks, she reaches toward him only to pull back her hand, whispering, "Don't, Will. I can't . . ."

"We got family, Lulu." He has recovered. "Still . . . But . . . Well, when I was here in March, when you wasn't talkin' to me or havin' nothin' to do with me, well, I wanted to ask you to come with me. Tour with me. I'm askin' you again, Lulu. I promise you I won't put you on the spot like I done that time on stage."

"Why? Why now?"

"For that family, Lulu. They want it. That's why Irma had us meet like this. Fight it out. Well, I'm plumb wore out from fightin' you. I surrender. Let's bury the tomahawk, sign the treaty."

"You can't change, Will."

"You can't neither."

Silence. She rises and moves to the window, pulls back the curtain, closes it, steps back. "I guess we do owe it to them."

He shoots off the divan like the twenty-year-old given permission to marry the girl he adores, not the sixty-four-year-old buffoon, making a beeline for the brandy.

"Let's have a drink, Lulu. It'll be the peace pipe. War's over."

"You're incorrigible, Will Cody."

"Damn right. Buffalo Bill's a man of his word." He fills two glasses.

She approaches him, tentatively takes the glass. His clinks against hers.

"And it's my last drink, Louisa."

* * *

January 10, 1917
Denver, Colorado

He lived up to his word too, she remembers, alone in the room with her husband. Lived up to it despite the hardships, losing Scout's Rest Ranch, losing just about everything, even his name, his show, perhaps his soul to that bastard Tammen.

Now it's over.

She feels it then, shocked by it, reaching up with a tentative finger, curiously tracing the trail the tear leaves as it rolls down her cheek. She squeezes the cold hand, hoping it will respond in kind, but when it doesn't, she chokes out a sob, maybe a groan, and she wonders:

Did she really love that old reprobate, or does she merely hate him for leaving her alone one last time?

Born to Be Hanged

Elmer Kelton

Author's Note: Old outlaws were never allowed to die. Just about every Western badman worth his salt supposedly survived his "official" death and was seen alive long after he was reportedly buried. These legends have grown up about such people as Jesse James, Billy the Kid, Butch Cassidy, and many others of less notoriety.

Judge Orland Sims, who wrote a couple of books about West Texas characters, told me once that he planned to write another to be entitled *Dead Outlaws I Have Known*. He never did, but he could have. One in particular who piqued his interest was "Blackjack" Ketchum. Blackjack first gained notice in the Knickerbocker community west of San Angelo, Texas. Even as a youngster, he developed a reputation for lawlessness.

The official story is that Blackjack was hanged in Clayton, New Mexico, in 1901, having been wounded and captured in an aborted effort at train robbery. During his long imprisonment, the many appeals and delays, he was fed well and gained considerable weight.

The generally accepted version is that the hangman did not take this gain into proper account and dropped Blackjack too far. The grisly result was that the impact severed the outlaw's head from his body.

The late Glenn Tennis told me that as a teenager he helped his undertaker father move bodies from the old Clayton cemetery to a new site. They found Blackjack's body well preserved. He said the features still looked like photographs he had seen of Blackjack. Moreover, the head was indeed separate from the body. Nevertheless, a couple of San Angelo old-timers who had known Blackjack were convinced that the hanging was rigged to allow him to survive. One told me he was sure he had seen Blackjack ride up to his brother's ranch house near the Pecos River some years later.

Though I am confident of Glenn's account, it is interesting to fantasize that Blackjack survived through some arrangement with the local law. For those who believe in the inexorability of fate, his story might have gone something like this:

Blackjack thought for a moment that he was indeed dead. The rigging hidden beneath his coat had absorbed the impact of the fall and allowed him to land on his feet atop a stack of sandbags, hidden from view behind canvas sheets that screened the bottom of the scaffold. But he had been unable to stand. As he lurched forward, the false noose drew tightly around his neck and choked him. A deputy posted out of sight beneath the scaffold quickly grabbed him. Holding the rope taut above the noose, he loosened its grip enough to allow Blackjack to breathe. He wheezed, struggling for air.

"Quiet," the deputy whispered urgently. "You want to give the whole thing away?"

Blackjack knew the crowd out there would not give him a second chance. They had come here hungry to see a hanging, and they thought they had. He managed slowly to fill his lungs. His neck burned, blistered by the rope's rough caress. There was an old saying that some people would complain even if they were hanged with a new rope. He wished this had been an old rope. It would have been more pliable, and easier on his neck's sensitive skin.

"Hold steady," the deputy whispered. "We've got to keep this rope tight till the crowd breaks up, or they'll know somethin' is haywire."

Presently the deputy was joined by another, and by a doctor who had been brought from out of town because the local physician was too honest to be involved in this kind of subterfuge. They removed the noose and let Blackjack ease his bulk to a sitting position on the sandbags. Blackjack heard the rattle of trace chains. The hearse was pulling up next to the scaffold.

The second deputy said, "You'd better play real dead, or somebody out there will see that things ain't on the up-and-up. Then there'll be hell to pay."

Blackjack held his breath as the doctor leaned over him, pretending to make an examination. "I detect no breath," the doctor said. "I pronounce him dead."

One of the deputies helped the undertaker carry a plain wooden casket beneath the scaffold. "He's too heavy for us to lift," he said. "Mr. Ketchum, you'll have to crawl into the coffin yourself." He looked back to be sure no one could see from outside the canvas.

The thought of lying in that casket brought a surge of nausea. Blackjack wished he had not eaten the hearty breakfast they had brought him as a last meal. He feared he would vomit, but knew he must not.

"Take a deep breath," the undertaker told him. "Then

hold it till we get you into the hearse. A lot of people will be watching."

He noticed that one of the deputies was scattering a red liquid beneath the scaffold. "Chicken blood," the man said. "There's a good reason for it."

Though Blackjack's eyes were closed and a thin cloth was laid across his face, he was aware of the bright sun as the coffin was lifted and he was carried out into the open. He heard excited murmuring from the crowd that pushed in for a look. His lungs burned like fire, but he could not afford to breathe. He was aware of darkness as the lid was placed over him. Even then, he feared to take a deep breath. He opened his eyes, but saw only black. Feeling suffocated, he fought against a sudden panic that threatened to engulf him. He had always hated tight places. This one gave him a stifling sense of being buried alive. He fought against a desperate desire to cry out, to beg for someone to open the box and set him free. Judgment prevailed, and he managed to hold silent, though his lungs threatened to burst.

He felt the coffin sliding into the rear of the hearse. In a minute, the horses moved and the wheels were rolling beneath him. Sweating heavily, he pushed the coffin lid up just enough to let in a little light. Black curtains did not allow him to see outside, but on the other hand, they kept bystanders from seeing inside.

The hearse pulled into a shed that he surmised belonged to the undertaker. Someone closed the outside doors and said, "All right, you can climb out now."

Blackjack trembled, his legs threatening to collapse. The undertaker gave him a half pint of whiskey. Gratefully, he downed half of it without pausing for breath. It helped relieve the cold knot that had built in his stomach. On a wooden slab he saw what appeared to be a body covered by a sheet. "Who's that?" he asked.

The undertaker said, "A hobo. He fell trying to catch a freight. As far as anybody needs to know, he's Blackjack Ketchum."

Blackjack had made a specialty of robbing trains. He shuddered to think how it would be to fall under the wheels of one. "Must've been an awful mess."

"It was. That's why we scattered the chicken blood. We gave out a story that the noose pinched your head off."

The deputy who had waited beneath the gallows said, "You'll have to stay here till after dark. Then I'll bring you a horse. We want you to ride as far and as fast as you can go, over Raton Pass and into Colorado. If anybody around here was to recognize you, you'd go right back on that scaffold, and the rest of us'd all be in one hell of a fix."

Blackjack was puzzled. "Why go to all this trouble for me? I've got no money to pay you with."

"A feller up at Trinidad has got a job for you. He's paid us good to keep you alive and kickin'. We had figured on buryin' some rocks in your coffin, but that hobo was a lucky break. If anybody ever takes a notion to dig you up, they won't know but what he's you."

Blackjack shuddered. "That's a damned grisly thought."

He had slept but little last night, dreading the morning and the strangling grip of the noose, knowing he was on the verge of a long sleep from which he would never awaken. They had not told him of this scheme until just before they took him out of the cell. Now he stretched out on a cot and made up for lost time, sleeping through much of a long day, awakening eager for night so he could put this oppressive town and everybody in it far behind him.

At dark, the deputy brought him a little money and a

plate of food. "Eat hearty," he said. "It's a long ride up to Trinidad."

"Several days. What do I do when I get there?"

"You won't go into town till dark. After midnight you'll find a saloon known as the Colorado Miner. After it closes, you'll knock on the back door. A gentleman will be expectin' you."

"What's his name?"

"You don't need to know. He'll know *you*. Just listen and do what he says. When the job is done, he'll give you travelin' money. Afterward, if I was you, I wouldn't stop ridin' till I got to Canada, or maybe whatever is north of that."

Blackjack was uncomfortable about going into a mission without even knowing what it was, but he swallowed his misgivings. He considered himself deeply in debt to the unknown benefactor who had saved him. Without that help, he would by now have been buried in the coffin the hearse had carried out to the graveyard.

Thank God for unlucky hoboes, he thought.

He finished his supper and took a long swig of whiskey. "Now where's that horse?"

Keeping off the roads, he took several days to ride from Clayton up through the high pass and down the long slope to Trinidad. There weren't many towns of consequence between there and Montana that he had not seen at one time or another, including this one. He thought he remembered the Colorado Miner, though it was but one of many dram joints in town. He waited as instructed until he judged midnight to have come and gone. He had no watch. His had disappeared along with most of his other personal possessions during the two years or so that he had languished in jail. It seemed that no matter how much everybody had hated him, they had been eager to collect whatever souvenirs they could get their hands on.

He tied the horse to a fence in deep shadows behind the saloon and rapped his big knuckles against the back door. He listened to the floor creak as someone walked across. The door's hinges squeaked, and it opened just enough for him to see one eye peering out suspiciously. The room was dark.

He asked, "Are you the man I'm supposed to meet?"

"Step inside quickly. The blinds are down. I'll light a lamp."

In the dim glow Blackjack took a long look at the face, and in particular at squinted eyes that seemed to bore a hole through him. The man appeared well-to-do by the cut of his clothes. He said, "You probably do not remember me, but I was in the courtroom, watching your trial. And I was present when you dropped through the scaffold. I have to say right out that I believe you deserved the sentence they gave you. You appeared to be a man born to hang."

Blackjack felt offended. The man was contemptuous of him, but not so much that he would not use him. "Then why go to the trouble of gettin' me out of it?"

"Because I saw that you are not a man who flinches easily. The task I have in mind is simple, but it requires a determined man who will not flinch or let soft feelings stay his hand."

By the tailored suit, Blackjack made a wild guess that his benefactor might be a banker. He had known of a few who arranged the robbery of their own banks to cover up shortages, or simply for self-enrichment at the depositors' expense. "You got a robbery that needs doin'?"

"No. I have a man who needs killing."

Blackjack frowned. He had killed, but it was not a thing lightly undertaken. He said, "You could hire any thug who happened to drop off of the train. You wouldn't have to go to all the trouble and expense of savin' my neck."

"But if such a man were identified and caught, he would gladly betray me to save himself from the hangman. In your case, you have the strongest possible incentive not to let yourself be captured. You've already felt the choking of a noose about your neck. You will do anything to avoid another." The man poured Blackjack a drink. "Moreover, no witness could properly identify you. Everybody knows Blackjack Ketchum is dead."

That made sense. "What're you goin' to pay me?"

"You've already been paid. I have bought you your life. Nevertheless, I will pay you three thousand dollars when you are done. That should get you at least a thousand miles from here before you stop for breath."

Single robberies had netted Blackjack more money, but under the circumstances he decided it was not appropriate to quibble. At least he was not six feet under the ground. "I'll do the job for you. Who is the hombre I'm supposed to kill?"

"His name is Wilson Evans. He's a prosecuting attorney."

Blackjack warmed to the notion. He had been at the mercy of more than one prosecuting attorney. He had lain awake many nights, dreaming of artful ways to help them shuffle off the mortal coil. Unfortunately, he had never had the opportunity to carry out any of these schemes. "I suppose this Evans is givin' you trouble?"

"Let us just say that this man has shown far too much opposition to certain areas of my business. You see, I own this establishment and several others of similar nature. It is his fervent desire to see my businesses ruined and myself housed in the penitentiary at Canon City. I do not find that prospect appealing."

Blackjack poured himself another drink without invitation. "Any special way you want the job done?"

"I am interested in the result, not the means. My only stipulation is that you do it thoroughly and elude capture. I would regret seeing you back on the scaffold."

"Not half as much as I would." The whiskey was not strong enough to shut off Blackjack's terrifying memory of the noose tightening around his neck. It was a death he would not wish upon a sheep-killing dog. He asked, "Where will I find Evans, and how will I know him?"

The man gave Evans's address to Blackjack and described his appearance. "He is tall, and he usually wears a black swallowtail coat and a black wool hat. I judge that he is about forty years old."

"That probably describes a lot of people."

"I would not advise your doing the deed in the heart of town. Too many law enforcement officers would be quick to respond. I would suggest catching him leaving home or returning there. You could be well on your way before anyone could organize an effective pursuit."

"Home it is then."

The man handed Blackjack a few greenbacks. "This is on account. You will receive the rest afterward. And one more thing: You still have the beard you wore on the scaffold. You would look considerably different without it."

Regretfully Blackjack rubbed his chin. The beard had appealed to his vanity, but he could grow another when he was far enough away.

"I never did hear your name," he said.

"No, you never did, and you will not. You may call me Lazarus, if you wish."

"He's the one got raised from the dead, ain't he?"

"In this case, he is the one who raised *you* from the dead. Good night, Mr. Ketchum."

* * *

Clean-shaven, Blackjack took a room in a cheap hotel away from the center of town and tried in vain for a good night's sleep. He was haunted by a recurring dream which had him falling through the open trapdoor and choking to death at the end of the rope. He awoke wide-eyed and in a cold sweat.

Later, he caught his horse and took a ride up the street where Evans lived. He picked out a modest red-brick house with the number he had been given: 326. It stood next to a church. He studied it intensely, mentally picturing Evans coming out the front door, down the short steps, and into the dirt street, which would lead him a few short blocks to the town's center. Blackjack could waylay him anywhere along the route, though he had rather do it as near to his home as possible. A vacant lot on the other side of the church would afford him quick passage off the street and out into an undeveloped area, where he could lose himself in a stand of timber. By the time pursuit could be organized, he should be well ahead of it.

He would have to put in several days of hard travel when this job was over. He decided to give himself and his horse a day of rest before he got the town all stirred up. He remained in the hotel room all day except for mealtimes. He found that he slept well on his second night in Trinidad. He arose early, had a large breakfast, and saddled his horse at the livery stable.

He had lost track of the days and had not realized that this was Sunday. Evans would not be likely to go to the courthouse, though Ketchum decided it was unlikely he would remain at home all day. Ketchum rode up the street and dismounted where he could watch the front of the small brick home. Before long, people began moving toward the church. After a time, someone opened the front door of the house he was watching. As the man who called himself Lazarus had said, Evans was wearing a black coat and a woolen hat. Carrying a Bible under his arm and walking with a cane, he stopped at the church steps and began greeting visitors as they arrived.

Blackjack realized with a start that this man was a minister. The house in which he lived must be the parsonage. He swore under his breath. Why all that nonsense Lazarus had told him about Evans being a prosecuting attorney?

He knew one thing for certain: He could not kill a minister. He was sure hell must have an especially hot corner reserved for men who committed a crime that serious. He mounted his horse and rode back to the Colorado Miner. Tying the animal behind the saloon, he tried the back door but found it locked. He threw a heavy shoulder against it and broke it open. No one was inside.

He had nothing but time. He could wait. After a while, he heard voices and heavy footsteps in the front of the building. The saloon had opened for business. Though he knew his pistol was loaded, he checked it again to be doubly certain. He heard someone walking toward the office from inside the saloon. He drew his pistol and sat with gaze focused intently on the door.

Lazarus stopped in surprise, seeing Blackjack sitting in his desk chair. He closed the door behind him and said testily, "I've heard no shooting, no commotion in the street. I have to assume that you have not yet fulfilled your agreement."

"You told me Evans is a prosecuting attorney. Turns out you lied. He's a preacher. I never agreed to shoot no preacher."

"I told you that because I thought you might be hesitant about killing a man of the cloth, whereas you should have no qualms about a prosecutor. This man has influenced much of the town against me and cost me considerable business. His being a minister makes no difference. He is mortal like the rest of us. All his prayers and preachments will not save him from one well-placed bullet."

"You'll have to be the one that places it. I won't."

"All I have to do is to raise a holler that Blackjack Ketchum is still alive. The whole country will be down on you like a pack of wolves."

"But they'd find out how the hangin' was rigged, and who paid to rig it. You'd have to get out of town so quick that your shadow couldn't keep up with you." Blackjack pointed the muzzle at Lazarus. "You promised me travelin' money. I want it."

"You haven't earned it."

"Only because you lied. I figure you still owe me. Now fork it over." He poked the pistol closer to Lazarus's face.

The man's eyes widened in a mix of fear and anger. "I don't have much on me."

Blackjack had noticed a small safe in the corner the first time he was in the office. It was the sort of thing that always caught his attention. "I'll bet you've got some in there. Open it."

Grumbling, Lazarus knelt reluctantly in front of the safe. He began turning the dial, first left, then right, then left again. "You won't get away with this."

"I'm bettin' I do. What're you goin' to say, that a dead man robbed your safe?"

Lazarus swung the safe's door open. "No, but I can say that he died trying." He whirled around, a derringer in his hand, and fired.

Blackjack felt as if a horse had kicked him. By reflex he fired the pistol. Through the smoke he saw Lazarus fall back against the safe, shock and disbelief in his eyes. Blackjack fired again, and Lazarus slumped to the floor.

Blackjack took a long step toward the safe, eager to

grab whatever money he could find and get out of here. But his legs betrayed him. He fell forward on his knees, then on his face. He rolled half over and placed his hand over his stomach. It came away bloody. He tried to rise up, but could get no farther than his knees.

A derringer might be considered a woman's weapon, but its bullet could kill a man. He realized Lazarus had put one through his lower chest. It burned like the furnaces of hell.

He heard excited voices in the saloon. The door burst open, and half a dozen men rushed in. Some almost knocked others down in their haste. One wore a bartender's apron. He shouted, "He's shot Diamond Joe!"

Blackjack presumed that was the name by which people knew Lazarus, not that it mattered. His vision was blurred, but he pointed the pistol in a way that he covered everybody. "You-all stand back. I'll kill the first man that comes any closer."

It was a hollow threat. Someone grabbed the pistol and wrested it from his grip, then used its barrel to strike a hard blow against the side of his head. Blackjack sank to the floor.

He heard the bartender say, "The safe is open. This jaybird was tryin' to rob the place."

Someone examined Diamond Joe's body. "He's dead. Took two straight to the heart. Who do you reckon this man is?"

The bartender said, "Never seen him before. Probably dropped off of a freight and figured on grabbin' some easy money before the next train comes through."

"We'd better send for the sheriff."

"No, sir," the bartender argued. "Diamond Joe was a friend of ours. You know how bad the courts are about turnin' prisoners loose. We'll take care of this killer ourselves and tell the sheriff afterwards. Grab ahold of him. Somebody find somethin' to tie his hands with."

Blackjack struggled, but the wound had made him too weak to put up much defense. He felt himself manhandled by rough hands. His arms were twisted behind his back, and he felt the bite of a coarse rope around his wrists. He argued, "He shot me first. I just defended myself."

Somebody struck his face with a hard fist. He saw an explosion of light and felt the salty taste of his own blood from a split lip. He was jerked to his feet, then slammed back upon the floor again.

He cried, "It was him that fired first. I'm shot, can't you see?"

They might have seen, but it was obvious they didn't care. They began pulling him across the floor. His knees bumped painfully over the threshold as they dragged him out into the morning.

He had no strength to mount his horse, but rough hands lifted him into the saddle. They held him there as they led the horse down the alley to a telephone pole with crossbars that supported several lines. Through burning eyes, he saw someone pitch the end of a rope up in an effort to lay it across a crossbar. It took three tries to get it done.

Strong hands pulled him far enough down the horse's left side that the bartender could reach him with the open loop and drop it over his head. It chafed his neck as it pulled tight.

Tears burned his eyes, and his heart pounded in panic. Blackjack cried, "For God's sake, you can't do this. You can't hang me again."

He felt the horse fidgeting beneath him, caught up in the wild excitement of the crowd. This was the nightmare of Clayton all over again. His tongue seemed swollen and dry. He started to scream from deep in his throat when he heard a slap and felt the horse surge out from under him. His head seemed to explode. The scream was cut off abruptly at its highest pitch.

The crowd grew quiet, watching the body swing back and forth.

The bartender looked up in satisfaction at the morning's work. "Can't nobody blame us for doin' this. He had it comin'. Some people are born to hang."

Someone said, "It was a peculiar thing he said, that we couldn't hang him again. What do you reckon he meant?"

The bartender said, "There ain't no tellin'. One hangin' ought to be enough for anybody."